Morningwood

Morningwood

Morningwood

Kit Cox

Edited by Ilya Rostov

OAK MOTH

BOOKS

2017

First Printing: 2017

ISBN 978-0-9934535-1-9

Oak Moth Books
Derbyshire

www.kitcox.com

Dedication

To Sir Michael Caine CBE, who through my countless hours of film watching inspired everything about Morningwood; from the soldier doing his duty in "Zulu", through the tired teacher in "Educating Rita" but most of all, the down to earth spy that was Harry Palmer.

Also to my Father, Michael. Who is not a Sir, a soldier, a teacher or a spy but is still just as important to me.

Prologue

Embers filled the air, drifting like fireflies through the thick black smoke, before settling on the hard ground of the Winter battlefield and the cooling bodies of the dead.

The Dagda sat amongst them; his giant frame glistening with the sweat of battle, his great war club, steaming with the blood of the slain, resting by his side. Despite the cheers of victory that echoed from every allied mouth, he didn't take his sorrowful eyes off the sword, buried to the hilt in the solid ground before him. He could have pulled it free, it would not have resisted. It was, in fact, unremarkable as swords go; just one of many wielded that day and as the saying went "Draw your sword against the king and be prepared to throw away your scabbard." They chose to live by that creed; they threw away their scabbards to defend the innocents until the end of days. An eternal army, always ready for battle.

The sword upon which the Dagda gazed had been wielded by the Guardian of the Early Morning Woods, the spirit tasked with chasing the harbingers of darkness from the sacred places. The Guardian had been the first to raise his voice up in anger against the injustices heaped upon the innocent mortals whose lands they invaded, bending them unrelenting to their will like cattle and easily discarded playthings. The Dagda had heard the call and along with many others, had rallied to that battle cry. The Guardian had been an inspiration to all; a leader of immortals, a god to the innocents but with his chaotic nature he could already see too clearly that lessons were never really learned and a new oppressive dominion would simply replace the old. The cages from which he chose to release them were already being forged again in blood and fire.

The Dagda had tried to argue their cause, explain how their way would be shielding the innocents from harm. His words had instead pushed the Guardian's resolve too far and in defiance the greatest of protectors rose up with righteous anger, sheathed his sword in the very Earth he had chosen to defend and walked unmolested from the field of battle.

Morningwood

The Dagda knew, without his guidance, the other warriors would succumb to their true nature or fall in battles defending the path he had set. They could certainly survive without him; he just wasn't sure how long.

The carrion birds were already circling.

Chapter One

The two men stood over Jonathon like crows. Their suits were predominantly black, a perfect match to their demeanour. If their presence here was meant to be comforting, it had missed the mark by a very long chalk and only enhanced the situation recently unfolded in the room.

In contrast, Jonathon Moore was a slight man with thinning brown hair and NHS glasses. He was so shocked by the conversation, he hadn't even noticed when he had gone from standing up to seated and the knot of nausea that had built within him was threatening to come to the surface. As he regained some sort of sense, he found he was still fully aware of the serious reality of the situation, even if it felt like a surreal nightmare. He raised his wide, questioning eyes to one of the official-looking men stood in the room and for the first time saw a kind of compassion etched across the wearied features. He couldn't find the words and opened his mouth silently like a fish, trying to speak.

"Will you be okay Mr Moore? I can phone a family member to sit with you if you would like?" The man's words came across in a practised, almost robotic way and did little to throw light on what had brought about Jonathon's current state.

"I'm sorry. I don't think I quite understand what's going on?" said Jonathon, his voice not rising too high above a whisper.

The officials looked at each other as if trying to agree on a next step without words and the more gruff-looking of the two gentlemen, seeing it as his turn, stepped forward; as if he could make the situation more understood with a firmer hand and no hint of emotion to cloud the words, "Your daughter is dead sir."

Jonathon felt the nausea rise again and with it the situation swam into clear focus. These men were police, all be it of the plain-clothed detective variety, but still police. They had appeared on a dark grey, rain-soaked weekday morning, as Jonathon prepared for work and had calmly explained how it was their sad duty to inform him of the death of his only child. Not an accidental death, that alone would have been difficult to come to terms with, but the horror of a premeditated

Morningwood

murder. They had explained how his twenty-year-old Alice had fallen in with a fairly unlikely bunch and it had been the undoing of her. They spoke of stupid occult rituals, fads that had taken hold of the younger members of higher society, whilst high on mind-altering drugs. They also talked about several people already being in custody, as if that would make up for the fact his precious little girl was no longer going to be walking through his front door.

They had said all of this as if it would make sense to the forty-five-year-old engineer and seemed content that just telling him the facts would answer all his questions and make things right with the world. Offering to phone a family member seemed their only form of comfort, but that would mean speaking to either his brother or ex-wife. Seeing as they had run away together over fourteen years ago, leaving him to raise a daughter he wasn't entirely sure was his own, their comfort left very little to be comforted by.

Jonathon stood slowly, rising numbly from the kitchen chair, walked to the front door, turned the latch and opened it to reveal the harsh British weather and grey landscape beyond. He didn't say a word. The policemen, taking the hint, just looked at each other, then filed past him, pulling up their collars as they left, the relief of a difficult job done and yet still a whole day to attend to. Jonathon closed the door with a morbid click and went quietly back to sit in his favourite chair, facing the decoratively tiled fireplace, with its four-bar electric heater, turned off and cold, the mantle above decorated with pictures of Alice from toddler to teens and he wept uncontrollably.

***

It wasn't quite as open and shut a case as the police would have one believe, but it made a lot more sense than the actual events that had unfolded in the grounds of the stately Sussex house in the closing hours of a late August night of 1965.

The lady who crouched next to the crime scene was being watched by several members of the Sussex Constabulary. She was certainly causing a commotion amongst the uniformed officers of the law, as comparisons were made to a certain comedic film star already famed for her ample curves and giggling persona, although a call for a blond wig had put a few of the officers present into the bad graces of their superior. He was finding the idea of his crime scene being disturbed by an outside agent upsetting enough, without adding into that it was a woman and one who supposedly resembled a ditzy blond from a Carry On film about spies.

Mulberry was neither ditzy nor blond. Her dark hair was cut into a sensible pageboy bob and her senses were keen enough to search the crime scene thoroughly, as well as discern what the gathered policemen were discussing behind her. In the chauvinistic eyes of the sixties male, this definitely wasn't a world for women with its blood and violent death. It was certainly far more acceptable for them to picture the women in the trench coat as light entertainment, rather than a skilled practitioner of her craft. Doing in all likelihood a far better job than the men who had already tramped most of the evidence into the ground, with their police-issued boots.

She had seen all she needed to when the superior officer of the attending police walked forward, his patience finally spent.

Inspector Burkmar was a well-built man, tall and broad across the shoulders, as a good copper should be, but promotion had seen some of that build moving towards his belly and now his chiselled, clean-shaven features had become round and softened, although his temperament was moving towards the harsh.

"So Miss have you found anything new or can my boys get on with the job in hand?" he asked gruffly.

Mulberry fixed him with large green eyes and at once he felt uncomfortable in their unfaltering gaze, "And what job would that be Constable? The continued ploughing up of a crime scene. Or the effective police cordon preventing the general public access to a murder scene on private grounds, a good mile from the closest public highway?" her voice was stern but mocking and it had the desired result of infuriating the police officer beyond the restraint he thought he could hold.

"I'll have you know Miss –"

"Mulberry" she added helpfully.

He continued, his anger growing, until spittle-flecked his lips, "My Officers were doing a fine job before you showed up. In fact, they had followed a line of good questioning and fine police work and were here as the atrocity unfolded. We have several felons in detention as we speak and a fairly open and shut case of ritual murder at the hands of some very twisted individuals. We even have our victim's name, and agents of a more helpful agency will have already informed her next of kin, well before you even turned up and started poking about."

That last piece of information surprised even Mulberry, who had certainly felt very confident she knew where the police were at with their investigations, but then again, another agency might be more dynamic than the rigid structure of the police, however wrong their information might be.

She pointed at the darkened area where a great fire had raged, "You informed that victim's next of kin of her demise, already, despite the lack of identifiable remains?

The officer faltered at the confident address and for a moment doubted his sources. The fire went from his voice, although not the displeasure of talking to the woman before him, "Our perpetrators all identified the victim's remains as one Miss Alice Moore. I think they should know who they burnt to ashes and bone," He said with less confidence than he had hoped.

Mulberry raised her eyebrows at the comment before she turned and walked to the detritus of the dead fire. "Follow me if you will," she said with the strict tone of a governess to her voice.

The policeman obliged, curious as to how the woman was going to make her case against the already definitive crime scene more plausible. Mulberry stopped and looked down at the remains of the fire. A rib cage and long leg bone seemed the clearest evidence of the presence of the victim, standing stark and white from the still warm smouldering ash, although other bone fragments also lay hidden amongst the warm embers.

She pointed at the obvious remains, "Capra aegagrus hircus," She said with an unshakable belief that her Latin was up to scratch, despite not using it for some time. "Or the domestic goat, as I feel you may know it."

The officer leant forward, shock etched across his features, as Mulberry continued, "In fact what's left of the body. The head, of course, they have set up on their altar."

She pointed at the gathered mess of clichéd relics placed on the stone altar, including indeed a goat's head on a copper tray. "The body lay in the grass over there, for quite some time, although the light sprinkling of blood by the indented grass suggests the beast had already been drained of blood some time earlier. I should imagine the blood was kept and used to paint symbols or simply drink as part of their ceremony."

The officer stumbled over his words, "They told us they had done for her, told us in great detail, in fact, the horrible little runts."

"Yes, that's certainly a problem with the criminal-minded they don't seem to feel they have to tell the truth too often, it comes with the territory," Mulberry looked around. "There is very little evidence in fact that Alice Moore was ever here, despite your line of good questioning and fine police work."

She smiled at the officer who was suddenly deflating like a balloon, all pomp gone from him, allowing her to continue unabated, "I'm not saying they haven't 'Done for her' but they certainly didn't do it here... Well, not last night. If you only have your goat remains and confessions to go on, I don't think you'll keep your prisoners much longer, the lorded gentry tend to have good solicitors and I very much doubt killing a goat is considered a crime."

Mulberry started to walk away, she had very little else to find from the crime scene she hadn't already discovered. Although she would certainly need to come back after the police had gone and hoped her little pep talk would see them depart within the hour, tails between their legs.

The police officer turned towards the departing woman, words had failed him but the gathered policemen had certainly heard enough to know his words would soon return in an angry outburst directed at them and a shoddy investigation. Those that had something else to be getting on with quickly found it. The embarrassment had certainly seen that the suspected crime scene soon abandoned, with all superficial evidence quickly gathered and taken away in bags.

***

Mulberry had sat patiently waiting in a lay-by overlooking the estate and watched the departing police cars through her binoculars. Finally, happy she could now investigate unobserved; she returned before the night had fully drawn in and walked unmolested to the darkened spot of the fire. Without the gathered police, it was easier to see the lay of the land. She felt bad for deceiving the officers, they had been on the right track, but too much information and jumping to conclusions had led them to make assumptions. It was unlikely they would ever have discovered the real truth however.

The area of landscaped grounds had been made to look like a Greek ruin. The stone altar was, in fact, an ornately carved plinth. Now devoid of its velvet cloth, black candles and severed goat's head it could easily have been a table to receive a tray of refreshing Martinis for a summer's garden party. A few fake columns on either side framed the flattened area where the fire had been. At the far end, facing the plinth and sealing the rectangular folly, was an ornate fountain with its shallow pool beneath. The fountain was still, it's mechanism turned off, but the water glistened cleanly in the pool beneath, showing constant maintenance and reflecting the dark clouds above.

Mulberry approached the stone-rimmed pool and glanced at the shallow waters. Her eyes took on the grey colour of the reflective surface and she smiled. She could feel the weakness in the air, the thinning of the veil from the ancient ceremony and was happy how easy this would make her task.

She already knew she was alone and unwatched but she stole a glance around the quiet grounds anyway, as dusk muted the green. Content with her solitude she kicked off her shoes and placed her bare feet on the cool grass, before unbuttoning her coat and sliding it from her shoulders to reveal her full naked breasts and curvaceous hips. With a graceful leaping dive, she was in the water, the tiniest of ripples marking her passing. The fountain's water showed no sign of her and was as shallow as it had been on her arrival.

***

She swam down into the great waters, between worlds towards the bubble she had perceived so clearly from the stately grounds and the ornate fountain's tranquil pool. The bubble was big and hovered unmoving, as if caught in an invisible net; it pulsed gently as Mulberry swam around. Her bobbed hair washed in the movement of the liquid surrounding her and grew with the currents until it was difficult to tell where the hair ended and the water began. She placed her hands on the bubble and swirls of delicate blue light moved beneath her skin.

The bubble contained the silent, naked form of Alice Moore. She was daubed with blood-red symbols and her eyes remained closed, her chest rising and falling as if in a dreamless sleep. Mulberry swam beneath the bubble and pushed up, but it merely contoured as if pushed against glass and she stopped, frightened it would burst. She swam above it, unheeded in her progress by the force that stayed the girls prison and gently laid a hand upon the bubble's surface, it moved downward with ease, it's decent growing in speed. Mulberry swam beneath it and moved the bubble upwards towards the point it stopped and swam back, leaving it to rest.

Her suspicions had been right, the men arrested had indeed been carrying out an age-old ritual that would promise them riches and rewards if they had been answering a request from the denizens below. She very much doubted the young socialites could have stumbled upon the arcane magic without help and she wondered who could be responsible for the second-hand knowledge. Then again, the socialites had been interrupted by the very excellent work of the police, who it seemed were a very effective force in stopping the mundane aspect of the crime; if a little lacking in knowledge of the true nature of the crime they were stopping. Their interception had halted the ritual half-way through and although not their fault, the girl was now trapped half-way between worlds. Of course, a woman as fair and untouched as this would be a gorgeous and succulent treat for any of the many recipients that could be waiting at her destination's end, but she was already across the veil and there was no way directly back to The Above from here. The fact no one had come to collect such a treasure from its drop off suggested the ceremony had in fact been one-sided. So if there was no recipient, why had they seen fit to send her this far? It could only mean the agents who had instructed the socialites had a more Earth-bound reason for her despatch, one that required the girl remained in an undetectable position for some time, if not indefinitely.

It felt wrong to leave the girl behind but she was safer here than being pushed into the wonderful world beneath. She was indeed a delicious morsel and even Mulberry could feel her mouth moisten in her presence. To begin with she had to find out why the girl had been kidnapped and used in the ritual, but then she also had to work out how she would get her home. The land below the water was a dangerous place to any mortal but to a treat such as this, it was a gauntlet impossible to run unprotected. Mulberry was just a Nymph; she wouldn't be able to defend the girl against even the most delicate of attacks. Of course amongst the mortals she was as strong as the tide and as constant as the sea, but in the land beneath she was just another spirit, easily dismissed.

She swam up, away from the bubble and the sleeping girl to formulate a plan. The fact other, more knowledgeable eyes could be watching the unfolding events hadn't escaped her; she could easily be in just as much trouble above as below if her involvement was noticed.

As she neared the surface, she kicked her legs hard and sprang from the water like a salmon, landing on the cool grass now darkened by the night. Her body drank of the moisture on its surface and she stood instantly dry, the hair on her head returning to the elegant style of a professional woman. She quickly covered her body with the trench coat, hiding her curves and soft curls beneath the heavy fabric, her eyes more aware of the shadows around her.

As she pulled on her shoes, her attention fell on the ornate fountain. The ornately carved column had at its centre a sculpture of the god Pan, draped in twisting vines and grapes covering his modesty, his goat legs allowing him to rise up with a great trumpet pressed to his lips from which water would have issued if the fountain was turned on. As she inwardly criticised the crudeness of the modern interpretation of a Greek favourite, her mind found its solution. She didn't have to face these dangers alone and she knew just who to turn to, despite the long years of silence. Pulling the trench coat's belt tight around her waist, she hurried off.

***

Jonathon Moore had not left the house; he had not answered the ringing phone or the inquisitive knock at the door around noon. He could still somehow feel his girl in his heart and had decided the police must be wrong. Until they gave him proof, he was happy to hold onto any hope that may arise. The house had grown dark with the departing sun and yet he had still not moved to turn on the lights. He simply sat and watched the shadows grow.

Another knock came at the door but when he failed to answer it, he was surprised to hear a key slide into the lock and the door open. He spun around, his heart leaping, his girl was home! He had been right to doubt. He went to run into the hallway to greet her, to share the terrible events of the day, but his path was blocked. The shadow clearly wasn't his daughter; it was a man, possibly thin, certainly wearing a brimmed hat and holding his daughter's bag dropping her key back inside.

"How nice to have found you in, Mr Moore," The man said with an educated voice that spoke of breeding, "I would have hated the need to hunt you down." The threatening tone of the comment made Jonathon back up, he had no idea who the man was but there was an implication to his words that set the engineer on edge.

"I have a little job for you, you see. One I was led to believe you would turn down in normal circumstances." The figure placed the handbag on the hall table and moved its handles as if to make it tidier, before looking back at the frightened father, "I do have your daughter, however, so I believe I'm in a quite a strong position for reasonable debate."

The outside door suddenly slammed closed and Jonathan for the first time that day wished he had turned the lights on. The hallway was plunged into darkness, hiding all detail of the man before him, leaving only the chilling voice behind, "Shall we begin our negotiations?" It said coldly.

Morningwood

Chapter 2

The spires and halls of Oxford were legendary in their grandiose architecture while the University Colleges themselves boasted as much elegance inside as they did out. The room had possibly been quite sizeable and elegant in its day, but many years of hoarding had seen the walls close in and the elegance become obscured with clutter, including a large heap of empty birdcages, ranging from the ornate to the mundane. It was big enough to boast two great windows, although one had its interior wooden shutters closed. Judging by the pile of books that stood before it, opening them was a function that had remained obsolete for quite some time. The walls were lined with many bookcases, but they appeared to hold as many bottles as they did works of literature. Numerous books were subsequently stacked on the floor or resting on tabletops and chairs. The largest of the chairs was a great leather Chesterfield that stood central to the room facing the non-shuttered window. It was well-worn in the cushion area and free from books, suggesting it was regularly used for its intended purpose. Alongside it rested an air rifle with a black metal barrel and heavy wooden stock. An open tin of air rifle pellets lay on the chair's distressed right arm; while the left arm supported the lid of the pellet tin, full of various cigarette butts, roll-ups and an ancient looking half-smoked cigar. A dark oak desk took up the greater part of the available floor space and behind it, asleep in a captain's chair, reclined a man of middling years. His face was lightly tanned and dark-bearded, his hair trimmed and yet unkempt. He wore a rumpled shirt with rolled up sleeves, a tartan tie and light brown corduroy trousers held up with braces. A tweed jacket was thrown across the desk and on top of it were two magnificently cobbled brown shoes with a black sock balled up inside each one.

A knock came at the door, gentle at first but then after a pause, louder. Another, greater pause and the door opened and a man in his early sixties with a finely trimmed moustache and neat blue suit entered.

"Sir!" The man uttered quite commandingly, hoping to rouse the sleeper behind the desk without leaving his position at the door, but to no

18

avail.

The man entered, leaving the door slightly ajar and approached the desk with a regimented stride that suggested some kind of military background, "Sir!" he said louder from the far side of the desk. The figure stirred but didn't wake.

"Professor Morningwood!" The man continued, his voice losing some of its regimental tone and the figure woke, blinked bleary brown eyes and turned his head to look at the interloper.

"Who the hell are you?" The Professor mumbled, his deep voice croaky from sleep.

"I'm Kensington Sir, the Head Porter." The man spoke with no element of weariness in extolling his position.

Morningwood coughed, clearing his throat, "Christ, what happened to Peterson? I liked Peterson."

"He retired Sir, close on four years ago now," Kensington's voice contained the measured unsurprised tone of a man who had gone through the theatre of this conversation many times before.

"Jesus, how long have I been asleep?" Morningwood sat up in his chair and noticing his shoes for the first time removed them from the table and brushed down his jacket.

"According to the ledger, you arrived promptly at five this morning and came straight to your room, so it could only have been a maximum of six hours, Sir," the statement of the porter contained no element of judgement, just a simple laying out of the possible facts.

Morningwood leant forward as if finding a chink in the porter's statement and wanting to push his advantage he raised a questioning finger, "You say six hours? But I can't remember Peterson retiring?"

"You bought him a cottage as a retirement gift… in Cornwall. He was very grateful for your generosity, sir."

"And so he bloody should be Kensington, and you should take note too, I'm a generous man not taken to being woken when I am clearly in the stages of very deep thought." Morningwood sat back in his chair, a sign that the conversation was to move on to other matters.

"Precisely sir, but there is a woman who wishes to see you urgently and she is not amenable to our requests to call back later after you have finished your morning thoughts."

Morningwood took his jacket from the table and laid it over the back of his chair, "Is she a looker Kensington?" Morningwood offered up the question whilst scanning his desktop as if looking for some lost item, before fixing his eyes firmly on those of the porter's.

"The lady is not without her merits sir," said the man with little emotion.

"Then send her up. Who am I to deny a pushy lady with merits from a Head Porter."

"I shall 'escort' her up sir."

The porter bowed his head slightly and departed from the room, leaving Morningwood to open a drawer of his desk, remove a bottle and glass from within, pour a good shot of rum; before downing it in one with a healthy shiver and replacing all back inside the drawer. As the drawer closed, so his study door was knocked again and Mulberry entered, not waiting for permission to be given. A smile crossed her lips as she read the gold lettering on the door as she passed within.

"Professor Morningwood… it's been a long time." She fixed her green eyes on the figure before her and her heart ran fast in the presence of one she felt she would never see again. The smell of the room was earthy and full of the warm notes of the forest trees and at once it felt like home.

Morningwood stood promptly behind the desk and gave the Nymph a wide toothy grin, "Mulberry you little cracker, I haven't seen you since Noel's little post theatre party."

Mulberry raised an eyebrow, slightly impressed at the memory of a fellow who could recall a party over forty years ago but would often forget the name of a dinner companion by the second course, "There's good reason for that as I'm sure you can well recall," the Nymph replied.

Morningwood gave a single moment's thought before breaking down in fits of laughter, "Oh God the Peacock. You never saw the funny side of that did you old girl?" He chortled causing a blush to rise to Mulberry's cheeks. "You've forgiven me then?" He continued, the twinkle not leaving his eyes.

"No Early, I have not forgiven you. However, I do need your help and if our friendship still has any meaning at all, you will see it as a way of making amends." Her voice had become stern and robbed the laughter from the Professor's lips.

Morningwood threw his arms open wide, bringing attention to his studious surroundings "I am a Professor of Wisdom, like the Oracle. Ask your question and I shall furnish you with knowledge."

It was Mulberry's turn to laugh, "A Professor of what exactly?"

Morningwood gave a sideways smile as if about to let an old friend in on a very personal joke, "The Greek Classics."

Mulberry's laughter grew, "And do many pupils attend your lectures?" she enquired through the mirth.

"God I hope not, I sure as hell don't." He thought for a moment his face becoming serious, "But it's a living and that's something I need to remember."

"I don't want your knowledge Morningwood; I require your strength and speed," the Nymph stated simply but felt an uneasy shift in the fellow before her as he replied earnestly.

"If only you had come sooner my pretty flower, the battle days of this old Satyr are behind him."

As Morningwood walked around the desk to reveal the average frame of a man in his middle years, the sight took Mulberry aback, "You've lost your legs," she stammered.

Morningwood patted the trousers in which he stood, bare feet on the worn carpet, ten wide toes scrunching the faded fibres beneath them "Not Lost, my little Nymph, merely traded."

Mulberry couldn't take her eyes from the very human appendages, "But why? You had found acceptance, excuses and stories and that doesn't include the myriad of ways you hid them." Mulberry was gobsmacked, she had known a Satyr with goat's legs for centuries, bluffing the world around him, challenging the mortals to make their own excuses for his appearance whilst other of his kind hid.

"I am old and tired and whereas I once wished to see the world question its very existence I eventually lost the appetite for the game." The Satyr announced, with no sense of the loss the Nymph was feeling, he had come to terms with his decision and it was now as natural to him as putting on the right jacket for the weather.

"I don't believe you. You are Early Morningwood. You have been unashamedly Satyr amongst mortals since the beginning of history. You have blasphemed in the face of the one true prophet. You have lain with the lion and the lamb and made the Vatican grant you access to the kingdom of heaven. You've whispered in the ears of Kings and warmed the beds of Queens. You can't lose your appetite for the game. You are the game!"

Mulberry had no real idea where her rhetoric had sprung from but

Morningwood

as one living a lie amongst mortals, she had always looked up to Morningwood for his unadulterated resistance to hide and it was that strength of conviction that had led her back to him now. She felt her cheeks flush as Morningwood started a slow clap.

"Bravo my dear, there is fire in that belly of yours despite its nature. But when a game is over the best players know to leave the table. This world and the one below are drifting apart and one day they will separate entirely and those of us who opted to exile themselves here will remain until the sun burns out and the crops die. The kingdoms below reached stalemate centuries back and neither side is prepared to tip its King.

"As for the mortal world, well, it has created Kings of its own and they play a game that makes everyone paranoid and looking for differences, to judge one another upon.

"We are creatures, dearest Mulberry, captured between two cold wars and if you want to see the final curtain you have to make sacrifices. For me, it was my legs and horns, which I'm a little upset you have failed to mention, and for you, it was everything you stood for."

The words hurt even though Mulberry knew they were true. Becoming an exile amongst the mortals she had sacrificed everything the moment she rose through the waters. She had wanted to taste the brief bright lives of the world above, feel the passion of man, revel in his creativity and she had paid highly, but she had seen the error of that life and had made changes, changes that had led her back to the Satyr before her.

"That's why I'm here. We no longer sit back and let that happen, we police the mortals, in a hope it will end our war and theirs."

Morningwood looked intrigued, "We?" he asked sitting on the edge of his desk.

Mulberry felt herself grow in stature before the Satyr, "I am an Agent of the F.A.E."

Morningwood's eyes widened as if in shock, "I'm not even going to ask what that stands for, I'm just going to tell you it sounds ridiculous."

Mulberry bristled, "We protect the mortals from the corruption below. Subterfuge and espionage our weapons, to slay any would be rising beast."

Morningwood laughed derisively, "Immortal spies. What happened to the good old days, when we simply convinced a Jingoistic soldier to wade in, all guns blazing?"

"They were your methods Morningwood. We have matured somewhat from your games of monsters and soldiers," Mulberry added as if talking to a child.

"You haven't matured far enough then. You simply put your armies in the shadows, like the two courts before you." Morningwood walked up until he was stood toe to toe with the Nymph, who stood a few inches short of his height and looked deep into her eyes.

She could feel him move inside her head, sorting through old memories, touching experiences that made her ache and yearn and then he broke off and walked past leaving her breathless and confused. By the time she turned, he was already sat in the Chesterfield facing the view beyond the window.

"The Redcaps still roam," she said to the seated figure who appeared already lost to her.

"Of course they do, it is their calling, like it is yours to swim and beguile and it is mine to drink and dance." His words seemed hollow.

"Your calling is to protect the innocent and guide home the lost," she said forcefully. "You're still releasing the birds." She had noticed the cages long before she had noticed the wines and spirits displayed prominently in the room.

"There are more bottles than cages, Mulberry my dear. Learn to use your eyes if you hope to be effective in espionage," he said, not taking his eyes from the window.

Mulberry sidled up behind the seated Satyr and bending she wrapped her arms around his neck in a loose embrace, bringing her lips close to his ear, "I noticed the bottles too, but many of them are still full, whereas all of the cages are empty. You haven't changed Early; you have simply started to hide like the rest of us."

The Satyr reached up and took the Nymphs delicate hand in his, "Then I have to assume you come to me to release someone you feel you cannot."

Mulberry smiled, she had broken through, "Oh I can release them without help; I just can't guarantee I can protect them when I do. I need an old Goat to butt heads."

It was Morningwood's time to smile, the Nymph smelled of fresh rain on a summer day and he was happy to be drawn in by the intoxicating perfume, "Where do we begin?" He said softly.

Chapter 3

Mulberry glanced across at the man in the passenger seat beside
her. She was having a difficult time seeing him as a Satyr now, with
his straight legs neatly placed in the foot well of her Mini. He hadn't
spoken much since she had picked him up, but then he had very little
to say. He wasn't the type for small talk and she remembered he was
always happier with his own conclusions than those of others, so
asking her for the low-down on what was happening was going to be
an alien concept to him. Back at Oxford he had asked simply if they
were looking to protect a mortal. On confirmation from Mulberry that
the whole thing was to involve the rescue of a twenty-year-old party
girl called Alice, he had simply started to bumble about the room and
when she realised he had stopped listening she stopped talking. He sat
thoughtfully pulling on his socks and shoes, before quietly tying the
laces with the concentration of a child still fresh to the process. He
rolled down the sleeves of his shirt and looked for the cufflinks that
he eventually discovered had rolled onto the floor, and finally he
pulled on the tweed jacket. Mulberry wouldn't have said he fell into
the category of a typically handsome man of the Sixties, his face was
bearded and the younger men favoured a clean shave or a simple
well-groomed moustache. No, he wasn't of the time, but the well-
tailored jacket and smart appearance certainly gave him a look of a
more dashing older gentleman. On finally dressing he had gone to the
door and unhooked a beige Mackintosh from a peg and with a
winning smile had asked where they were off to.

The Mac was now across the back seat of the car entwined with
Mulberry's. She had dressed since her swim and wore a simple shift
with a bold black and white zigzag stripe. It was short in design, as
was the fashion, and showed off her sculpted legs as she drove.
Mulberry had always been pleased with how her legs could distract
men so easily but Morningwood had been more intent on examining
the car as they drove, pulling down the sunshade and moving it about
as if trying to define how many positions it could have. He had
opened the glove box and slowly closed it until the light went off
before opening it fully again and then closing it with a satisfying

click.

"Have you never been in a car before?" She asked sarcastically as he started to fiddle with the seat adjustment.

"Plenty, just the first time in a Mini. They're deceptively TARDIS-like aren't they?"

"They're what?" Mulberry was used to Morningwood trying to be the cleverest man in the room and she knew the game was not to pretend you knew what he was saying but ask so he could enlighten you with his intellect and wisdom.

"Roomier on the inside," he added with a certain amount of pride.

"What language is that from?" This time, she was actually curious about the answer.

"It's an acronym; it's from a Television show on Saturday night just before I step out to the pub. You'd like it. It's about history and monsters... well, perceived history anyway."

"I don't tend to watch television, FAE has kept me fairly busy since its popularity has grown," she said, flicking a switch on the steering column, filling the car with a rhythmic clicking sound as she started indicating to pull out into the faster lane of the dual carriageway.

"Shame, you'd like it, they certainly like an over thought out acronym; and you'd love the Avengers," Morningwood delivered the last comment as if he had won some kind of inner debate. "So will I know any other members of your club?"

Mulberry glanced at Morningwood before moving her eyes back to the road, "You would have met all of them I imagine. Whether you remember any of them however, that depends on how much they piqued your interest." She pulled back into the slower lane, thinking the conversation possibly called for a steadier drive, "I very much doubt we will meet any though. Agents of FAE tend towards the secretive. You don't hide amongst mortals if you want to let everyone know who you are."

Mulberry was regretting her lane change as the car in front was slow-moving. Its exhaust was smoking quite badly and the smell was drifting into the Mini.

"We formed when it started to become evident that the Redcaps had become more organised, using their exile to gain favour in the land below by influencing the world above. The thought of them being able to return fills me with grief. While the damage they are capable of

Morningwood

individually amongst mortals has made History, as a collective they could destroy the world if we choose to let them," She could stand the car in front no longer and overtook.

Morningwood turned in his seat to face the Nymph, concern etched on his features, "How long have the Redcaps been a collective?"

"Who truly knows, I find it difficult to believe they haven't been behind all human atrocities to be honest."

Morningwood laughed, "Trust me humans don't need Redcaps to create atrocities."

Mulberry continued, "To answer your question, FAE was formed around thirty years ago to combat the growing Otherworld problems and we've got quite good at intercepting and thwarting their plans, as well as limiting other incidents between our worlds."

Morningwood turned to face the windscreen and fell silent for a moment, before speaking, "Seems even our world is changing. I've certainly seen the interaction between us and the mortals ebb and flow over the years. I've battled side by side with men fully aware of who we all were and what that meant. I've acted as secret confident to those of the human world who wished to suppress our existence and I've stepped back into the shadows as the likes of Crowley painted a world that was so far removed from the one I knew existed, I didn't even want to be part of the lie. I never thought we could become so mythical that we could carry out our antics in front of the humans so openly that they would be more likely to blame each other, rather than believe in us."

Mulberry removed her hand from the gear stick and placed it on Morningwood's leg for comfort, once again she was reminded of his change, "Did it hurt?" She asked, aware she was changing the subject.

Morningwood snorted, "It hurt like Hell. I'm pretty sure the pain was sufficiently bad for you too when you made the change. It was never going to be easy, I knew the cost."

Mulberry removed her hand realising how intimate the action was, "It certainly wasn't without its discomfort, but I changed as I came through; though it was more like a rebirth than a mutation. You waited so long, you battled the change and I've heard from others, the longer you wait, the greater the pain."

Morningwood placed his hand on Mulberry's bare leg and she slightly swerved the car at the contact causing a beep from a passing cab. "Good thing I know where to find distraction then isn't it?" He laughed and the sound filled the small car and for a second the Nymph was lost in the moment.

She removed his hand from her leg, "I'm trying to drive," She said, slightly regretfully, as his hand had left a spreading heat.

The next few miles were spent in silence until Morningwood removed a crumpled box of Lucky Strikes from his pocket and tapped a cigarette gracefully upwards, removing it fully from the packet with his lips. He patted his pockets noisily and on finding no matches, leant forward and pushed the button of the cigarette lighter on the dashboard.

"Do you want one?" He offered the pack towards the Nymph, causing her to chuckle.

"Can't get them to stay alight, I'm afraid. Some aspects of me will always remain, at heart I'm a water spirit, what you see is mainly cosmetic."

"Well, the powers that be did a good job," he grinned taking the freshly popped lighter from the dash and placing the glowing disc against the cigarette with one hand while rolling down the window with the other.

Although the gentlemanly gesture had been there to save Mulberry from the smoke, it merely blew it across the car to her side, so with little thought she opened her own window and despite the smoke they were suddenly very refreshed from the cold blast of air that came into the car.

"I'm guessing you think Redcaps are involved in this little mess were planning to sort out?" Asked Morningwood.

"Maybe, it certainly isn't a mortal matter," she added, in all honesty she couldn't really say who was behind the Alice situation at present; she just thought the girl should be released and brought back home.

"Possibly worth finding out first, don't you think?" Said Morningwood, as he inhaled deeply, causing the cigarette tip to flare.

He had been thinking about it ever since Mulberry had told him she needed his help. Surely the girl was just a commodity to the folks of the Underworld, closer to smuggling narcotics than kidnapping and if you took away the contraband, the smuggler would either source more or try to get back his shipment. Of course to Morningwood the girl was the most important aspect here, but he still wanted to stop it happening to others and at the same time protect himself from

Morningwood

recrimination.

Mulberry gave him a long look, it hadn't really appeared as if he had been interested in the whys and wherefores but the sudden questioning of her plan suggested otherwise, "I just thought you'd help me release her. That bit won't be easy of course; she's all the way through. I left her where she was because it was the safest place but it certainly isn't as safe as getting her home."

"You know for sure it's not as safe as her home do you? I mean that suggests you checked out her home and the motivations of the people who put her through in the first place. Don't forget the people who put her there," he inhaled and blew out a cloud of smoke, "They're still over here with us. Releasing her will either put her back in the game or send your Immortals elsewhere for goodies."

He drew in the last of the cigarette and threw the spent butt out of the window to spark on the road behind, "Maybe you best tell me everything you know so far and I'll decide if it's safe to go get her straight away."

Morningwood had been protecting innocents from the moment the worlds had met and he knew his motives were purely in favour of the girl's safety. He couldn't vouch for the Nymph however; like all exiled immortals, she had a past.

Mulberry bristled; she was suddenly reminded of why she hadn't made contact with Morningwood in what would be considered by most mortals a lifetime. He was full of his own self-worth. At parties, he always had to be the centre of attention even if it was a celebration for another and in life he always had to be the one calling the shots. The whole bird thing he did, although in his nature, was a real magnifying glass on his psyche. He would buy a bird in a cage or steal it if the one he set his mind on wasn't for sale and then release it back into the wild. Perfectly aware that most caged birds wouldn't survive the first cold night or over-curious cat, the action was to prove he had demonstrated his control over things and that was often all he cared about, he'd ticked the first box; the rest was up to someone else to sort out. This situation with Alice was no different. The moment he knew it was a girl and worked out she must be in the world below (or else Mulberry wouldn't be coming to him) he was on board but he would have realised over the course of the drive that he was simply a tool in the whole release procedure. Therefore, he had no real control of things, so he had to add his little angle to show he was still in charge. It appeared, in this instance, the angle was going to be whether or not he was releasing her somewhere safe. Okay, if he wanted to play that game she would let him. She had been playing the espionage game now for a long time and had made a lot of educational mistakes, it was about time she got to see him out of his depth and maybe even see him picking up some humility along the way.

"Okay, Early. What exactly do you want to know?" She asked keeping her voice calm.

"Who's the girl, where does she come from, who put her there and how exactly did you find out about it?" He wound the window up with a shiver, a small involuntary movement that prompted Mulberry to keep hers wound down.

"Well, the girl is your standard Carnaby Street princess who wanted to play with the rich boys. Sweet enough... well, very sweet in fact, to the point of untouched."

That fact alone suddenly had alarm bells ringing to Mulberry, now she thought about it. Alice wasn't your standard London clubber on the party scene, one night would normally have robbed a girl of any kind of purity in the fashionable clubs of Soho, it certainly wasn't a time where a girl held out for marriage anymore.

Mulberry put a pin in her own thought and continued, "The people who carried out the ritual were a bunch of young Etonians. You know the type, rich, privileged, looking for the next fad to wash over them. Far too young to have come up with the ceremony themselves so there must be another party behind it all. As for my involvement, well that's simple, FAE keep an eye out for any ritual ceremonies involved in crime and despatch the nearest free agent. Most turn out to just be crimes but every now and then we get lucky. I threw the police off the scent and went back later to follow up on the evidence I had uncovered myself." She looked at Morningwood who was still looking out the front windscreen "So what are your thoughts?"

The Satyr was clearly mulling things over and Mulberry was very aware he wouldn't have missed the unusualness of the purity angle; she was pretty sure he had taken his fair share of flowers in the last decade of free love. As he was sterile, like all of his kind and with a constitution that could battle even the toughest STD into defeat, he would have been a fool not to be cashing in on the bountiful crop of eager young lovers; it was the roaring twenties all over again.

"You didn't say where she came from." It wasn't strictly a question but somehow it needed answering.

"I don't rightly know. We're not actually that bothered are we?" She felt suddenly very much of her kind with the indifference the last statement had shown to the mortals. Yes, she was planning on saving the girl, but for the purely selfish reason of redemption rather than compassion.

"Aren't we? And by we, I'm assuming you mean the FAE?" Morningwood's words were harsh.

"No, I meant we, as in you and I. The FAE don't actually know this particular crime panned out into something more yet. I thought I would just get her out. Pretty simple case of rescuing the damsel." As always she was feeling a bit like an amateur chess player up against a master when trading words with Morningwood.

"And for this chivalrous action you came to the hermit in the woods rather than trust your fellow knights at the round table?" The Satyr looked at Mulberry trying to gauge her reaction to the perceived mistrust of her fellow agents.

"I just wanted to finish a case to the end without having it taken from me," Mulberry added quickly.

Although her reply was short it spoke volumes to the Satyr who knew an old boy's network ran just as keenly through the immortals as it did through any human organisation and he let the subject drop. "You see if she's as pure as you say, and I'm certainly not doubting that, then she can't be a big part of the scene, especially not one so rich with hedonistic Etonians."

He pulled his jacket collars up against the cold of the car, his breath coming in small clouds, "So she must have come from somewhere else and that means they must have sourced her. If there is a shadowy figure telling these misguided youths what to do, they must also have told them who to do it with and that might be important." He shivered, "Could you wind your window up, it's brass monkeys in here."

Mulberry hesitated at the request, still getting a small amount of satisfaction at the Satyr's discomfort, "I've been going all night it's helping keep me awake." She lied, starting to feel the cold herself through the flimsy dress, but she was certainly more robust to the cold than the Satyr and she was prepared to push it further.

"Right!" said Morningwood as if coming to a decision, "Let's swing past the police station that was called in to handle the original crime, see if they can't throw some light on who they think the missing girl might be."

Chapter 4

DCI Burkmar didn't like the men he currently had downstairs in the cells. He certainly knew his place when it came to the high rollers and he definitely tried his hardest to make sure they understood theirs, whilst trying to remain diplomatic enough in his approach to not ruffle official feathers. He'd had them in police custody now for over a day and none of them had seen a solicitor or even asked to see one, despite being read their rights. He was hoping the experience was making them sweat, left alone in their cells coming to terms with the fact that their prank may have backfired. What kind of idiot sets up a scene like that then tells the attending police they've killed a young woman when they hadn't? The woman, who had appeared on-site, had set the alarm bells ringing. Now he knew for sure they hadn't got a human victim, as she had suggested because he had the evidence bag on the table before him, containing the goat femur neatly labelled as such. Of course, he'd still had an element of doubt on leaving the grisly site and so had taken the bone straight to their evidence boys, on his return to the police station.

"What's that?" He'd said placing the bagged bone down in front of one of the awkward, suited men of forensics, disturbing him from his pack lunch. The thin, balding, officer, with a comb over, poked it with his biro.

"Besides a leg bone… I'd have to say a largish dog, maybe a sheep?" With all his heart, the man had just wanted to say "A bone." It was the sort of flippant quip that raised a laugh in the office and continued to raise a laugh at the bar after work as colleagues bought you drinks. However, DCI Burkmar had a reputation for not seeing the funny side of those kinds of quips. He was what was being thought of as "a modern officer" around the station and there was no room for humour in modern policing, especially when it came to bones.

"Could it be a goat bone?" Burkmar had asked, already quite sure of the answer.

"Possibly, it ticks all the right boxes but I'd need to examine it fully to give you a definite identification."

Burkmar picked up the bag "No you're all right, carry on with your lunch. Just needed to know it wasn't human."

The DCI checked the clock as he had walked from the room, to confirm it wasn't lunchtime. He was certain that on hearing the door, the forensics guys would instinctively pick up sandwiches, to make you feel you were interrupting and not hang around. It was the only way they could always appear to be eating but remain so thin.

Now that bone sat on his desk taunting him, a prop from the boys down in the cells. He looked through his door into the outer office.

"Hobson! Have we informed Mr Moore his daughter isn't dead yet?" he shouted to one of the men hunched over his desk scribbling notes.

The younger officer, who had been addressed, looked up at his boss's door before glancing around the office, as if looking for help and on gaining none, he resigned himself to answer.

He half stood and raised his voice in the sort of way someone does when they need to be heard but at the same time not loud enough to give the impression they were an expert on the matter and most certainly not someone taking responsibility, "Err! No sir." He looked around again, "We kind of thought, well we kind of thought we don't actually know she isn't dead, do we?" He didn't want to really question his boss, he hadn't actually been to the scene he just knew they had three men in the cells admitting to murder and as of yet, no body. Those facts didn't suddenly make the girl alive, just meant they hadn't found her.

"I've got a goat on the table says different," Burkmar continued.

Hobson felt uncomfortable with the distance this conversation was happening over, so he stood fully, walked to the door of his boss's office and spoke normally, making sure not to enter the room and somehow volunteer for something, "You've got what, sir?"

Burkmar nudged the bag, "I've got a goat. I currently don't have a girl and if policing has taught me anything it's that if you don't have a body you don't start crying murder."

Hobson was worried he was about to become the officer for this case. He was new to being a police detective, but he knew from a few years in uniform that you wanted to avoid any crime from the upper classes unless of course you were perceived to be on their side. It had a way of halting your progress and promotion.

"You want it to be chalked up as a misunderstanding then Sir, let the lads go?"

Burkmar looked out of his window, the day was as cold and grey as the rest of the week had been but at least it wasn't raining anymore. They didn't have a murder, what they had was a confession of murder from three separate sources. They had to assume it was true because of their independent witness, a girl who had made the distressed police phone call and got them there in the nick of time to catch the boys leaping around a fire. Not an anonymous witness either, but someone they had picked up and interviewed again when she was calm. Alice Moore had not been alone that night, she had sensibly been with a friend and with that security they had both gone to the big house together, after being favourably approached at a club, by the group of men now in Burkmar's cells. As it was three guys to two girls, it seemed legitimate and safe to continue the party in more opulent surroundings. The witness had admitted to taking drugs, she said it had been the main theme of everyone's intoxication that evening and had passed out because of them, to be woken some time later by the cold. She had found herself alone so went to the window; she had been drawn by the flickering firelight and noise, once there she saw what she called a ritualistic murder with blood, flames and her friend being tied and daubed with symbols. She had done what any sensible person would have done; she had run away, finding the nearest phone box to call the police.

They had come quickly and interrupted the ritual and made arrests but there was no Alice.

When asked of the missing girl's whereabouts, the blood-covered men simply admitted they had "done for her." The bones on the fire had been enough for the attending uniformed officers to make an arrest and when DCI Burkmar had finally got to the scene he took all that had happened at face value and gone with it, right up to the appearance of the operative from the agency showing up.

"Sir!" said Hobson trying to break Burkmar of his thoughts.

Burkmar continued to look from his window across the car park; a green Mini had just pulled in, "It's a tricky one, we have the testimony of a scared girl recently woken from a drug-induced sleep and the confession of three posh idiots. I have to admit I don't want to let them go, but I also don't want you guys caught up in an elaborate misunderstanding that the papers would love. We don't really have an alternative though, we have to plough on… Hang on, we may just have got our alternative."

The green Mini had just delivered Burkmar's salvation. The interfering operative with the fashionable bob and heavy eye makeup stepped from the car pulling on a coat. He could see movement in the car of another doing likewise, before a man stepped out of the passenger side, dressed in a long Mackintosh.

As the new man lit a cigarette, Burkmar was, for some reason, put in mind of both a modern day Jesus and the big bad wolf. "Looks like the case is about to be taken out of our hands Hobson, and if it isn't I'm going to make sure I hand it over anyway."

***

Morningwood looked up at the building, instantly noticing the man looking down at them from a second storey window. It wasn't difficult to spot a police detective; they had a way of not breaking eye contact. That this was the police headquarters of the county made the job of identification even easier. Morningwood nodded at the watching man who nodded back.

Mulberry was already up the steps holding the main door open, "Come on." She said tight-lipped, "And aren't you supposed to be doing this for me?"

"Deprive you of your rights? No, I'm a modern Satyr; I'll help you burn your bra if you want."

"Like I'm actually ever wearing one," she whispered playfully as he walked past.

As they approached the front desk, the phone rang and despite its obvious internal nature the desk serjeant picked it up rather than address the couple walking towards him. He raised a finger to them whilst not making eye contact as if to signal he would be one second if they could just wait. Morningwood almost chuckled at the small amount of power the uniformed officer obviously got from this moment of control. He took the time to look around, the entrance lobby was sparse, six wooden chairs, more suited to a simple dining room set, stood along one wall beneath a notice board of posters warning of the hazards of everyday life and notices of police events, with a few wanted posters dotted in between. The rest of the lobby was pretty much dedicated to the desk and tiled throughout, for easy cleaning. The desk serjeant put down the phone and addressed

Morningwood

Morningwood, a simple action of male deferral that wasn't lost on Mulberry or the Satyr.

"They want you to go up. It's through that door there, up to the second floor and someone will meet you." He indicated a door behind the desk and lifted a flap to allow them both through.

"You must have to lift this a lot during the day?" Commented Morningwood as he was passing through, happy to be pointing out the unimportance of the man's job, taking away his perceived power.

"Not really Sir, most people visiting come in through the back, this entrance tends to be a place for people with enquiries or information." The information was given in a way that suggested the desk serjeant was annoyed at the obvious dig and he wanted to point out Morningwood was somehow in the wrong.

"Do we not need to sign in?" Asked Mulberry, annoyed but not surprised she was being talked over.

"No Miss, I gather they know who you are or they wouldn't have phoned down. C.I.D. have their own records, Miss," He wobbled the flap to give the visual clue she just needed to go through and there was no need for conversation.

Mulberry shrugged and followed Morningwood through the door into the cold stairwell.

"Well, he seemed lovely," Said Morningwood, as they climbed, "Do you have to deal with the Police often?"

"We all try to avoid it, to be honest, they don't interfere with questions when they think you belong, but the FAE aren't exactly a government-funded organisation."

Morningwood nodded, "I was meaning to ask, who exactly do they think you are?"

As they rounded a corner, Hobson was stood holding a door open at the top of the stairs, "You must be from the Ministry of Defence, DCI Burkmar is expecting you," he smiled warmly.

"M.O.D." Said Morningwood with a grin as they followed into a well-appointed office of desks and filing cabinets, "This will be interesting."

Burkmar was stood by the open door of a side office, a more private space off the main room, a smile plastered across his face, "Welcome again, Miss Mulberry, I see you have brought a friend."

He held out his hand to Morningwood, who shook it silently and entered the room beyond. Burkmar shook Mulberry's hand too and when they were both inside he followed and closed the door, sealing them in a room of cheap office furniture and slatted Venetian blinds. There were two chairs in front of the desk and one behind. Morningwood decided not to buck convention and before being asked sat in one of the two chairs designated for guests and leant forward, taking a clear bag off the desk. Burkmar indicated Mulberry should sit and he went around the desk and positioned himself in the seat of respected authority, his mind working through the angle in which he was to palm off the case entirely and possibly save his department from embarrassment.

"Domestic goat, female about two years old," said Morningwood absently, causing all eyes to suddenly turn to him as he examined the bone through the clear bag.

There was a common misconception that Satyrs bore the legs of a goat. They, of course, had something similar in design and Morningwood had to admit there was certainly something goat-like about their entire appearance, but that was it. However, in a really long life he had studied goats quite extensively and could name breed, gender and age from just a single vertebra, just in case the topic ever came up. It never had.

"Bloody hell, are you all versed in livestock at the ministry?" Burkmar said, suitably impressed at the knowledgeable identification.

Morningwood looked up at the DCI, slightly bewildered at the question, before finding mischief in his heart, "Oh Yes! In the Farm Animal Emergencies or FAE, we pride ourselves on our knowledge of Livestock." Mulberry kicked Morningwood's ankle, out of sight of the DCI and stopped him drifting off into storytelling.

"I'm sorry?" Said Burkmar generally confused.

"Don't be," interrupted Mulberry, "We have brought Professor Morningwood on as an expert."

Burkmar smiled, this was obviously going to be an easier handover than he had at first thought. The MOD were bringing in experts and that was certainly a good sign that they saw the case as theirs, so he thought he would continue in that vein. He had no idea why the MOD would be involved at all, to be honest, but when wealthy families were involved it didn't take too much of a leap to just chalk it up to who knew who and those establishments who might

Morningwood

wanted any unpleasantness swept neatly under the rug for the sake of the old school tie. He had been proud of himself when he had guessed Mulberry's affiliations at the crime scene before she had the chance to show him papers; they weren't going to confuse him by sending a woman.

"We still have your suspects downstairs in the cells if you were looking to question any of them," he added hopefully.

This was going easier than Mulberry had expected too, so she was happy to go along with the case being handed their way. She was sure the friendlier approach the DCI was adopting was because he felt it had all been a big cock-up from beginning to end and he just wanted shot of it all. With both parties playing along, Morningwood, who had no idea about these things, just assumed it was normal.

"We didn't know if we should release them or if you would want a word first?" Burkmar added.

"Well, we really don't need to. We were actually coming in to get the Moore's address, speak to the father and find out where he thinks his daughter might have gone or if she's coming back home?" Mulberry said, not wanting to be too tied up with things.

"There's all the information we have," said Burkmar pushing the slim folder across the desk to be picked up by Mulberry, "I guess it's all yours now," he said calmly, trying to contain his inner joy at passing the buck.

"We will, of course, need to speak with the detainees before we go though," said Morningwood, prompting Mulberry to almost turn on him; she wanted out quickly, now they had what they had come for. Morningwood continued, "Could you set up an interview room with the one who was most covered in blood and release his possessions to us?"

"Of course, I'll go do that now." And not wanting to lose the upper hand over speed, Burkmar left the room quickly, leaving the door slightly ajar.

"What are you doing?" Hissed Mulberry "We just want the address, we can't hang about in case someone looks too deeply at our credentials."

"He's not going to check up anything, the man just wants this all off his patch and we've given him the scapegoat," he tapped the bag "Literally."

"Why do you want to interview the pawns though?" She asked

exasperated.

"Because when you're being played with, you nearly always see the player," he said with a grin, causing her to raise her eyes to the ceiling exasperated.

"Okay, we'll interview one but then whatever you find out we'll leave. Deal?" She held out her delicate hand to Morningwood, who took it in his like a precious gift.

"Deal," he said with quiet reverence.

The handshake was interrupted by Burkmar; "Right! I'm moving Nigel Rothborn across for you; he's the son of the estate owner, Lord Rothborn. His things will be outside the room. Do you need an officer or privacy?"

"Privacy," they both said together.

***

Mulberry and Morningwood had removed their coats before entering the room. The small bag of Nigel's personal items was already in the Satyr's hand and he was examining the contents carefully without removing any. The man himself was sat handcuffed to a chair as they entered. He was a surprisingly largish young man, in just shirt, beltless trousers and socks. His round face was stained with marks of old blood as were his hands and he had the smell of someone who had been drinking heavily, sweating profusely and not washing.

He laughed arrogantly as the duo entered, speaking through the chortle with an accent only found in the most aristocratic of English houses, "Oh, gracious me, it's Jesus Christ and Mary Magdalene. Have they had to get the church involved in our satanic ways?"

"Maybe you should look again," smiled Morningwood, handing the lad a pair of thick-rimmed glasses, from the bag of possessions. Instinctively Nigel put them on and was face-to-face with Morningwood's gaze coming into clear focus. Their eyes locked. "I think it's about to get Biblical," the Satyr said smiling.

Mulberry had no idea what Morningwood was going to do and actually hung back by the door so no one could just walk in without nudging her out of the way. She had been watching the Satyr carefully and as Nigel's eyes locked on his, she saw the briefest of flickers in

Morningwood

Morningwood's mortal form, a memory of the goat-like Satyr shining through and the boy recoiled momentarily in his seat. The lad looked physically shaken, as Morningwood turned his back on him. If you've been dabbling in the occult, the last thing you want to see in your police cell is the image of the devil. Morningwood was reaching into the bag again and removing an over-ornate gold ring, the type Catholic priests would sometimes wear although the iconography was all wrong.

"What a nice ring," Morningwood seemed to announce the comment to the room, holding it up to the light before trying it on his own fingers and finding it slipped snugly onto his middle one. The larger lad having pudgier fingers than the more toned Satyr, would have worn it on his ring finger. "Did you kill the goat?" Morningwood enquired turning back to Nigel.

"What?" The lad was confused and Mulberry didn't blame him, Morningwood was acting oddly.

"Simple question really. You were… are… covered in a lot of blood, it's either the girl's or the goat's." Morningwood's words were calm, measured and polite; it gave them a somewhat sinister edge.

"It's the goat's." Said the lad offhand, looking down briefly at the blood on his hands.

He looked back up to a blow that shot deep red colours across his vision. Mulberry almost moved to intercept as Morningwood's clenched fist struck the handcuffed lad so hard he took the chair clean off its feet and smashed it to the floor. After a moment's thought, she stayed put, knowing the door behind her needed to be protected now from interlopers more than ever. The crash to the floor took the wind from Nigel's lungs and he could feel a bloom of pain opening across his cheek, accompanied by a warm trickle of blood. A rich taste of iron was filling his mouth. Before the lad's lungs could fully fill with air, the weight of Morningwood was across his chest, as he straddled the prone youth. Strong, corduroy covered legs either side of Nigel's plump body pinning his arms securely to his sides, the glint of the heavy gold ring prominent on Morningwood's still clenched fist. With the other hand, he removed Nigel's glasses that had surprisingly survived intact and placed them folded in his own pocket.

"I think you can clearly see what's coming, without these," the Satyr bent down so his face was a mere inch from the panicked aristocrat's and whispered menacingly, "A few more simple enough to answer questions. Let's try to get these ones right."

Mulberry couldn't hear the exchange but each time the ring caught the light she winced. She always knew Morningwood was not what stories would call the 'good guy' but the brutality of the first punch and the threatening nature of his unheard questioning made her want to retreat from the room. It was pure morbid curiosity kept her at her post.

Eventually, the Satyr stood; an action that made the lad curl into a blubbing ball and Mulberry instinctively grasp the door handle of her only exit. With his back to her and looking broad across the shoulders, head hunched, Morningwood unclenched his fist and the ring slipped from his finger to roll across the floor and almost poetically come to rest at the side of the crying victim. Morningwood moved his neck tilting his head first one way then the other, a small click sounded and he shook out his hunched shoulders, turning back to face the slightly petrified Nymph, looking as normal and humble as he had when they first walked in.

"Right! Now we have the answers, it's time to go," Mulberry happily opened the door and they stepped quickly through. A uniformed officer rose from a chair down the corridor and approached.

"I'd give that one a minute or two to get his thoughts before you go in. He had a bit of a fall so he might appreciate a cup of tea, to steady himself. You can tell DCI Burkmar we have no need for them now, so when he's finished any paperwork he can let them go," Morningwood's smile was so cheerful, the young officer beamed back and with an unnecessary salute went off to tell the DCI and possibly fetch a cuppa.

Morningwood and Mulberry looked at each other as the officer departed and they were left alone. Quietly they picked up their Macs and walked to the lobby, raised the flap; before it was raised for them and stepped through, with a subtle nod of the head to the Desk Sergeant as they passed.

They were in the Mini and driving away before most people had even known they had left the building.

Morningwood
Chapter 5

They parked up in the shadow of a London tower block. The weather had improved greatly on the short drive to the capital's outskirts, the sun finally breaking from behind the sea of grey clouds and warming the car as they drove, improving the dark mood into which Morningwood had found himself slipping. Here, however, in the small car park at the foot of their destination, the tower block offered the unwanted, yet perfect, shade from the weak sun. Morning frost still glistened on some of the metal handrails, despite the lateness of the afternoon. Mulberry checked the address from the file again, this was certainly the place, it just didn't feel right. It was the sort of place good, working class folk lived; not the type of area you would expect to find the residence of someone hobnobbing with the Rothborns. The father of Alice was Jonathon Moore, her only traceable parent; although her mother was listed in the files as Margaret, she had been added with no contactable address. The typed notes on Jonathon included the address they currently stood at and his profession of Engineer, next to which, written neatly in pen, someone had put 'Nuclear'.

"This the place?" Asked Morningwood, stood beside the Mini looking up at the concrete monolith before them.

He had for some reason put on the glasses belonging to Nigel as they had driven along and kept looking at things through them, then pushing them back off his eyes and looking again.

Mulberry had the feeling this was what children must be like if they weren't given enough to distract them. She had to admit the glasses suited him and made him look even more academic than he had before. As they were an expensive brand of frame, they gave him a more fashionable up-to-date look than he had been showing in his Oxford lecturer's garb. Mulberry realised he was actually waiting for an answer.

"Certainly what it says in here," she tapped the manila folder.

Morningwood looked back at the building, "It's not very classy is it?"

"Maybe the flats are nicer inside, it's difficult getting property in London," Mulberry added, not sure why she was defending the look of the building, apart from the fact it reminded her slightly of where she currently lived and didn't want Morningwood with his Oxford estate to be judging her, later.

"Well onwards and upwards. I'm guessing he went for the view. So it will be nice to see it."

Morningwood marched off as Mulberry followed behind, feeling her case was somehow falling into the hands of the Satyr and she was just becoming an assistant to his whims. He was already mounting the stairs as she walked past and pushed the call button to the lift.

"They never work those–" Morningwood's words were cut short by a loud ping and the sound of the door's sliding open.

Mulberry felt stupidly victorious at being right, she stood aside as an old lady wheeled a tartan shopping trolley from the lift. She wore a floral headscarf and gave the couple an accusing look as she passed. Morningwood smiled and nodded at the departing woman before her watery grey eyes fell on Mulberry. The Nymph also found herself smiling at the old lady as if to placate her stare. The woman walked away muttering to herself about Jezebels, much to the amusement of Morningwood.

As they stepped into the lift, he watched her go, "I wonder why we take that kind of thing." He offered up as a statement rather than a question. Again Mulberry felt compelled to answer, like an eager student, trying to get Sir's attention.

"It's because she's old. We let the old get away with a lot because it might be all they have left." She pushed the floor number they needed and watched the doors close over the vision of the departing woman and her tartan trolley.

"She can't be much older than seventy," intoned Morningwood, bringing to the Nymph's attention how many more years older he must be.

She said nothing but smiled behind the Satyr, inwardly chuckling at how much he got away with in their community due to his great age, but, of course, no one would ever tell him and spoil his fun. The lift journey they took in silence, Morningwood had done all his talking in the car and smoked until he ran out, which was mercifully quite quickly.

Nigel, it turned out had been quite a talker too in the grand scheme of things, Mulberry wondered how much talking she would have done pinned beneath the Satyr but then realised if he'd pinned

Morningwood

her, it wouldn't have been talking on the agenda. Turned out Nigel
Rothborn and his friends had been approached several months back,
in a Soho nightclub, by a thin gentleman, leaning heavily towards the
camp. The man had been very free with the cocaine and bubbly and
they slowly realised he was the club owner after a couple of things
were quietly brought to his attention by staff. He had told the trio that
he had come to England with nothing, but soon got into the good
graces of dark unseen forces and they had given him power and riches
beyond his wildest dreams. The lads, intrigued, had indulged in some
of his occult meetings and seen stuff that proved to them, beyond all
shadow of a doubt, that he was telling the truth. The owner, however,
was worried he would tire of the boys before they got a suitable
reward; an honest admission the boys had found refreshing. He
offered them the chances he'd had, by instructing them of the ritual
that had brought him everything – a ritual that could only be secured
with the sacrifice of a virgin maid. The man even got them one of
those, telling them to hang out in his club every night, prepared for
the ceremony just in case and he would point them to the right girl
and even make sure she stayed compliant. It was all the background
Mulberry and Morningwood could have needed; it fit so perfectly
with the theory they had already set in place. The final pieces were
the name of the Club and the proprietor; The Scene, owned by
Howard Barrie. They couldn't trust the proprietor's name for
background information, it was most certainly a fake, but they could
look up the club when the time came.

The lift doors opened and, thoughts interrupted, they both
stepped out. Morningwood went straight to the balcony and looked
down, whilst Mulberry got her bearings on the flat numbers.

"Number four," she said, starting off for the door, only to realise
Morningwood wasn't following, he was watching something below in
the street. She looked over the balcony herself.

Several stories below the old lady from the lift was surrounded
by a small gang of scooter-riding youth, a selection of Vespas and
Lambrettas buzzed around her, circling her like wolves, reaching out
to touch her trolley as they passed. The harassment didn't seem to be
slowing the lady much who just kept moving stoically on towards the
pavement. However, it certainly looked like it would escalate and just
as the woman stepped up onto the kerb one of the scooters broke

forward, the rider grabbed the tartan trolley and drove off with it bouncing in tow.

"OI!" Shouted Morningwood and a sea of helmeted heads turned upwards, a couple flicked the V sign up at him and they drove off at speed. Morningwood turned towards the stairs but was stopped in his tracks by Mulberry.

"We have bigger problems to deal with than stolen shopping carts," she said with authority and as if by divine providence the door of number four opened and a man stepped out onto the walkway and turned to lock his front door.

"Mr Moore?" Asked Mulberry towards the figure and Mr Moore froze.

Slowly he turned to look towards the couple of Mac-wearing individuals, stood just outside his house, out of the view of his spy hole he had checked so carefully before venturing out. He couldn't believe his bad luck, he hadn't answered either the door or phone as he had been instructed and now he had walked right out into the presence of two police detectives.

"I don't have time," he mumbled and tried to walk past, but the bearded man put a hand on his chest and he felt that making a run for it would just arouse more suspicion.

"Not even for some information about your daughter's whereabouts?" Asked Morningwood, as compassionately as he could, not removing his hand from the smaller man's chest.

Jonathon felt his shoulders slump, he wasn't designed for all this, "I know she's not dead," he said meekly.

"Maybe we best talk inside," Mulberry offered, as Morningwood half guided the man back towards his flat.

***

Inside the living room, Morningwood pulled open the curtains and was finally greeted with the sunshine he knew was waiting on the far side of the building. Flooding the room with the warm light it very much needed. The flat was, in fact, a maisonette and as Mulberry had stated it was far nicer on the inside than it had been on the outside. The living room had a dining table with a light directly above that shone off the heavily varnished orange-coloured wood. Behind it was

Morningwood

the serving hatch that was open and showed through to the kitchen at the front of the building, overlooking the walkway on which they had arrived. The room had a Philco Predicta television in pride of place beneath the window and a small sofa and mismatched armchair faced it like devout followers of its magic. The fake fireplace (that would once have been the room's focal point) was filled with the type of four-bar electric heater that always smelt of cooking dust and the mantelpiece above was strewn with photos of just one girl, in various stages of maturity.

Mulberry picked one up as Jonathon watched her from the doorway, "Alice is a very pretty girl Mr Moore; you must be very protective of her?"

Jonathon just looked deflated from his stationary position, no real life left in his ashen face.

"You must be glad to know she's alive." Added Morningwood trying to get a response from the man, Jonathon simply shrugged.

Mulberry put down the photo and walked the short distance to the man in the doorway. Her voice was delicate and full of support as she spoke the next words carefully, "I will be honest with you Jonathon; she isn't out of danger yet, but she is no longer in the hands of those who are trying to blackmail you."

Morningwood listened intently; he was impressed with Mulberry's risky strategy, she could easily be making the wrong assumptions and then all would be lost, but if the gamble was right they would bound quickly along in their enquiry.

"Where is she then?" Jonathon asked his voice building in strength.

"We have her Mr Moore, she's in our custody," Mulberry didn't mind telling the distraught father this as it was in some moderate way close to the truth.

Jonathon exploded with rage, "THEN SHOW HER TOO ME. WHY DO YOU ALL PLAY SUCH MALICIOUS GAMES. SHE'S MY DAUGHTER."

Morningwood went to step forward, but Mulberry held up a halting hand. She stepped into the ranting father's space and embraced him tightly. Until the man's head was on her shoulder and he was sobbing.

"Put the kettle on Early, I think Mr Moore may need one of your famous brews."

***

Morningwood put the tea caddy back away in the cupboard he had eventually found it in, along with all the other bits required for making a brew. He adjusted the teapot on the tray alongside the three cups, filled with hot sweet tea, which Morningwood believed was the solution in cases when you didn't have any scotch. He was about to carry the tray through when he spotted a postcard on a corkboard. A bright sunlit day showing off the ruins of a castle on some Scottish hill. Although the actual ruin didn't look familiar, the shape of the structure did and he knew instantly where it was. He turned it over to read; *'Dearest Alice, I shall be home for the weekend. Dad XXX.'* It was simple enough and addressed to the house they were in, but Morningwood still slipped it into his pocket.

As he walked into the room with the tray of drinks in his hands, he saw Mulberry, a comforting look on her face, sat on the sofa with the red-eyed engineer. He offered the tray over and both took a steaming cup before he placed it down securely on an occasional table and took the last one himself, remaining standing. As he sipped he had to wonder how people could drink tea without sugar, but then he saw a lot of folks mix ginger ale in with their whiskey and that just made him worry for them, but then again, horses for courses.

Everyone drank silently for a while before Mulberry spoke.

"I'm afraid we won't be able to get her back to you for...?" She looked at Morningwood, who shrugged before holding up three fingers (in all honesty he had no idea, but it seemed to make Mulberry happy), "...Three days," she continued as if speaking to a simple child or elderly relative.

"I only have your word," chimed Jonathon and it was obvious he would take more convincing.

Mulberry looked thoughtful, for a bit, "I'm not going to ask what they have demanded of you but can you delay it for three days?"

Jonathon thought and then nodded. Mulberry nodded back reassuringly.

"Then continue as if you are going through with the instructions they have asked you to follow, but delay them three days. If we have lied and don't hand your daughter back safely within that time, you can assume they have told the truth and continue, getting your daughter back that

Morningwood

way."

Jonathon gave Mulberry a horrified look, "But it will be a catastrophe!"

She patted his hand, "No it won't Jonathon because we haven't lied to you. You will get your daughter back safe."

The man's face went ashen again and he looked towards Morningwood, who helplessly announced again, "Three days." Completely unaware what kind of game they were getting into.

***

As they left the maisonette, closing the front door behind them with a click, leaving Jonathon alone in his chair to decide his next move, Morningwood spoke.

"So, a right pickle then. Someone is using his daughter to blackmail him to do something catastrophic and we have given ourselves three days' grace to make sure it's not going to happen, and we have no idea what it even is or how catastrophic. Unless you happened to find out as I was making tea?"

They entered the stairwell and the sounds of Morningwood's Cuban heels on the concrete steps made it sound like he still had hooves as they descended.

"I just comforted him. You know a gentle hand on the back. If he had wanted to tell us anything it would have happened I think. We have three days' grace and there is very little damage one human can do to be honest despite our time limit."

Mulberry was confident they had given themselves some time, but in the grand scale of things she had just wanted the girl back to thwart whatever immortal schemes had been laid out, she didn't really care about the effect not getting her back would have on the humans.

Morningwood adjusted the glasses he now wore, he had no idea his sight had needed correcting since taking on this mortal form, but they certainly seemed to give more clarity and as his eyes were seeing better, in turn so was his brain.

"I kind of agree with you, that it takes more than one man to cause a problem. But give them a sword and they can, if lucky, assassinate a King. Give them a gun and they can take down a group or even a small army with the right place to hide. Give them a bomb and they can do all kinds of localised damage. You are right, one human has very little potential, but it all depends on the weapons to hand and giving him the desire to use them."

Mulberry gave Morningwood a look, she knew he was getting at something and he wanted her to make the connection, but she was lost, "He didn't have a weapon to hand though and I very much doubt he could use one if he did."

Morningwood smiled, pleased to still have a finger on the destructive capabilities of humanity, "I wonder if he could find a weapon in one of the Nuclear reactors, the ones across the country he regularly has to maintain and set safety limits on?" He added quietly letting the words sink in.

Mulberry's head whipped around, "What?"

She was stunned, it just hadn't occurred to her. She was a spirit of nature; her mind didn't move to the violent machinations of man. She went quiet, no words were enough. She spun around to go back up the stairs, following her nature; when water hits an obstacle, it turns, changes to an easier course. Morningwood grabbed her arm stopping her dead.

"We have to stop him." She said with horror on her features, "We can still rescue the girl, but he must be stopped." She hadn't felt like this since making the decision to leave the below world, rather than except death. It was the only course.

Morningwood released her arm, "Then go. Stop him." At his words, she started to bound up the stairs but he continued, "You know how to stop a man from saving his children do you? It often doesn't end how you would like it too," He said calmly and her feet slowed until she stood still.

She listened to the clip-clop of the Satyr walking up the stairs to her side and soon they were both by one of the open landings, looking out across the London skyline. Not the tourist bit with the domes and wrongly-named clock towers, but the true heart; with the smoking chimneys, high rises and traffic.

"He gave us three days," said Morningwood seriously, as if talking about a contract that could not be unbound.

"We could stop him right now," she said quietly, the implications settling in. She adjusted her comment, "YOU could stop him right now."

Morningwood

"I could, but I won't. We have three days; we can waste it watching the view or we could get a little girl back," The Satyr held out his hand palm up, Mulberry looked for a second before taking it and then hand in hand they continued their descent. She knew it was to be a very long way down.

***

They entered the car park and walked towards the Mini. Mulberry pulled the keys from her pocket and glanced back up to the high rise, discerning where Jonathon's flat must be, before turning back to the car where Morningwood was already stood by the passenger door. The sight, however, froze her blood and sent goose bumps along her smooth arms. She nodded at Morningwood directing his attention behind him. The Satyr turned, sat at the corner of the car park were the six mixed scooters, complete with fenders, mirrors and other over the top paraphernalia. On each of them sat its rider and behind two of the riders sat a passenger on the pillion. They at first appeared the fairly standard type of youth you'd expect to have a little gang on an estate like this, causing trouble upsetting the police. Dressed to shock, several of the riders wore suits, well-pressed and turned out as if mocking the fact they were actually the ragamuffins of old. Others were in fishtail parkas opened and designed to flap behind them as they rode, like drab crows. The girls had skirts so short they really shouldn't be straddling the seats on which they sat, flashing knickers to the world and wearing laddered stockings or long, striped pop socks. Surprisingly all of them wore helmets, the hard leather type designed to resemble the German helmets of the last war, adorned with goggles, patches and in two cases; the tails of animals. It was a quick glance before he turned back to the Nymph, who was still focused intently on them.

"They're kids. Ignore them, or did you now want me to have a word about harassing old ladies?" He said with honest questioning.

"Look at their faces Early," she said a taint of fear to her voice.

Morningwood turned his head back around and this time took in the faces of the silent scooter gang. At first they passed muster as the kind of faces you'd expect but then he saw the similarity, the mouths, all of them had clean looking scars that lead smoothly from the corners, sweeping upwards until they stopped an inch before the ears. The scars weren't added later in life as some gang initiation, although you would be forgiven for thinking so, they were, in fact, the imperfect healing that occurs when an immortal species with a wider mouth, like a frog, takes on a mortal form. Morningwood's eyes went back to the helmets, all were skillfully dyed red, although the dye had a way of leaving blotches and over time mellowing to a darker brown.

"Redcaps," Morningwood found himself mutter, before turning back to Mulberry, "Get in the car," he instructed.

Chapter 6

Morningwood took off his Mac and climbed into the passenger seat of the Mini, the leather creaking as it moulded to his shape. He put his mac in the back and slipped the glasses off and put them carefully folded in the glove box. He did all this as calmly as possible, giving him time to think.

Mulberry in the meantime was starting to feel fear creep into her bones and had focused on the gang in her rear view mirror. They just sat quietly watching like crows on pylons waiting to swoop down when they saw carrion to feast on. She put the keys in the ignition and felt Morningwood's large warm hand cover hers, it felt comforting, but she knew it was to stop her from turning the keys and firing up the engine.

He was now silently watching the group behind them.

Morningwood had dealt with Redcaps before but never in any great number, always alone and always in immortal form. They weren't beings of the greatest stature, never really topping more than five feet in height and they had a way of slouching and slumping, giving them an even more compact and twisted appearance. He remembered the heads of them, like large apples that had been left in the sun to shrink and wrinkle, until only the large lipless gash of a mouth remained, lined with tiny sharp tearing teeth, drooling as they watched you with small sunken black eyes. He had fought them along the Scottish borders when the British wanted territories and control. It seemed every landowner had his own pet Redcap to single-handily hold off intruders, but the English got themselves a Satyr and the tides changed. Legend had it they needed to kill constantly and keep their caps soaked in the blood of their victims or they would die. It was pure propaganda spread by the Scottish lairds wishing to keep the English at bay. There was nothing magical about their blood lust, at most the laird had acquired a psychopathic little bastard that just enjoyed killing and was bloody good at it. In fact, it was the reason they had been expelled from the land below. Long before the two worlds had become one, the antics of the Redcaps had seen to the death and imprisonment of all of their kind, but years of removal from society had made the younger generation of immortals unaware of their history. They started to question the incarceration of a whole race; leading to some of the grand debates that helped start the coldest of wars. When the chance to exile them arose, giving them a freedom of sorts, a world of their own to roam, it was seized upon by all sides instantly and the Redcaps were removed from below and put in the world above. Time was the best judge and after but a short while, this single act was deemed the greatest of mistakes and Morningwood had subsequently fought many of them to correct it, but they were always a solitary threat. Mulberry had suggested they were making collectives and although it had worried him, he hadn't really seen it as a thing the Redcaps were capable of. Too much in-fighting kept the Redcaps solo, but here was a gang of eight, youngsters, in mortal form but still the same spirits of chaos and destruction.

"They're not doing anything," Mulberry observed, interrupting his thoughts.

"Not yet. They have no idea who we are. I'm guessing they're just here to watch Mr Moore and being bored they are looking for trouble," Morningwood didn't take his eyes off their reflection.

"If they don't know who we are, we should just drive away. They're clearly no threat to Jonathon just watching him," she added.

"They are waiting for us to drive and that's when the violence will begin and I doubt we can take on eight of them. I think we'll struggle with two." He looked at Mulberry, gauging her response and he could see the fear on her features. She was not built to do battle, her type were designed to stay in deep water or high trees and watch in safety, but now the fight was coming to her, "We need to split them up and for that you're going to have to be brave."

Mulberry turned on him, anger now on her lips, "How dare you –"

"Use that fire," he interrupted, "You're going to be alone. You need to drive to Greenwich. Just off the main road there is a major bombsite, beside it stands a row of three boarded-up shops, massively overgrown. Stop the car and wait there."

"What do you mean? Alone?" she said, her anger disappearing.

"Start the car," he answered.

Mulberry instantly responded, doing up her seatbelt quickly and turning the key. As her engine fired, it was met by the sudden whirring noise of the scooters starting behind her.

Morningwood

In a sweeping movement, Morningwood opened his door and stepped from the car, his last words before the door closed were simply, "Drive."

She didn't want to pull away at first, but she knew the whole reason for having Morningwood with her was for moments like this. If she didn't trust him here, how would they cope below. Morningwood's form blotted out her view in the mirror as he walked behind the car and she drove.

***

The Satyr had walked from the car, making sure to keep eye contact with the gang. He was well aware they had no idea of his nature and the possible reason for their intimidating stance was purely his shout from the walkway earlier. They had confidence in their position, they were tough and there were a lot of them ready to ruck. Morningwood was hoping he had pre-empted their form of attack, he needed them split up. He had little time to make his move if he was to protect Mulberry.

He noticed the almost indistinguishable nod given by the Redcap in the smart-pressed grey suit and straight tie. He had his leader, as three of the other scooters broke off and went after the Mini, taking the two pillion riders with them, leaving him with just three Redcaps. Suddenly Morningwood felt his muscles ripple beneath his shirt as if they were sensing it was time for battle.

The leader didn't say a word, no witty quips or one-liners, it was silent threats only and that was the thing that made this real. Morningwood knew the moment someone spoke the battle was off, words were distraction not action. Another nod and the lead Redcap's two outriders came forth circling the Satyr, like hyena moving in on their prey.

The leader of the Redcaps was a self-assured youth who went by the name of Spades because in a pack spades meant death and he was the ace. He was more than happy when the man stepped from the car, London was full of old men in suits who believed youngsters needed to be taught respect because they hadn't fought a war. He had half-expected to see the tweed jacket of this history teacher appear in the car park following his shout and was somewhat disappointed when it hadn't happened. The later revelation that he was with a woman, several years his junior, the dirty old man, put instantly in the Redcap's mind the conversation that must have happened on the balcony, *"Leave it, John, they're kids, they're not worth it."* He thought of all mortal men as John, because to him they were just nameless bodies. Now this history teacher hero had stepped from his car to teach them a lesson, the Redcap wondered if the ill-planned encounter would give the John a quick trip to the hospital or the morgue.

Morningwood didn't watch the scooters circling him, he was aware he had inherited both the Redcaps with tails attached to their helmets and it was easy to think of them as dogs waiting for their master's order to attack. This being the case, he only watched the master.

The Redcap leader didn't like the silence of the man before him and the gaze that never left his. Could he not see the danger about him? But whatever the reason for the man's inability to look away, it was acting as a great distraction, as the stare had continued, his soldiers had slipped weapons unseen from their coats – a metal bar and a wrench now circled the quiet man. Spades had had enough of the man's inappropriate arrogance and gave the signal to attack. He knew his boys would do it with force and speed.

Morningwood saw the order and heard the engines that had settled into a steady buzz turn into an angry screech. The scooters both turned in to attack, they would pass either side of him like knights jousting and as expected, one would reach him first. The angry face of the wrench-wielding Redcap was on him and the heavy tool was swung for the Satyr's chest. He dropped with speed, passing unharmed beneath the swing, falling onto his back and, hooking his foot on the rear of the passing scooter he was spun like a top to face the opposite direction and the other approaching attacker. The metal-bar-wielding Redcap thought his colleague had hit the man with both weapon and vehicle, knocking him to the ground and his arm relaxed, until with a graceful spring, the "victim" was back on his feet in a crouched position; one that looked like a well-practiced, battle position. The Redcap's arm tensed again and he reached out to strike, although the lapse meant the blow would contain a lot less strength.

Morningwood

Morningwood gauged the speed, threw himself forward and grabbed at the striking arm, not the weapon, as that could easily be dropped and he wanted to hold on. He had made good contact, the Redcap was stunned at the iron-like grip, his wrist was held as if in a vice, his arm trapped, sandwiched between the man's body and bicep. The thought of escape was upmost in the creature's mind and the velocity of the scooter came too late. Morningwood pivoted, sending the scooter and rider around him in a graceful arc, until it was on the same course as the wrench wielder, before pushing back and down on the captured Redcap. He came off the back of his scooter with force, slamming into the tarmac of the car park, his scooter went soaring into the air gaining speed as it lost the restricting friction of the road. The wrench-wielding Redcap turned, on hearing the strange noise of the scooter engine behind him. The underside of the flying Lambretta caught him full in the body, the impact sending his scooter flipping forward, it's bank of headlights and mirrors shattering on the hard ground, scattering diamond shards of glittering glass across the grey surface before the mess of scooter and Redcap left the fray in sprays of blood and oil.

The lead Redcap had to react, he had no idea what had happened even though he had seen it unfold with his own eyes. One of his soldiers, his loyal attack dogs, was down and still. The other was struggling beneath the grip of what still looked like a geography teacher. The leader gunned his scooter forward, he wasn't going to rely on a weapon, he was going to ram the bastard.

The charge was anticipated and the man stood, the Redcap soldier still trapped by his arm but now also held by his leg. Then like a contestant at the Highland Games the man spun and the body was thrown, squealing at the oncoming vehicle.

The leader swerved, his soldier's flight path wasn't accurate and he flew past to hit a parked car with a crump. It hadn't unseated Spades, but it had changed the angle of the charge, taking the intended victim out of harm's way.

The leader dug his foot in, swinging his Lambretta around in a burning crescent of rubber to face the man.

The two warriors faced off.

One a smartly dressed youth on a gleaming Italian steed, the other a tweed-wearing gentleman who stooped to pick up the lead bar by his feet as if it was a sword. Giving it a couple of trial twists in the air to gauge its weight.

The Redcap not wishing to be outdone, reached into his smart tailored jacket, pulled forth a large flat blade and grinned at his opponent. He was starting to enjoy this guy, and to think moments earlier he'd expected the geography teacher would be a push over, another have-a-go hero. He was even more pleased when the man took up a stance like a baseball batsman or samurai warrior, his iron bar held to one side in both hands, pointing to the sky.

Morningwood however, was feeling the strain of the battle, this body was not as good as the one he had traded it for and he realised if these Redcaps had been more mature and still in immortal form, he wouldn't have stood a chance. His only advantage seemed to be that the Redcap still had no idea of Morningwood's true nature. He had to wait until the Redcap moved and act based on that, he no longer had the energy to attack. He didn't have to wait long, the engine was gunned, the small back wheel slipping side to side before finding traction and shooting forward.

The Redcap was learning from Morningwood's actions, his blade was clasped firmly against the handlebars of the scooter, allowing Spades to keep both hands on the steering, giving it more control if the man chose to side step. He planned to go the weapon side so if he missed, the man could not swing easily into his back as he passed, therefore the blade was held on the right-hand handlebar and the Redcap was prepared to strike low if his victim ducked.

Morningwood waited. Gauging the dip of the blade and the direction of the charge, he stooped slightly, to the Redcap it looked like he stumbled and in a way that was true as he misjudged the new legs not yet used to battle. Then surprisingly, he sprinted forward to shorten the distance quickly on the incoming Lambretta, throwing off the Redcap's angle of attack and jumped. He jumped high, pulling his legs up, a great salmon leap of old. The surprise of the Redcap was glorious as this human left the ground, acrobatically turning in the air above him and he passed beneath. Morningwood swung the metal bar down, hitting the Redcap on the side of his head hard and sending him flying from the scooter as it tipped onto its side and slid to a halt against the previously downed Redcap.

Morningwood landed badly, his ankle twisting painfully. He

Morningwood
wasn't used to fighting without sturdy hooves yet, but he still had to be pleased with the results. As he walked past the stirring leader of the Redcaps, he straddled him and swung the metal bar like a golf club, repeatedly into the creatures back until it was still. He then limped over to the fallen bike and pulling it back onto its wheels he checked for damage then gave chase after Mulberry.

***

Mulberry had left the car park, completely unaware of what was to happen next. From here she knew the rough direction to Greenwich, it was an area she liked to visit with its big park so close to the water. She believed she even knew the bomb site that Morningwood had spoken of, it was quite close to a Shell petrol station she had often filled up at. Of course London had its fair share of bomb sites, the Blitz had been a couple of decades back, but the capital hadn't quite recovered from the constant raids of the German Luftwaffe. Whole communities had suffered and in some respects were still suffering from the blighted undeveloped lands, although they did make good areas for kids to play in.

She soon heard the familiar noise of the Italian scooters as they weaved through the traffic to join her. She had made a decision to not drive fast, give Morningwood time for his plan to work out and she certainly wasn't the only Mini in the London traffic, it was a popular new way to get around the urban sprawl. Who knew, maybe the simple action of just not making herself stand out by panicking might even work to hide her. Mulberry didn't want to tangle with Redcaps whilst alone. She hadn't much wanted to tangle with them whilst they were together.

The mechanical insect-like drone of her pursuers was getting closer and she checked her mirrors. One was driving along the white lines in the centre of the road, getting the occasional horn blast from unhappy motorists coming the opposite way. The other two were slowly working up the gutter side. So she had three following her, Morningwood had done a good job of splitting the pack. She was, however, a bit disconcerted when she realised she had the two scooters with passengers, almost doubling her numbers of pursuing

Redcaps. It seemed she was lucky; they had clearly not taken too much notice of her Mini when it was parked as they were slowing down to examine all the similar cars in the traffic behind her.

A red light before her stopped her progress and the street was suddenly full of pedestrians, holding the hands of children who stared at the traffic rather than looking in the direction they walked. Mulberry smiled when she noticed the old lady from the flats pulling her tartan trolley behind her, the Redcaps obviously hadn't taken it far and she'd got her possessions back. The lady was passed and the lights had started making the quickened bleeping noise to hurry on pedestrians who struggled with the visual image of a flashing green man, and then she was surrounded. The scooters pulled up on all sides. The Redcap on the white lines without a passenger leant down and grinned at her through the side window. She could see his teeth were small and sharp and she hoped it was something he had kept from his change, rather than a conscious effort to file them back into points. On her passenger side, the scooter with the girl in striped, thigh-length socks was parked by her door and behind her the final scooter slipped into the column of traffic. Apart from her forward view she was completely surrounded. It was like having a police escort and she was grateful they hadn't sent a fourth to box her in completely.

The lights went green and she pulled off perfectly, flanked by the accompanying Redcaps. It started to dawn on her, what exactly could they do? She wasn't going to leave the urban sprawl and all these faces watching. Surely they wouldn't, or couldn't lift an aggressive finger, against her? Had that been Morningwood's plan? Send her out from a fairly hidden car park to be safe in the traffic of London? Then she remembered the papers of last year, mods and rockers had taken the time to go down to the beaches of the South Coast and riot. She remembered the pictures, the violence, the arrests, but most of all she remembered the crowds of onlookers, not one lifting a finger and getting involved. She tried to convince herself it wouldn't happen here in the capital. Who would not find it in their heart to stop a gang of youth harassing someone violently? Then her heart sank as she remembered she had done just that with the old lady earlier. If it had been up to Morningwood, the protector of the innocent, they would have been back down in the car park to rescue a tartan trolley, but there were very few Satyrs in this world looking out for people. She looked to the crowds on the pavements of London, a mishmash of preoccupied youth and older folk with heads down. If the Redcaps attacked she was on her own, she'd just have an audience to watch.

The thought process had led her to the next set of traffic lights. They were currently showing amber reminding her it was almost time to stop. She slowed and as the light turned to red, sped up, shooting across the junction. The scooters fell in behind and followed across despite a small blasting of horns. The traffic ahead was congested with no way through and soon she was surrounded again, except that this time the scooter that had been on the inside, moved quickly in front, blocking the car in. The female Redcap, on the back, turned, gave Mulberry the V sign and stuck out her tongue. Mulberry was now their prisoner, the Redcap on the white lines loudly rapping the roof of the Mini and gesturing that she should take the next road on the left.

She was being corralled into a quieter part of town.

The scooter in front slowed until their back wheel was on her bumper, guiding her like a cowboy would a prize cow. They were coming up to the turning when she slammed on her brakes. The scooter behind hit her with a crump, the sudden impact and extra weight of having a passenger tipped the scooter over. Mulberry revved forward, ramming the Lambretta in front past the turn, although they kept their balance and she took the turn at speed. The road was narrow and though she could soon see all the scooters behind her gaining ground, they would not be able to pass. If she could only keep to the narrower roads she had an advantage and could come up with a better plan.

She took a hard blind right and the moment she was out of sight around the corner she stopped. As expected the lead bike took the corner fast and went straight into the back of her parked car. The driver flew over his handlebars, his face smashing the glass of the rear window, causing Mulberry to scream and speed off down the narrow ally. She then saw the other scooters, turning the corner slower with passengers, swerving to avoid the fallen Redcap, the alarming upward bump of one of them suggesting they had ridden over the arm of the casualty, before continuing.

She took the next right turn. It wasn't much wider than a

footpath, but the Mini fitted where so many other cars wouldn't. She didn't stop again, a trick rarely works twice, but instead she sped up, the close uneven walls removing both her wing mirrors and scrapping her paint. She sounded her horn as she neared the exit back onto the main road, a steady blast clearing the path of pedestrians and allowing her to shoot back onto the larger road, take a left and fly. The scooters didn't waste time with horns, they shot through the entrance one after the other to a scramble of people and screams. They had gained a certain amount of speed despite their engine size and thanks to the traffic that Mulberry had to negotiate, they caught up quickly. As one pulled alongside, the passenger jumped onto the back of the Mini. The Redcap in torn stockings was now clung on to the gap where the rear window had once been, she tore off bits of the broken glass and hurled them forward at Mulberry.

Mulberry cursed and swerved the car from side to side, hoping to shake the tick, but to no avail. With the female Redcap in her rear-view mirror and her wing mirrors gone she couldn't see what was going on behind at all. That the swerving had almost taken the, now single occupant, scooter off the road was lost on her, but she could still hear and she could tell from the many sounds, that there were more than two scooters behind her. She cursed again, realising the fallen rider in the alley was also back on her tail. The other Redcaps had heard a third scooter's approach and on an initial glance into their mirrors, had only seen the ride of their leader.

As they passed over the rise of the railway bridge the single rider, a Redcap by the name of Wings, turned to greet his boss. What he got instead was a fist to the face. It wasn't that hard a punch and one a Redcap would have been easily able to bounce back from, but then Morningwood had meant it more as a shove than a punch. The scooter, mounted the path, hit the wall that made up the bridge's sides and the rider was thrown from his Vespa into the railway cutting below. The Redcap missed the live rails and instant electrocution by landing sprawled on the hard sleepers between the tracks, the wind taken from his lungs. The cutting was one of the many that let air into the tunnels of the underground – a brief break of sunshine for the driver before diving back underground. He blinked his eyes open to see a sea of concerned and shocked faces looking down at him, some shouting. He sat up to witness a silver fronted tube exit the tunnel at speed.

The crowd above witnessed the impact, the explosion of meat meeting metal and the shuddering stop of the tube as the engine entered the other tunnel, its breaks screaming.

The other Redcaps were suddenly very aware this new rider wasn't one of their own.

Morningwood saluted and gave them a beaming grin; he was loving the fight despite the lancing pain in his leg. He pointed at the front wheel of their scooter and both Redcaps looked instinctively at the perfectly working device when their quizzical faces looked back up they saw the Morningwood now held a metal bar in his hand, he winked and jammed it in their spokes.

The bike didn't throw them as expected, but the front wheel disintegrated, the scooter fell and the occupants slid along the road like rag dolls, allowing Morningwood to race off and catch up with the Mini and Mulberry. As he approached, he could see the legs of the Redcap girl disappearing through the back window.

In the car Mulberry had the arm of the Redcap girl around her neck, pulling her backwards, choking her, stealing the air from her lungs. The girl was trying to bite off her ear as well, but so far only hot, wet lips had found the lobe. Mulberry put her hand to her waist feeling the cold metal of her seatbelt buckle, the moment her fingers touched it and reassured her mind, she pressed her foot hard on the brake.

The feeling of the Redcap girl flying past was distinctly unpleasant. First her hand came quickly from around Mulberry's neck her nails scraping the exposed nape. Then a heavy belt buckle tore the fabric at her shoulder and left a gash along the soft skin beneath and finally the Redcap failed to break the window as Mulberry had hoped, but instead bounced around inside the car. Several hard impacts against Mulberry's body followed and she felt decidedly roughed up.

The car slowed to a stop and Mulberry's door was pulled open, strong hands came inside and grabbed the Redcap girl, dragging her from the car. Morningwood, slammed the girl against the side of the Mini, hoping to wind her further. The girls arm struck out and a lightning blast of pain went through Morningwood's chest. He saw the glint of broken glass stuck through his jacket and into his chest. He stumbled backwards, the heat of pain growing through his limbs.

The Redcap girl walked forward a booted foot came up fast between Morningwood's legs and he fell to his knees as the nausea rose.

The girl undid the straps of her blood stained leather helmet, red-haired spilled out to her shoulders as she took Morningwood's tie in her hand, pulling him closer in a choking movement, she kissed him passionately and the Satyr could taste her blood on his lips. She stood above him still holding him steady by his tie and raised the helmet like a club above her head.

"You put up a good fight old man," She said with a voice like honey before she flew unexpectedly sideways.

Mulberry stood behind her with a tire iron in her hand, "Bitch." The Nymph snarled.

Morningwood

Chapter 7

Mulberry parked the Mini on the bomb site, beside the boarded up shops as instructed. The street lights were already on and giving everything an eerie yellow glow. As she stepped from the car she surveyed the damage and couldn't help but think by the cold light of morning the Mini would look like it had been abandoned rather than parked.

Morningwood struggled from the passenger seat and joined her. He looked at the car for a bit before moving off.

"I think she'll live, can't say the same about me though." The glass in his chest was causing all kinds of new sensations of pain as it moved with rhythmically with his breathing.

Mulberry sighed and followed the Satyr. The Mini was a brand new car and now it was in bits. It certainly wasn't turning out to be her best day as the Nymph stood next to a blood-soaked Satyr in front of a row of boarded-up shops.

Morningwood fumbled in his pocket and produced a bunch of keys whilst standing before the outside of a cobbler's shop. He unlocked the door and entered the dark interior.

Clearly there had once been a business here and a work bench-come-counter had the indications of product logos and the remnants of stock still evident. Faded patches where machines had once stood were the biggest sign the business was over. Morningwood walked through the shop to the back door and opened it out onto an overgrown garden.

Mulberry followed the Satyr as he walked through the small shop, she closed the front door behind her with a loud click as the deadlocks fell into place. As the shop plunged into complete darkness with only a rectangle of light remaining, like a portal onto the garden beyond, it felt like going home. Then she stepped through and could hear the traffic on the main road again, passing by in front of the shops. The garden was, in fact, the outdoor space of an old London townhouse, protected from the road by the row of shops and the large advertising billboard that had been erected on top of them. The house itself was quite grand, sweeping steps led up to the heavy black wooden front door, flanked by two stone carved female fauns, delicate deer legs and Rubenesque upper bodies. Morningwood placed his hand on the breast of the faun to the left of the door and Mulberry half expected him to press a secret button. She soon realised it was a comfort thing, one of those familiar actions performed to show you're home, as he placed a key in the door and unlocked the house.

"Welcome to my London retreat," he said beckoning Mulberry inside.

The Nymph stepped inside, only slightly disturbed by the bloodied hand print left on the statue, but all thoughts of that were eradicated when the Satyr turned on the light, flooding the hallway and revealing the most beautiful images. It was decadence personified. The walls were decorated with hand-painted frescos, picked out with gold leaf and Gothic swirls. The ceiling was hung with a myriad of ornate birdcages, the doors removed and glass crystal eggs placed within, reflecting the electric light around the walls like the play of sun across rippling water seen through the branches of ancient trees. The tiles on the floor were shaped to appear like interlocking lizards and the sweeping staircase was adorned with an elegant driftwood bannister, washed bone white by the sea.

All this opulence and they hadn't left the hallway. Mulberry was entranced.

Morningwood had already started to climb the stairs and was halfway up before she noticed and started to follow. He was dripping blood on every step and she felt annoyed with herself at how upset she felt at him soiling such beauty. When he reached the top, he pushed open a gleaming white door and painfully reaching up pulled a cord, illuminating a bathroom of colourful ceramic and brass.

Mulberry continued her ascent then leant on the doorway looking in. Morningwood sat on the edge or a roll top bath with bronze, cast lion feet. He was gently touching the shard that protruded from his chest; it had lost its shine and was stained red.

"I think I'm going to need your help," he said with a wince.

Mulberry approached, she didn't really do other people's blood, water had a great way of washing away your sins.

"Should I just pull it out?" She asked unhelpfully, causing Morningwood to give her a long look before answering.

He wasn't sure if she was asking for instruction or mocking him for not just doing it himself.

Morningwood

"I very much doubt I will be able to take my jacket off over it." He said as if giving her a guideline and when she failed to move, he continued. "Just pull it straight out, don't twist it… And use a towel, I don't want you cutting your hands."

She had to smile that even with a shard of glass in his chest the Satyr still thinking of the well-being of others. Mulberry grabbed a monogrammed hand towel from beside the ornate sink then hesitated to use it around the blood.

"It'll wash out or I'll buy new ones," He said quietly when he saw her pause.

Mulberry wrapped the shard in the towel, the blood instantly seeping into the pale fibres as she took a firm hold of the object within.

Morningwood gasped, causing her to let go.

"Oh God, did that hurt?" She said concern etched across her features.

"Of course it bloody hurts. Just get on with it." He hissed through gritted teeth.

Morningwood's anger at her made it easier to carry out the task. Her lips tightened, she could imagine she was stabbing him. She took a firm hold and pulled.

Outside the bathroom window, two roosting pigeons took to the air and flew into the park for a quieter night as Morningwood let out a howl of pain and profanity. He was bent double, waving his free hand at Mulberry clutching his chest with the other. When she failed to get his meaning, he snatched the towel from her, shook free the shard of glass and thrust it into his shirt pressing down on the wound.

"How was I supposed to know what you needed?" She protested as he flashed her another look.

He pointed towards a semi-circular floor to ceiling length cabinet, "There's a first aid kit in there, could you bring it over, please."

Mulberry looked, before walking over like a sulky teenager, "I've been hurt too you know," she mumbled as she pulled open the double doors revealing shelves of towels and one of the general detritus that gathers in a bathroom, even ones as grand as this. She saw a large old beige case with a red cross on it and pulled it free.

"That's it." She heard behind her.

Morningwood had removed his jacket and as she turned, she was shocked how much of his shirt was now red and shining with moisture.

"Oh God, she really got you good." The concern in her voice caused Morningwood to raise his eyebrows.

He painfully slipped the braces from his shoulders and started trying to undo the rest of his shirt buttons. Mulberry watched for a moment before coming over to help, she moved his hand away before her delicate fingers plucked the buttons gracefully from their holders.

Soon the shirt was unbuttoned and she teased it from his trousers so it fell gracefully open revealing his deeply haired chest. She ran her fingers back up through the soft curls to his throat and slid the shirt off his broad shoulders and down his powerful arms, revealing a torso athletic with muscle and marred by scar tissue. She threw the garment onto the floor and opened the case, impressed at the array of bandages and sutures. She selected a needle and thread, stepping past him into the bath and pulling him up to his feet till he too stepped inside and they stood together in the bathtub. She pulled the pale fabric bath curtain around them and removed the hand and towel from Morningwood's chest.

The blood didn't pump at first but oozed like syrup from the jagged cut. Mulberry turned the tap beside her and the shower started to pulse cool water over them both. The blood on the wound broke up and washed slowly away, turning the water pink, revealing the deep pale cut in his chest, so close to the heart. Mulberry effortlessly threaded the medical needle and ran her fingers gently over the wound, biting through the thread as she did so with perfect white teeth. She looked Morningwood in the eyes and he looked warmly down into hers. A small wince passed across his face as she pushed the curved needle through his skin and she playfully growled at him before turning her attention to her work. Her fingers were delicate and skilled and the gash was soon sealed.

Morningwood ran his fingers across her work with a smile, then pulled her beneath the water and wiped the blood from the graze on her shoulder. She flinched at his touch, the wound was sore but shallow, he turned her around so she faced away from him and moved her already growing hair away from the scratches on her neck. They were already close to healing, but he leant in and kissed them anyway.

With the water soaking her dress and bringing about her true nature, the touch of the Satyr sent warmth through her body and blue

Morningwood

swirls of light spinning beneath her skin. She sighed and leant back into the strong body of her former lover. It had been so long since she had felt him this close, this personal. His familiar hands encircled her waist, fingers linking above her naval and pulling her closer, his kisses moving slowly around her neck, till entranced she tipped her head back. The water cascaded across her face and the heavy makeup of her eyes ran in streaks, while his hands ran down her body, pressing the wet fabric of her dress smoothly against her curves. Soon they were on her legs, the warmth of her skin beneath his palms, she sighed as his fingers ran tantalising rivers back up her inner thighs, touching the soft fabric between her legs and sending instant waves of yearning through her. She spun around in his embrace, her hair, now grown half way down her back, whipped behind her and their faces came together, their lips locking in a passionate, heady kiss that robbed them of both breath and senses. His hands cupped her buttocks and lifted her slightly, into the passion of their locked lips before lowering her back to the ceramic bath, his hands rose quickly finding her zip and loosening her dress so it slipped from her body, clinging briefly to her aroused nipples as it fell. The thrill of her naked skin against his chest was intoxicating, she leant back, supported by his strong embracing arm, her breasts thrusting skyward, he sank his head down to take one of the perfect buds between his full lips whilst his tongue flicked playfully; she felt his arousal grow.

The kisses descended down her body as she played in the water. He soon crouched before her, the passion of his kisses focused on the drenched fabric of her knickers. The heat beneath them building as he eased them aside, his hot tongue and questing fingers exploring her body. The joy in his heart rising once again to have his mouth hungrily buried in her soft womanly curls. She felt her legs turn to jelly at his expert touch and leant back against the cold tiles for support. The heat and cold both bringing instant and different pleasures to her skin. She ran her hand through his wet hair, half guiding, half for support.

Her breath started to come in gasps at his continued attentions until she felt the tides move inside her, passion building in waves until she could see only swirling colours. She gasped once more, enjoying the continued sensation before she pushed him breathlessly away. He took the sign and rose back up, lifting her in his arms. She swung hers around his neck and they kissed so deeply she could taste her passion on his lips as he stepped from the bath. He moved from the bathroom and with his foot opened the door to a bedchamber. As he walked into the darkened room illuminated only by the streetlight, he looked as if he were made of bronze. Gently, he laid her on the ornate wooden bed and she playfully wriggled up to the cushions before sliding off her knickers and throwing them at him. He smiled as he removed his footwear then stood to drop his trousers and stand proudly masculine before her. She purred as she remembered the perfect dimensions of his member and how well he had used it, as he crawled, grinning up the bed. She threw her hands above her head, crossed at the wrist as his kisses came. Working their way up her body, making her back arch again and her breath come in short and excited gasps, she couldn't help but giggle uncontrollably at the fun to come.

Chapter 8

The Scene was one of the happening nightclubs of Soho, it didn't have the celebratory ownership of say *Esmeralda's Barn* or the status and clientele of the *Flamingo Club,* but it was still considered to be a happening place and one regularly frequented by those in the know. Tonight it was quiet, a handful of businessmen and wanderers, not in the know, were keeping the waitress staff busy, but the management knew something was up on the streets of Soho and The Faces were staying well out of harm's way.

Howard Barrie was the owner and proprietor of the club and he watched the comings and goings leant up against the mirrored window of his office, head in his hands. After a long while, barely moving, he pulled his fingers down his face, stretching his mouth wide open and yawned, before turning and walking back to his desk, where a larger man sat trying to eat an overfilled sandwich without getting too much down his shirt. Barrie wore a tailored, dark pink, pinstriped suit, yellow shirt and cherry-red cravat. His hair was white and swept about on his head like ripples of ice cream. His face was clean shaven and heavily lined with age. To everyone who knew him well, he was simply "Camp Barrie".

The man in the seat struggling with the simplest of snacks was Johnny Bare and despite the more obvious nickname towards the ursine he was known as 'The Troll'. His suit was also tailored but as a man whose waistline was moving into the realms of moonlike, it looked more off the peg. His dark hair was severely chopped down at the back and sides giving him a mop that sat on top of his head like a nest and he complimented this with a pencil moustache he was extremely proud of because he thought it made him look dashing.

He was Camp Barrie's bodyguard and as far too many suspected – his lover.

"What are you eating?" Asked Barrie with disgust.

"Samidge," replied Johnny, with a spray of crumbs through a mouthful of food.

"I'm assuming you mean sandwich and I could already deduce that from the doorsteps you're grasping so tightly in your beast-like mitt. I was enquiring as to its filling." Barrie continued, his voice a lilting play on words and accent that many would consider estuary speak.

Johnny looked at the offering in his hand as if he hadn't really considered the content of his food before, "Turkey… Or pork?" He added hopefully.

"Well, that's reassuring then." Said Barrie shaking his head.

His thoughts were interrupted by a commotion in the club and he stood and returned to the window. He smiled, his glorious Redcaps had returned. He left the office and wandered up to the booth into which they had all crammed.

They weren't the best of employees – getting them to do the simplest of tasks was a struggle, but on quiet nights he revelled in their gloriously devilish antics. Only five of the normally eight-strong crew sat around the sculpted red table and he could see as he approached that they were far from unscathed. His pace slowed. Now Barrie didn't mind them going off-piste, once in awhile, but only if that meant it didn't interfere with his interests. A beaten and depleted gang was cause for concern.

"What's this?" He said sternly, the camp tone slipping from his voice, his meaning obvious.

"Leave it out Barrie, we've not had the best of days."

The retort came from Spades, the well-dressed leader of this motley crew and Barrie fixed his gaze on the adolescent Redcap. His clothes showed traces of wear and damage not normally present in the Redcap leader, despite his frequent scraps and scrapes. He had a long, dark purple bruise to the left-hand side of his face, and his left eye was bloodshot and red. Barrie's eyes assessed the rest of the pack. Pippi and Zippo, a fairly inconsequential male and female of the species, just seemed sheepish, as if the wind had been taken from their sails. William was actively trying to avoid eye contact with his boss, but a plaster across his ugly nose and two black eyes showed he'd taken a blow to the face and the tailed helmet he held in his fidgeting hands was deeply dented on one side. Finally, Robyn; she was certainly Barrie's favourite, the daughter of a former employee. Her flowing red hair had been shaved to a crew cut on only one side of her head and four, dark black stitches held together a recent head wound.

"Where's the rest?" Barrie asked slowly, a threatening tone seeping into his voice.

Spades leant on the table and fixed Barrie's gaze with his one good and one damaged eye, speaking almost sarcastically, but in the way someone does when they don't really understand sarcasm and instead see it as threatening, "Wing's is dead. Ringer and Harold are in the hospital and they don't think Harold will last the night." The last comment seemed to make William wince and fidget even more. "We've also lost four scooters, so we'll be putting in an order if that's good with you boss?"

His statement made, Spades sat back in the plush padded booth, leaving Barrie stunned momentarily into silence.

"Who did this to you?" He finally found himself say.

"We did it to ourselves," came the voice of Robyn, a bitter tone to her words, before she clarified her answer, "We took on someone we shouldn't have."

Barrie's eyes whipped angrily around to his favourite hired psycho,

"Someone?" He said quietly.

"Some. One?" He said again, his eyes opening wide, his voice becoming manic.

"Some… One?" The Redcaps were used to this irrational voice when the boss got angry.

"Somefuckingone?" He practically screamed, his body shaking and twitching as his voice became like the screeching wind.

William, who was closest, retreated like a dog with its tail between his legs. Suddenly large arms wrapped around their boss. It was The Troll. The large man was whispering calmly the whole time, pulling the twitching Barrie back to the office as he ranted, the patrons of the nightclub watching, until the door shut and the eyes fell on the table of Redcaps. The curious eyes then thought better of their wandering and went back to enjoy the other spectacles of the club.

After a while, Spades snorted and pushing William out of his way walked towards the office, followed by Robyn. They knocked and waited until the door was opened by The Troll. He nodded his head and they both entered. As Robyn walked past, she pointed to a big splodge of pickle on his lapel, as he looked down she flicked her finger up into his face making the gatekeeper of the office feel stupid in the presence of the Redcaps. She was always very careful to make him aware that in the pecking order they came directly below the boss and he was very much below them. It was something Johnny already knew well, he was aware of the nature of his employer and of his employer's henchmen. Johnny was one hundred percent mortal and as for the nickname, 'The Troll' he wasn't sure if it was meant as a compliment or an insult. He assumed the latter. He couldn't talk to any of the other mortals about his knowledge, just the mention of Faeries and they assumed he was talking homosexuality and closed ranks. Continually surrounded by people, he had nevertheless become lonely and isolated in the world, until the small nuggets of affection thrown to him by his boss had made him a loyal hound. The only one who could calm his master when anger took hold.

Johnny never really liked the Redcaps, they made him uncomfortable. He had seen their dangerous ways and how their simplest of actions could inspire biblical rage in others. It was the girls that bothered him most, they could incite whole rooms to battle and then just sit up on a high vantage point throwing bottles into the fray as if they were blowing out kisses. He certainly didn't like them around his boss, they brought out the worst in him, but that didn't stop them being his boss's favourites.

Camp Barrie was sat at his desk, a glass of fine scotch held in his hand as the couple approached; he loved how the Redcaps had been integrated so long into the world of men that they openly bred here. Every year, more little psychopaths entered the school system and changed the course of humanity. Sure, they still had their own change to go through, but they did it quickly and now the stunted soldiers he had enlisted in the Highlands were almost indistinguishable from the youth they grew up amongst, some never really knowing their true nature. Of course, none of them ever grew to be big strapping lads, every time Barrie heard someone described as having 'small man syndrome' he wondered if they hadn't just encountered a Redcap male. For all the anger of the men, the females of the species were most definitely deadlier than the male. The naturally petite Redcap stature was more suited to the body type of mortal woman and it was certainly in vogue, the waspish figures with shapely legs. As forthright and angry as the males, their feisty mindset certainly gave them a step up on all current female attitudes and politics.

Spades was the leader of the pack, he had grown up on a bad estate and would have become a wrong'un, even without his Redcap parentage. He prided himself on his appearance at all times and Barrie knew how much his ruffled suit must be hurting him at the moment. Bruises were badges of honour but poorly turned out threads were a slip in control and showed weakness in the Redcap's eyes. Yes, Spades was tough but he had only known this urban sprawl. If this had been the wilds, he would have had to have watched his back at all times against the upcoming alpha female who currently stood by his side. Robyn was the kind of girl men went wild for. She wasn't a glamour puss or a porcelain doll you had to wine and dine and treat with kid gloves, no, she was a hellcat. One of the lads wrapped up in pretty paper. She had passion and she understood exactly how to use all the gifts that had been given to her.

Barrie was calm, but he still took another big sip of the scotch before addressing them, "Tell me slowly, so I don't miss the fine details. How exactly do I have two of my troops in hospital and one in the morgue?"

He refrained from pointing out how beaten up the rest looked, as they were all painfully aware of that fact.

Spades seemed to be looking for a place to spit out something in his mouth, but on seeing the raised eyebrows of Camp Barrie he swallowed instead before speaking.

"We took on the wrong hero." He said as if the sentence contained all that was needed to be known and the conversation was over.

Of course it wasn't over and Barrie took a lit cigarette from his ashtray, inhaled and blew a cloud of smoke towards the pair before him.

"Enlighten me," he said, his voice starting to take back on the more effeminate tone, from which he took his name.

Spades raised his hands in an elaborate shrug, not sure what more needed to be said and Barrie turned his eyes to Robyn. She cocked her body and put her hand on her jutting hip.

"Like Spades said, we took on the wrong hero."

Barrie threw his glass at the girl, it struck her shoulder and splashed both of the Redcaps with scotch and ice cubes.

"Don't fuck with me." He hissed, "I don't like to be fucked with."

Spades took the cue to answer in greater depth, casually wiping the liquid from his face and clothes.

"It was just some arse from the high rise, proper little have-a-go. Didn't like us messing with some biddy's bag. He just was a little tastier than most of the idiots that step in to impress their girls."

"A little tastier…" Barrie mused, "He's killed one of you, not to mention breaking the rest."

"As I said," continued Spades, "We took on the wrong hero."

Barrie looked at Robyn, who was wiping scotch from her face with a single finger and sucking it clean. He despaired of Redcaps at times, the adolescent ones were the worst.

"So nothing to do with our Mr Moore then?" Asked Barrie as Johnny placed a fresh tumbler of scotch on the desk.

"No idea," said Spades, "You told us to watch from the car park, make ourselves known, make ourselves obvious. If you wanted to know who the geezer's visitors were, we would have sat in his lounge, in the warm."

"This whole affair rests on that man, if he gets nobbled or persuaded otherwise of his actions, then nothing will happen and we don't get our rewards." Barrie took a big swig of scotch and smacked his lips.

"The hero's gone. I stabbed him. Can't see him surviving the night with a wound as deep as I went," added Robyn with a fake pout.

The news cheered Barrie right up, he thought his Redcaps had gone soft, but it appeared they had killed their attacker after all.

Seeing the pleasure in Barrie's face Robyn added detail, "I stabbed him in the chest with a long shard of windscreen, and broke his manhood with my boot before I kissed him and left him for dead."

Of course, the ending wasn't quite the same, but Redcaps weren't known for their sworn statements of fact.

Barrie smiled further before his lips dropped back to a quizzical frown.

"You kissed him? Why did you kiss him?" He was hoping there was a perfectly logical explanation for the very un-violent action.

Robyn's eye sparkled, "Because that's what us girls do with Satyrs, they kind of set you aflame in all the best places."

Morningwood

Chapter 9

Mulberry awoke. She was alone in the bed, but it was still warm and comforting like a cocoon. She hadn't realised how much she had needed the passion, the feel of an immortal inside her. His heavy woodland musk still filled the air and she smiled and kicked her legs happily beneath the sheets. The passion had lasted until the streetlights dimmed and the sun rose. She felt revitalised, her hands went up to her once again short, bobbed hair and traced back over the contours of her body, chasing the fire that still sparkled through her aroused flesh.

She sat up, letting the sheets fall from her, and swung her legs from the bed. With the cold floor under her feet, she walked across to the door, stopping briefly when she noticed her small case had been brought in from the car, a change of clothes ready for her inside. Instead, she slipped naked from the room and descended the stairs, running the sea-worn wood beneath her hand. Its ancient imprisoned salt sparkled against her palm and soon she was back down in the entrance lobby. A smell of food was drifting from an unseen room, further into the house and she followed her nose until she could hear the crackle of cooking and the fragrant smell of wood smoke. She pushed open the door and revealed Morningwood as he stood by the Aga, cooking a fry-up on an impossibly large skillet. He wore a paisley dressing gown but she could see from the dangling belt it was undone. She had to admire his bravery as the pan spat with the cooking fat. She slowly walked into the room and he turned and smiled, appreciating her naked form as she came up behind him and wrapped her arms around his waist, looking into the pan to see a selection of sausages, bacon, egg, mushrooms and black pudding turning brown. She ran her fingers across the neat stitches to check they were still intact, then slid them down to circle his manhood, happy at the warmth in her hands.

"Would you like me to do you some?" He asked, his voice still deep from recent sleep.

She shook her head and went over to the butler's sink, turning on the tap and placing her soft lips beneath and drinking deeply.

Eventually, she filled a glass and waited, sitting at the scrubbed wooden table, until he did up his gown, tipped the skillet's contents onto a plate and placed two slices of bread into the pan to soak up the fat before he turned and sat opposite her. She watched silently as he ate, a proper appetite, worked up from war and desire.

He retrieved the fried bread before he had finished the plate, filled a mug of tea and continued through the mountain of fried goods until his plate was spotless, wiped clean with the crisped bread. She sipped her water as he placed his cutlery on the plate like Vercingetorix at the feet of the conquering Romans.

"Let's go get Alice," she smiled.

"Not yet, we have one last stop before we go. Those Redcaps were practically children and born of this world, there's no way they could have devised a plan, beyond keeping watch of that man's house. I want to go to *The Scene*, find out who's behind them." He stood up and walked to the sink, picking up something from the worktop, before coming back over and placing the postcard of the ruined castle in front of Mulberry.

She could see blood on it and realised it must have been in Morningwood's pocket the night before; apart from that it just looked like a Scottish ruin.

"Is this meant to mean something?" She asked, picking up the postcard and reading the back.

"Look again, but don't see the castle, see the shape," he instructed, pouring himself another tea from his enamelled pot. Mulberry looked closer.

"Is that the Unseelie Court?" She asked, not quite sure.

Morningwood beamed, "Technically it's the ruins of Dounreay Castle in Scotland but yes, it's the mortal echo of the seat of the Unseelie Court."

"Well! That is interesting, I knew when things caused a great impact in either world they created a ghost in the other, an "echo" as you nicely put it. I've seen a few as I've travelled about – most have been small, but the Unseelie court, that's quite a spot."

She went to hand the postcard back to Morningwood but realised she had missed something, the penny dropped instantly, "Jonathon's been there, which means there's a reactor close by. I bet the folks of Scotland gave the building of that a lot of thought and I bet it has an echo below."

She looked at the postcard again, "But surely that wouldn't work?"

She asked, not really to anyone. "That can't be his weapon!"

"Who knows," Said Morningwood, "But I bet if we go have a look at *The Scene* nightclub we might get a better idea of who would benefit if it does."

***

The Mini parked, Morningwood and Mulberry walked the streets of Soho until they stood before the entrance to *The Scene*. During the day, it was an uninspiring door set between two shops, with a fashion boutique to the left called *Hi-Life* and a bookstore to the right, with dark windows and no name. The doorway was covered by a dark red awning, popular with nightclubs; although they always put Mulberry in mind of a pram's concertinaed cover and felt inappropriate. 'The Scene' was written in white in an easily readable font on the material, and either side of the door was a thin-shaped conifer in a sculpted stone pot. This was an attempt to give the entrance class, but cigarette butts littered the soil around the conifers and robbed it of any class at all. The door was closed but not locked. Morningwood opened it and beyond a flight of stairs went straight up. He adjusted the glasses he had put back on and ascended, followed by Mulberry. It was a moment where chivalry was not high on the agenda of appropriate behaviour.

As they reached the top of the stairs, they were met with the club's interior decor. It clearly spread out over several of the buildings below and possibly across the shops on the street behind, as it went back a fair way. Dark red, velour seating booths and flock wallpaper, dotted with a myriad of ornately framed mirrors of all shapes and sizes surrounded them. The dance floor was of a simple hardwood with a stage off to one side and the bar was an ancient-looking wood that had been varnished to a high sheen, with several pump handles secured in place. Behind the bar, the optics were lined up, with rows of the more unusually shaped bottles standing free on glass shelves, the amber and coloured liquids within reflecting back rainbow light.

As they stood in the middle of the dance floor, Morningwood called out a simple, "Hello?"

Almost instantly, a door marked 'Gents' opened up at the side of the dance floor and The Troll exited, struggling with his zip like a child. He became even more flustered when he saw the pair stood before him, Mackintosh coats and an air of authority in their stance.

Before he could speak, a door behind the bar opened and Camp Barrie entered, still wearing the same pinstriped suit from the night before.

"Well, well, well, this is turning out to be a morning. First off I have Ronnie at the bar for shared cups of Joe and Rosie, and now I've got the Horns of Thermopylae in my little club. I gathered after some of my sawdust Caesars limped home last night I might be expecting a visit from a few folk, but it seems I've hit my celebratory wish list. Oh, look at your face cherub... You weren't expecting to see me now were you? And in such fine spirits, and you so far off your perch. Now, what were you doing last time I looked, oh! That's right, helping young boys with their Greek classics. Now, how would I get into that line of work?"

The Estuary speak was back in full flow and Barrie loved the theatre of it all.

Morningwood was none the wiser as to who the mincing man coming out from behind the bar could be, but he hadn't been called the Horns of Thermopylae in a very long time and certainly not since he had taken on mortal form.

"I had no idea you were moonlighting as an agent of FAE" Barrie continued, looking carefully at Morningwood's face as if seeing straight through to the Satyr beneath. His attention shifted briefly to Mulberry, "Oh look they've equipped you with a gadget of your own, how very James Bond. What does it do, warm your bed, then disappear by morning? They think of everything now don't they, that must save you so much time."

Mulberry bristled and surged forward, "I am the agent. Professor Morningwood is here in an advisory capacity only."

The moment she had spoken she knew she had said too much; her buttons had been pushed by an expert. Morningwood hadn't even moved when a gun was placed against his neck, he turned his head slowly to look down the barrel of a service revolver into the round face of The Troll. The face was unmoving and Morningwood didn't doubt for a second the gunman had all the steel needed to pull the trigger.

Morningwood

Mulberry stopped, the words caught in her throat as Morningwood turned his head back to look at Camp Barrie, "You have me at a disadvantage… Sir!"

Barrie laughed, "As I would have been with you if it wasn't for that fabulous musk that entices our female folk so. Little Robyn bobbed home all perky and moist and when she said she'd kissed a Satyr, I knew instantly who it would be."

He took in a deep theatrical breath and tapped the back of his hand against Morningwood's legs, "You've changed so much since we last met." He stopped squarely in front of Mulberry, looked her up and down and sniffed the air, "You don't smell as good."

He turned his back on her and walked away, "You can hide from the mortals Morningwood, but not us. If only your kind liked sharing the same space, I would have had more names to choose from when my little Robyn told me she'd been out playing."

Barrie turned to look at his visitors and stared straight into the grinning face of Morningwood, he had the revolver to the side of The Troll's head and his arm around the big man's throat.

"Oh for fuck's sake Johnny!" Barrie spat, his face contorting as if he was about to cry at the change of command.

"Sorry boss," The Troll almost whimpered, "I don't really know what happened."

Morningwood spoke calmly, "Don't blame yourself. I've been doing stuff like this for over two thousand years. I think you might be new to the game," Morningwood wrinkled his nose, "Although you don't smell so fresh."

The Satyr seemed to have a moment of thought, "Mulberry you wouldn't be a dear and go and lock the front door, please. I'd rather our host's other friends didn't wander back in."

Mulberry grinning again, ran to the door and threw the latch. By the time she returned to the club, Morningwood had sat the two mobsters down on the far side of one of the booth tables and stood with the gun hung down by his side. No need to cover them, it was fairly obvious he could raise it and fire before they got out.

"They're all yours," said the Satyr, pleased with his input so far.

He wasn't an investigator like Mulberry, he wouldn't really know what questions to ask and he had a feeling the Nymph was going to try and dig herself out of a hole and that was clearly an FAE matter.

Mulberry was grateful for the opportunity she realised her partner was giving her.

"Now!" She began strongly, "I believe Professor Morningwood has pointed out we have no idea of who you are and as an agent of FAE it is my duty to find out. You need to know when you despatch Redcaps to cause mischief you're going to get a house call."

"I wasn't aware I needed a licence for them," Barrie said smugly.

Mulberry gave a coy smile as if thinking, 'Hmm! Not a bad idea, Redcap licenses. I'll bring that up at the next meeting.'

Then her face became serious and she fixed Barrie with a stare, "The thing is, we exist on a delicate tightrope on this plane and Redcaps have a way of throwing that off and making it difficult for all. If we get a tip-off to go check on a little gang of them, we don't expect them to be so out of control that they'd try to kill us. Now as you know, at FAE we like to police our own kind and although we have no power over you, Professor Morningwood does have a gun. So I will ask you politely only once. Who are you?"

Morningwood was impressed. She'd done an excellent job of throwing the attention away from Mr Moore, whilst still giving a plausible reason why she needed to know the nightclub owner's immortal identity. He was pretty sure if it had been left up to him, he would have already moved onto beating it out of the nightclub owner.

Barrie shifted uncomfortably.

"I'm known around here as Howard Barrie or Camp Barrie if you like a nickname... which I do." He pointed toward Morningwood, "But he knows me as Conand."

At this name, Morningwood burst out laughing and approached the table, looking close into Barrie's eyes before stepping back with recognition and a grin on his face.

"Is this your new tower?" Morningwood motioned somewhat disparagingly to the club around them, "How the mighty have fallen!"

Mulberry gave Morningwood a look, hoping he would enlighten her. The Satyr was happy to oblige, "To steal Conand's moment of grandstanding, which I know he loves so much, let me catch you up on the history of 'Camp Barrie'," He said the last name as if it was something now to be ashamed of.

"Our host here, and Redcap wrangler, is none other than Conand, former Lord of the Formorians. When our planes first met, he was one of

Morningwood

the many who came across to settle in these lands, but he wasn't a good landlord and his mortal people rose up against him and took his immortal life. Now you would have thought that would be the end of our friend here, but he was too proud to move onto the next life. He chose to join the ever-circling spirits of the Sluagh, the restless dead. When that didn't fill his desires for power, he inhabited the cadavers of those recently deceased and lived their lives."

The Troll gave his boss a new look as if seeing him for the first time and feeling slightly disgusted. He looked back at the man telling the stories to find out just how disgusted he should be.

"I first met him in the body of William De Soulis as he languished in the luxury of Hermitage Castle with his little Redcap assassin," continued Morningwood, "I think that life ended when he betrayed Robert the Bruce, and as far I know from then on he has had a history of underhand crooked little lives. Our paths have crossed occasionally, but now, look at the splendour."

Morningwood chuckled, he placed the revolver on the table top, much to Mulberry's surprise and started walking towards the exit, "I don't think he's worth your precious time Mulberry, his affairs are and always will be in the world of men."

Mulberry looked at Morningwood as he descended the stairs, then at the revolver and finally at The Troll and Camp Barrie.

She didn't quite know what to say, so she quickly ended what the Satyr had started with a stern admonishment, "Try and keep your Redcap's under control."

She walked briskly after Morningwood, joining him in the street.

"Keep walking," The Satyr said when she joined his side, "Don't look back."

The Nymph could see the sense of this but had questions, "Why the hurry?"

"Because he is most definitely our guy and as much as we may have bought ourselves a few hours, it won't be long before he gets twitchy and starts to think about moving Alice. Don't forget he knows where she is," Morningwood spoke quietly as they walked, his voice barely audible above the clip clop of his shoes.

"So his schemes aren't just based in the world of men then?" She asked, although she was already quite sure of the answer.

"Far from it. He's been trying to get back into The Court's good graces since his death." They reached the car and climbed in.

"Are you ready to go home?" said Mulberry looking carefully at Morningwood.

"Not really. But I don't see another choice."

***

In the nightclub, the office door opened and Barrie's Redcaps filed out quietly to form a semi-circle in front of the table behind which he still sat, thinking.

"So do you think he's onto you?" Said Spades, annoyed he had been ordered to wait in the office watching silently through the one-way mirror.

Barrie looked the Redcap up and down, he had changed since last night and wore an even more tailored Italian suit. One that would have looked magnificent if the Redcap hadn't insisted on sticking a circular cotton dressing across his bloodshot eye with a cross of medical tape. He looked like a Mod Pirate.

"Of course he's onto us. That girl said he was here as an expert. The only thing that old goat is an expert in, is how to get the knickers off the likes of her and protecting so-called innocents."

"Seemed pretty tasty at getting the gun out of The Troll's hand… and he can have my knickers off any day," added Robyn, with a dirty laugh and high-fived Pippi, who seemed to be on the same carnal wavelength as her Redcap sister.

Barrie gave the girls a look and they came to some kind of order although their lustful giggling continued.

"Spades, I need you to go to the Rothborn estate, find out where those posh idiots actually put her and take her all the way through, and well… finish her. If you see either Morningwood or that girl, finish them too. Let's not take any risks this time."

Barrie could see his plan slipping away if he didn't take charge of the situation quickly and the Redcaps were the best security he had.

Spades smiled like the cat who had got the cream, he loved this new plan, it was far more up his street, so much better than hanging out in a car park.

"Can we kill the posh blokes too?" He asked hopefully.

Barrie knew his psychopaths well and could almost have predicted that question, "If you have all the information, you can eat them if you want, then dye your hats red in their entrails. In fact, I insist on it."

Spades glee was building and now he too was lustfully giggling. It was Ringer that spoke up next. He felt a few steps behind, as he'd only just got out of the hospital that morning, his arm was plastered and in a sling and he'd had to deliver the bad news to William that his brother Harold had died in the early hours.

"How exactly do we get into the Underland?" He asked, hoping the question hadn't been answered whilst he was away being patched up, "We were exiled, one-way ticket deal."

The comment was the first sensible one any of the Redcaps had made in a while and it brought them to silence, all eyes on the nightclub owner.

"Well that's the beauty of it, they'll think you can't. However, your race weren't exiled as a species; the humiliation was to be that of every individual, so it was done on a personal basis. Your ancestors were exiled, each and every one of them. We say 'The whole race' because it was, but on a technical loophole you reprobates were all born here so you can return anytime you like. Just nobody told you," Barrie announced triumphantly, it was knowledge he'd held onto for just such a happy occasion.

The Redcaps all started grinning.

"How do we break the veil though?" Asked Pippi.

The Redcaps all started nodding to each other, the knowledge was old and lost to their generation.

Barrie grinned evilly, "Delight in your carnage my dears. You tear those rich boys apart well enough in that weakened area and the veil will fall off the bone like well-braised steak."

Chapter 10

Morningwood sat with a large leather satchel open on his lap, looking thoughtfully at the contents inside, going through his mental checklist.

"You've been very quiet," interrupted Mulberry, "are you worried you've forgotten something?"

Morningwood closed the bag, "Only my common sense," he added with a touch of sorrow to his voice.

The comment stopped Mulberry's attempts at conversation dead, she had no idea what must be going through the Satyr's mind. He had been self-exiled, as far as she was concerned, since the first moment the two planes had met. A Satyr's nature had always been curious, they were wanderers and the moment they had new worlds to wander they took the steps needed to explore. It had not been the first time their plane had passed another, but it had been a long time. When the world of the mortals first joined with their world, the stagnation for many of the livelier of their kind was evident; they just had to get out, like kids seeing a glimmer of sunshine after a long rainy day indoors. The Immortals had always been creatures of nature, they hadn't needed a name for everything, to the point that they were no good at naming things, categorising a world that just – was. But the mortals had named everything they came in contact with and by doing so changed everything. It was most intoxicating to the Satyrs to be given names and to be made unique by these bright lives that burned out so quickly. The simple act of naming had been a gift so great it had made them unquestionably loyal to the mortals. The mortals became known as the innocents, their lives too short to be anything but that, and the Satyrs became their protectors.

War had also not been known amongst the immortals, they had lived side by side in peace for aeons. Only the Redcaps took lives, as it was their nature to destroy. This was deemed wrong and the Redcaps were rounded up and imprisoned before being banished to the new plane. To everyone, this should have been the end of it. However, with each new name given, they became gods to the mortals and in turn to themselves. This perceived power gave them something to fight for and a great war started amongst the ones who called themselves Seelie and the ones who did not. The Seelie accepted the godhood that was thrust upon them by the naming and the Unseelie rejected it. The plane that had no name became the Below, the Underworld or the Otherworld and for the first time in its endless history it found unrest. A brutal war that inspired the wars of men as it seeped into their dreams. Eventually, a truce was founded and the Seelie chose to depart their Otherworld home to live forever on the land of man. They walked amongst the mortals, introducing knowledge and taking mates amongst them. These unlikely unions produced offspring that were tainted. Great malformed giants started to walk the land, feared by the mortals and protected by the immortal parents. The occupation of this plane became so one-sided in its relationship, some of the mortals questioned the Seelie being amongst them at all and rose up to drive them back to the Underworld. The Seelie did not wish to go and were too hard for mere mortals to fight. So the Men turned to the Satyrs for help and they joined the armies as great warriors and teachers and drove the Seelie back to their own plane and banished the giants to a distant planet.The two courts of the Otherworld agreed the Seelie had become overly arrogant amongst the mortals and they accepted their defeat and chose to stay below. The Satyrs chose to stay above as a deterrent against either court returning to the world of mortals, pledging to remain until the last days of connection or beyond, protectors of the innocent. They were neither considered heroes nor villains in the Below world, they had simply followed their nature as was expected. Even so, it was believed by many, that every Satyr held in their heart a sadness that they had risen up against their own. Mulberry knew this, every Otherworld spirit knew this and right now Morningwood was choosing to travel back into that land to save just one innocent and perhaps by association all of the Underworld.

"It'll be okay," she said, almost unconsciously, "I'll be with you."

Although he said nothing, the words were a comfort to the immortal Satyr.

They drove into the grounds of the Rothborn estate. Gravel started to crunch beneath the tyres until they were parked at the front door of a large sandstone coloured country pile. Mulberry had not used this entrance before, preferring to take a gateway that led straight onto the estate, a field where the deer grazed by the edge of a dark wood.

She had chosen to avoid the splendour and walk across the landscaped gardens to the incident, but Morningwood was all for the front door. He had insisted on it. He wanted the young Nigel Rothborn to know he had come to sort out his error, his act of hedonistic pleasure for unknown treasures.

As they got out of the car they were instantly hailed by a voice behind them, a posh female voice.

"Hello there!" It said in a friendly greeting and they turned to see a young woman of about Nigel's age walking across the manicured grass before the house.

She wore a sensible jumper, tight jodhpurs and riding boots. She was plump in a pleasant way and kept warm in the late autumn sun with a flat cap and body warmer.

"I saw you coming up the drive," she said happily as she approached and upon reaching them put her hands on her hips, thumbs into the small of her back and arched dramatically with a happy breath-filled sigh, thrusting her ample jumper covered bosom forward. Morningwood smiled despite himself. "Just been brushing down Samson, took him on a long, energetic ride this morning and thought I'd end it with some pampering."

The words were said in the wonderful way Morningwood felt all girls of privilege spoke, as if you were already privy to one hundred percent of their life and, therefore, needed no explanation or details. It did leave Morningwood wondering if Samson was her horse or her stable boy and by the rosiness of her cheeks it could easily have been either.

"We're here to see Nigel Rothborn," Mulberry said with seriousness, cutting through the chit chat.

The official tone of her voice prompted the woman to look at them properly for the first time.

"What's Cousin Nigel been up to?" She asked almost knowingly, as she walked past them towards the side of the house. "Always causing problems whilst his Mother and Father are away. Seems to think it makes him Lord of the Manor and he can get up to any old tomfoolery." She carried on walking, "You best follow me, he's in the kitchen."

Morningwood made an elaborate gesture to Mulberry that she should go first and the two of them followed the woman through a side gate and down an alley until they reached an ordinary door at the top of two stone steps.

"I doubt Uncle Bart will ask you to remove your shoes, but I'd give them the once over with the boot scraper before you go in. Aunty Flick is a bit funny when it comes to mud on her floors." The woman pointed at a piece of ironwork beside the door and dutifully the couple ran the soles of their shoes across it, despite having only just arrived by car.

All three entered a hallway and the young woman removed her riding boots, calling out as she did so, "Uncle Bart, Nigel has visitors."

A deep posh voice called out from quite close, "We're in the

Morningwood

Kitchen Millie, we have the dogs with us." The last part of the shouted response sounded like a warning.

The woman now identified as Millie turned around with a smile, "You're not afraid of dogs are you? It's just Benji is a bit of a bounder and likes to jump up."

Both of then shook their heads in answer and then followed Millie into a door on the right of the hallway.

Inside, the room was very similar to the kitchen at Morningwood's townhouse. A cooking range on one wall beside the sink and draining board, a big window overlooked a sculpted private kitchen garden and the room was dominated by a big table. At the far end of the table sat a very stately looking country gentleman, wearing a jumper most people would have seen as rags, showing the mustard plaid shirt beneath, through its many holes. Beside him at the table was Nigel, a big colourful bruise on his cheek. He was cradling a cup of steaming liquid in his hands and turning to look at Morningwood and Mulberry his eyes opened wide in shock, begging the question; how much had he failed to tell his father. Also in the room were two other lads, both gangly and posh looking, they were leaning against various bits of furniture and they both had their heads bent as if in the middle of a scalding. A big black Labrador with a grey muzzle stood up from its basket in front of the cooking range and plodded over, a more excited younger dog of the same breed appeared from under the table and approached at speed. Morningwood raised a hand and both dogs sat before him, much to the surprise of all.

"Well I never," said Lord Bertram Rothborn, genuinely taken aback, "Never seen them do that before. I see my dogs as free agents, but it seems even they know authority." He looked at the pair stood in his kitchen, "And how may we assist you today officers?"

Morningwood realised the FAE must go from one place to another just expecting people to accept they were meant to be there and he had to admit it seemed to work.

Mulberry spoke, "We're sorry to interrupt Lord Rothborn, but we need a word with your son," she said, nodding her head towards Nigel, suddenly aware all of the boys could be his.

The lord spoke happily as if this would take a great load off of his plate.

"I was just giving them a talking to myself. You don't expect to return from Switzerland to find you have had the police on your property, tends to give a bad impression. No, you go ahead officers; I'll take the dogs for a stroll." The lord stood awkwardly and walking past the dogs he gave a cheery, "Come on boys!"

Neither of the dogs moved until Morningwood gave a subtle nod of his head and both shot after their master. Morningwood looked at Millie, who was staring intently at him, a distant look in her eyes. She noticed he was looking back at her and suddenly snapped out of it standing bolt upright, blustering and blushing.

"Yes… sorry… I'll go with Uncle Bart," she said in confusion and started to move, "I'll just close this behind me," she said, pulling the door closed, leaving the duo in the room with the would-be occultists.

This time there was no cheek, just faces looking down at shoes.

Mulberry continued as if the asking the lord to leave had all been part of her conversation, "Right gentlemen. Although I don't believe you to be gentlemen; I am even struggling with the fact you might be men. We have spoken to Howard Barries at The Scene and he confirms your story. He added, however, that it was an elaborate plot to later try and extort money from you all."

The lads in the room shifted uncomfortably.

"The girl was handpicked by Mr Barrie because she was in on the whole ruse. They were going to tell you they had the remains of the girl you believed yourselves to have killed, and then they were going to threaten to give them to the police if you didn't pay up."

One of the lads started to sob quietly.

"Now, unfortunately, because of the quick involvement of the police, we cannot arrest Mr Barrie for blackmail as he had failed to actually blackmail you. We have however given him a rap across the knuckles and we will be watching him."

Mulberry was enjoying the effect her words were having on the gathered lads and really started to fall into her storytelling role.

"This time you have been very lucky. A cocktail of clever conmen and strong narcotics led you down a bad path and you did something stupid. You will not do anything like this again, you will not try to contact Mr Barrie or return to his club or any other clubs in Soho. Do I make myself clear?"

The boys all nodded sheepishly.

"I'm sorry, I didn't hear you. Do I make myself clear?" A series of

Morningwood

mumbled yeses followed.

"Good. Now my colleague and I are going to have a brief chat with Lord Rothborn and then spend the day searching the grounds for something that may incriminate Mr Barrie further. Whilst we are doing this we do not expect to see any of you at all. Is that clear?" She said firmly and again came the mumbled yeses.

For a moment the room was quiet, then in a more upbeat manner Mulberry spoke again, her sudden snappy dialogue made one of the lads jump, "Right! Let's go search the grounds," she briskly opened the door and left the kitchen, a proud and smiling Morningwood in tow.

***

Finding Lord Rothborn and Millie was easy; they were only just outside on the raised patio area throwing a ball for the dogs. They were with Lady Rothborn, who had clearly been already outside, sat at her wrought-iron, garden table reading a book. The couple explained that the incident of the other night would require another search of the grounds and also told the concerned parents how the boys had been led astray. They asked for privacy and also asked if Mulberry's Mini could remain here for a day or two as they would be meeting up with officers at the bottom of the grounds and would be unable to return to pick it up for awhile. The Rothborn's were more than happy to oblige, even saying they would get their son and his friends to give it a thorough clean and wax. With this all agreed the family had retired with the dogs inside leaving Mulberry and Morningwood to explore the gardens.

***

Morningwood was admiring the fountain's central plinth, "You have to admit they do like to see a cheeky Satyr in their art. I think it's an acceptable form of pornography for well to do ladies – to get a well-chiselled torso and distracting phallus amongst their roses."

He turned to face Mulberry, she was stood in the most out of sight area she could find and was stripping from her clothes. He watched happily until she made eye contact and stood up in just her striped knickers, hands on hips.

"Are you going to get ready?" She asked, "This is the thinnest part of the veil, made thinner by their ritual. You were the one that said speed was important... Remember?"

Morningwood stood, prompting Mulberry to carry on and slip from her knickers, standing as naked as she could get.

"How exactly will you pass through?" She asked, genuinely curious.

"Same as you, by succumbing to my nature, of which I have two, both involving a full bush," he grinned.

Mulberry shook her head, "Well you'll have to use the leafy variety because this bush is going for a swim. She smiled, "I'll see you on the other side handsome." And without waiting, she dived into the fountain and was gone.

Morningwood was once again alone, he had been dreading this part but was glad Mulberry wouldn't be around if he hesitated. He removed a dark blue tunic from his satchel and stripped from his clothes, happy to feel the play of the cooling air on his skin. He slipped the simple tunic on, a fold of cloth went over one shoulder and a skirt that covered his torso. Picking up his and Mulberry's clothes he placed them all in the satchel, before standing before a great, small leaved privet hedge behind the fake Greek columns.

He took a deep breath and then stepped forward. For a second, the hedge had the same solid feel as you would expect of any well-maintained garden shrub but then it seemed to sense what was pressing against it and it opened, embracing the figure before it, pulling him in as he walked. It wasn't easy, it was still pushing through tightly grown branches and interlacing leaves. The lower branches which had grown thicker and stronger, hooked his legs, grazing his skin and tripping him. The smaller upper branches tangled in his hair where they pulled and tugged, turning his head one way and the other but he still forged on.

Soon the leaves grew darker in colour, larger in size and alien in shape. His leg hooked once more on a low branch that held his foot tightly, he pulled it free and stepped forward. What hit the ground were no longer the sensitive toes, but a firm graceful hoof. Morningwood smiled, he had missed the elegant, strong appendages more than he could say, he stepped forward and again the same pull on him produced another hoofed limb. He ran his hand up to push a

Morningwood

stubborn branch from his head, but instead found tangled in the leaves his horns, curved and ridged and with one powerful thrust of his strong neck they were free and he was walking happily, unhindered by the foliage around him. He raised a hand to his face, the features subtly changed, the nose swept more smoothly up to his hairline with no dip before forehead, his eyes were slightly more almond in shape and his face angular. His skin had become darker, no longer a play of the shadows but browner and with swirls like the bark of wood. He stepped from the bush through which he had passed, to stand beside a great, still lake. Twisted trees grew thick down to its sides, their roots exposed like gnarled legs, as if the forest was a vast walking herd come to drink at the tranquil oasis. He was stood on a jutting ivory rock veined as marble, protruding like a broken tusk above the cool waters, a fantastic, handsome creature of the alien forest.

He smiled at the familiar rich orange light, the smell of the glorious air, the myriad of strange seeds and bizarre insects that floated above the dark waters, casting shadows and ripples as they dipped down into the still waters of the deep lake. He threw back his head and bellowed like a rutting stag and the birds and beasts of the forest rose in a crescendo to welcome him back.

***

Mulberry had hit the water with glorious purpose, her dive had been grace personified and as she swam down through the layers that divided the worlds, her spirit shone through. The water caressed her hair out into dark tendrils that flowed around her. Her shapely body became smoother and swirling blue lights moved within her flesh, illuminating the space around her with a delicate inviting light. Her fingers became gossamer-webbed and her ankles developed beautiful fins.

The bubble lay before her, illuminated by her glow and she drifted alongside it, gentle flicks of her legs keeping her in place, as she placed her webbed hands against its surface and examined the woman contained peacefully within. Still the girl slept, as perfect as a slumbering child. The arcane symbols of blood daubed on her body seemed to pulse with their own organic flow, as if a heart still fed the life-giving liquid. Mulberry could taste the perfection of the girl even through her prison walls. Her own body reacted, a shiver ran up her spine and the skin along its length beaded as if pearls had been placed beneath the surface. From each, a sharp point pushed up until a dorsal fin that would have been the envy of any angel fish, moved in the water like a cape.

If she were alone with the girl much longer, Mulberry could not guarantee her actions, so she started to push. The bubble sank lower or rose higher, depending on your perception, and as it did so, Mulberry pressed down her fingers playing into its surface. It was like flesh beneath her hands, malleable and warm – the more she massaged, the more she wanted to tear it apart like an overripe fruit, desperate to get to the soft flesh beneath. She pressed her fingers in sharply, the bubble burst with a pop, water rushing to fill the space. The shock was like a slap in the face to the Nymph, the fin disappeared from her back, instantly pulled back into her spine like an anemone retracting its feelers. The water cold and circling, washed the blood from the girl's pale skin, swirled her hair and brought her to her senses.

Alice awoke.

For a second the girl was in darkness, unaware what had happened. What fevered drug induced dream she had woken from? Was she still sleeping? Was she awake in an unfamiliar room? She felt weightless, she felt cold, then her senses told her she was in water, submerged, disorientated… drowning. She panicked, a scream issued from her lips as a stream of shapeless bubbles.

Then she saw the light, an angel come to take her, to save her?

Mulberry was startled at first, the panic was an alien reaction to her for water was a friend that held you. Then she gathered her own senses and swam forward, placing her hands on the girl's shoulders, an unknown face but with calm eyes. It occurred to the Nymph that Alice might not make the surface now she had robbed her of her protection. She pulled her close until their bodies became almost one and pressed her lips against the girl's, giving her air, filling her lungs, tasting her purity. Mulberry fought her hunger for the innocent with all her strength as she kicked her powerful legs sending them both to the surface. Her eyes wide, her heart beating fast, Alice felt she must still be in a dream, a perfect specimen of femininity holding her tight,

Morningwood

keeping her alive as they rose up in the sphere of blue light. The water grew warmer, lighter. Mulberry broke free of the air-giving kiss and they ascended together, towards the surface.

***

Morningwood, revelling in the welcoming smells of home, stood watching the giant green disks of the native foliage, drift lazily about the dark sinkhole of the mouth-like pond. He saw the bubbles break first on the calm surface, sending circular ripples to crash gently with each other like tiny conflicting tides. Then the shapes beneath the water rose rapidly and two beauties broke the surface, gasping for air, heads thrown back like the greatest cries of pleasure and the Satyr smiled as once again the forest answered.

Mulberry swam quickly over to the panicked girl, gently brushing wet hair from her face making eye contact and flashing a warm, friendly smile. She wrapped a supportive arm around the girl's waist in case she couldn't swim, but as she felt the girl's legs instinctively kick and her hands circle she gracefully let her go. No words had yet been spoken, but the girl's eyes opened wide, a mix of fear and wonder as she looked past Mulberry towards the bank, causing the Nymph to turn and marvel herself on the Satyr for the first time. He was magnificent and she swam over to greet him. He crouched to meet her, like a knight bowing before his lady and she took his arm in her hands.

"How were you?" He asked supportively, reminding her how much he knew and causing her to blush.

"I almost…" she started to say but tailed off embarrassed

"You did well to control yourself," he looked up at Alice and smiled; she smiled back despite herself. "She is indeed a treasure."

Somehow comforted but still confused, Alice swam over, she knew it was a dream but it felt so real, "I'm Alice." She said, hoping to sound friendly and both the creatures of mythology turned to face her.

"We know," said Morningwood with a grin, "We're here to protect you."

Alice looked between the smiling faces, happy at least one spoke

English.

"Is something after me?" She asked looking fearfully behind her to the dark water.

"It's in front of you that the problems lie and that, I'm afraid, is your only route home," spoke up Mulberry, making Alice even happier that both her dream companions spoke.

"Like Dorothy in Oz?" Alice smiled.

"I would have gone for Alice in Wonderland," laughed Morningwood, "but then I can often be accused of being too literal."

He reached down and pulled the naked form of Mulberry from the water. She practically skipped onto the rock beside him and then he reached his arm forward to Alice.

"But I'm naked," she said blushing.

"I'll try to control myself," said Morningwood with his continued laughter. He patted the satchel, "I also have clothes."

Reassured, Alice grabbed the offered arm and the strong Satyr lifted her from the water. She covered her embarrassment with wet arms. For some reason, she felt drawn to the horned creature and she would prefer his first view of her were not parts she'd rather reveal later… alone.

Morningwood handed the girl a pre-folded arrangement of fabric not too dissimilar to a toga and like the gentleman he certainly wasn't, turned to face the water whilst she slipped it on. Alice tried to make conversation to hide her blushes.

"So nothing is after me then?"

"Oh, I wouldn't say that," Mulberry said, helping adjust the tunic for modesty, "Just nothing that can follow us."

Morningwood
Chapter 11

The night was already starting to draw in on the rolling countryside around the Rothborn estate. The road that went past the front of the house always got darker earlier than the rest of the surrounding area, as the trees had grown into a natural tunnel above its winding curves. Through the night, a sound like swarming bees echoed around the tightly packed trees and then a single light appeared at the far end of the darkness, quickly joined by three more. In the gloom, it was like two great insects with glowing eyes were flying down the woodland tunnel just above the tarmac. As they got closer merriment and laughter could be heard and indistinguishable voices shouting excitedly over the sounds of the engines. Spades was riding in front, he had been let off the leash with his masters blessing and he planned to hurt all in his path. His scooter was unscathed, but it felt soiled, knowing someone else had been behind the handlebars.

He never let any of the others ride his scooter. Robyn and Pippi weren't even allowed to ride behind him on the long seat. Harold had once sat on that seat when they were parked and Spades was away relieving himself. On his return, Spades hadn't said a word but almost killed his gang member for the transgression, leaving Harold with a scar he had taken to the grave.

William, Harold's brother, was riding Wing's old vehicle, its rider gone to wherever Redcaps go when they die. He hadn't wanted to ride at all, but Ringer had his arm in a cast and had asked to ride behind the recently bereaved brother, in a show of solidarity.

Zippo and Pippi still rode together, as had always been the way, but in a change to the lineup Robyn was now on a ride of her own, she had claimed the scooter that had killed Harold – William's old Vespa. William had refused to ride it ever again, in a sentiment that almost had Spades slit his throat with a switchblade for showing weakness.

Spades didn't like the fact Robyn now had her own ride; he didn't like her independence. She was already a loose cannon, but he wanted blood more than he wanted to stop a challenge to his leadership and he was very aware she wanted to be the boss. They hovered briefly by the entrance of the Rothborn estate, bunching in a little group by the open gates. There were no markings or indications what estate it was as most landed gentry didn't feel it was good etiquette to announce your presence on the landscape. Spades made the decision this was the right place and drove straight in. He didn't care if it wasn't; he knew they were close enough to the weakening of the veil and he was sure that enough carnage wherever they were would open the Way Through.

The broken green Mini however, was all the proof they needed that this was indeed the right place.

Inside in the living room, Lord Rothborn stood up and walked to his radio, turning down the volume and standing still until Lady Rothborn looked up from her book.

"What is it, Barty?" Even the dogs were looking at their master, happy confusion on their faces.

"Just wondered what that awful noise was," said the lord, still straining his ears.

"I think they call it Jazz." Said Lady Rothborn, leaving Lord Rothborn to wonder if she was making a joke, was truly just adding an opinion on his musical taste, or repeating a fact she had recently learned. He was about to turn the radio back up when there was a loud knock at the door.

Lady Rothborn turned in her chair, "Who could that be?" she asked as if her husband would know the answer.

He simply shook his head, "I'll go check, shall I?" He said sarcastically, knowing if it was anyone important or invited it would be for his wife, but heaven forbid she would answer the door.

He left her alone in the room for the first time that night and instantly she crossed to the radio, taking the opportunity to shut off the noise that was disturbing her reading.

The announcer in a perfect radio voice and despite the low volume could still be gently heard to say, "…the ukulele styling of Cliff Edwards."

Lady Rothborn stopped, her hand resting on the dial, "Oh, I like him," she said wistfully as the music started to play.

***

Lord Rothborn was walking across the hall, beneath the sweeping stairway hung with dark old paintings. He had already realised it couldn't be a friend of his at the door as they would have just walked in through the back and shouted out. It either had to be a friend of his wife's or heaven forbid, a salesman. Although salesmen often had more sense than to call on the big house, everyone knew the big house had no real money, that's why he was answering the door himself.

A voice hailed him from the stairs, "It could be for me, Uncle Bart." The lord turned to see his niece Millie waiting on the stairwell, he had forgotten she was in the house. She had accompanied his wife on a skiing trip to Switzerland while he was doing business in the country and had decided to stay with them on her return. The lord stopped his approach to the door.

"Do you want to get it then?" He asked, not sure why he had been stopped in his tracks if she didn't and pretty sure what she was wearing wasn't appropriate to be receiving guests in.

Millie twisted on her bare feet, "Oh no Uncle, that wouldn't be polite, it's your house."

The lord turned back towards the door, shaking his head, he wasn't sure what it was with aristocratic women and their inability to answer doors. He had travelled the globe and every woman below aristocracy saw it as their duty to answer the door, so their husband was not disturbed from his radio programmes. Apparently that luxury was reserved for the middle and working classes only.

The door was knocked loudly again.

"Hold on, I'm coming," Lord Rothborn said sternly. He was rather hoping it was a salesman now so he could give him a piece of his mind at the impudence of a double knock.

He opened the door.

Spades didn't like to be kept waiting, so the moment he saw the face of the older man appear at the opening portal, he hit him and he hit him hard. The brass knuckles he wore were his favourites and the moment of violence, like all these actions to the Redcaps, slowed down so they could savour every second. The older man's face hadn't changed; it didn't even get a chance to register surprise. His mouth had been open as if he was about to speak and the vicious weapon broke the exposed teeth sending a spray of blood up the man's face to add a bit of colour to the drab paleness of his features. Spades was happy that somewhere beyond the doorkeeper someone else had been watching, which meant his entrance had not gone unnoticed as a womanly scream filled the air.

His Redcaps flew past him on both sides, throwing the door wide as the man fell and Spades bent to punch him at least once more before he hit the floor, bringing his fashionable winkle picker shoes in for several sharp kicks after he had landed.

"Search the house," he bellowed at his Redcaps and was pleased Pippi was already dragging down a fleeing girl on the stairs, laughing hysterically like a hyena bringing down a wounded antelope, "I want them all," he shouted gleefully.

Spades grinned as his Redcaps dispersed. He bent down beside the whimpering Lord, pulling forth his nasty blade as he crouched, "I'm gonna open you up," he whispered. "You're my door now," and he rapped his knuckles playfully on the scared man's forehead.

***

Spades liked this room. It was perhaps a study or maybe a reading room. He didn't actually care. He just knew it wasn't one the family used. You could smell the dustiness of it, the stale air. Even the window shutters were permanently closed giving the impression the room had not seen sunlight for months. It was, therefore, *his* room, a cocoon of darkness he had opened up and flooded with violent light. The fire in the grate burned fiercely, stoked with the books from the shelves and anything that his Redcaps had broken, which was turning out to be much of the room's contents. Spades now sat in the only remaining chair, the one that made him believe this was where people came to read. It was high-backed, leather-upholstered and had drawers in the arms where game's pieces were neatly stacked.

Spades had on his lap a box of dominoes, open and half-empty. The rest of the rectangular ivory pieces littered the floor before him. Also, more importantly, before him were three young men, one weeping girl and a stoic Lady of the Manor who refused to break eye contact with the Redcap as he sat like a king on his throne. All of them were on their knees and each of them had a Redcap stood beside them.

Lord Rothborn was in a display cabinet. The shelves had been broken out and thrown on the fire and the glass door stood wide open, showing the lord hung by his hands in its interior, his shirt open and

Morningwood

his bare chest already bruised and bloodied.

Spades took another domino from the box and surveyed the room as he turned the piece over in his fingers. The glass eyes of many taxidermy animal heads looked down at him. A large tapestry of a man in a pith helmet, shooting a leaping lion, graced the far wall, the openly racist portrayals of his native camp followers showed them huddling in fear behind the great white hunter, whilst a final dark-skinned body lay face down beneath the leaping lion, it's obvious victim. Spades turned on the lady of the manor and flicked the ivory domino from his fingers so it struck her on the cheek, causing laughter to ripple through his soldiers.

"A family bathed in blood," the Redcap said pulling another piece from the box, "How fitting."

He looked around the kneeling prisoners, all in a state of bloodied and bruised dismay and flicked the second domino, striking Nigel, "Bring me the fat one," he commanded.

Ringer was stood beside Nigel, the aforementioned fat one, the Redcap half dragged him to his feet and threw him forward so he landed sprawled before the leader.

Spades didn't even look at him, he just spoke, "Tell me fatty. How did that ceremony go again?"

Nigel said nothing at first but then words started to flow, mumbled into the floor. Spades shook all over with excited energy at the power this prone lad made him feel, he could barely hear what the boy was mumbling into the ancient carpet but didn't care. He knew the ceremony off by heart, as the original plan had been for Spades and his pack to kidnap the girl and push her through into the Underworld. As a plan, that had shown no finesse and left too short a chain back to Camp Barrie. Barrie had an ancient vendetta against the Rothborn's from a previous incarnation, so he had cruelly chosen them to be his fall guys if anyone came sniffing around.

The boy stopped his mumbling, causing the Redcap leader to look down, realising he'd missed it all, "So to recap, you beheaded a goat and marked yourself with its blood, drawing on your human sacrifice the arcane symbols to open up the Underworld. All the time under the watchful eyes of its severed head…" As Spades spoke, Nigel started again to mumble into the floor like a holy man speaking in tongues.

"…with this very blade?" Continued Spades, pulling a long curved knife from beside his throne and standing beside the lad.

Taking the blade in both hands, he struck down with force, his eyes burning with an inner rage and the mumbling stopped abruptly.

Lady Rothborn's voice rose up in dismayed protest, causing Spades to turn, the fire still burning in his eyes. The dripping blade pointed first at her and when it looked like she would carry on her protestations, it was pointed towards Millie, sending a steaming red line of her cousin's blood across her sobbing form and causing more hysteria in the girl. Lady Rothborn fell silent and finally bowed her face to the ground. Spades picked up the head of the heir to the estate and placed it on the mantle beneath a trophy head of a great boar. The Redcap leader's pupils were now so large with excitement his eyes looked black.

He turned to Pippi, "Draw the symbols on our lord," he giggled insanely.

Pippi sprang eagerly forward and dragged the headless corpse back to the display cabinet, where she used her fingers and the pooling blood to dab images across the senseless man hung before her.

Spades sat down in his throne and fondled the new blade, "I want this whole room bathed in blood," he looked around one last time at the sobbing victims.

"Rip them apart," he said, looking straight into the eyes of Robyn, who grinned happily and blew her leader a kiss, before descending with the others on the gathered aristocrats. A sticky wet slaughter unfolded before Spades eyes as his pack set to work, laughing manically at their task.

***

It was difficult to tell who was who and what was what as the Redcaps stood before the cabinet. They all dripped with blood, their clothes soaked and shining, their hair matted and stuck to their heads in great gory dreadlocks. Only Lord Rothborn remained alive, his mind broken. From his insane eyes, he could see only six red figures stood in a room that seemed to bleed from its very walls. The figure at the front held in both hands, a heavy curved blade. Spades lifted it

Morningwood

silently above his head, pleased to see the lord's eyes follow its path upwards.

Lord Rothborn was mesmerised by the steely polished gleam, standing out so vividly in a world that smelt of death, tasted of iron and looked like hell. He wondered at its purpose as it fell towards him with enough violence to split him from crown to groin, his internal organs spilling out across the floor as his carcass separated, his spine holding the two halves together like a hinge.

"Open sesame," grinned Spades, stepping into the corpse.

***

Down in the Underworld, above a great alien forest stood a sandstone outcrop. It was almost geometrically regular in shape, carved with vast images long weathered by the elements. It pulsed and moved and then unexplainably started to bleed. At first small trickles of blood oozed from holes but then the ooze became rivulets of red, breaking down the sandstone in lumps and washing them into the forest until a waterfall of colour broke forth and washed away the very rock itself.

Figures stepped through the waterfall of blood, coming away from its surface as clean as if they had stepped through the purest of water. Soon, six figures stood by the outcrop, the blood dripping from the scarred surface of the rock behind them, but no passage remained. The figures, four males and two females, were naked, their skin mottled grey, their limbs thin and wiry with muscle. Their mouths were wide and lined with rows of sharp pin-like teeth, their black tongues licking constantly across the points. Small red eyes blazed as they surveyed the strange new landscape and nostrils flared and sniffed at the air. Each of them wore a red, blood-soaked, leather helmet on their round head. With an almost unperceivable sign from their leader, they shot off as one, down into the forest below, a forest that seemed to hold its breath as they passed.

Chapter 12

It was a winter's sun that shone through the forest's canopy, pale but welcome and every leaf seemed to drink of the gentle, coloured light. The forest itself was ancient. Trees grew into trees until trunks had become as imposing as buildings and irregular as the fevered dreams of surrealist painters. They formed arches so high it felt as if you walked through the river-carved tunnels and caves of a vast mountain. In places the canopy parted, allowing distant views of the alien sky, seemingly so far away that Alice felt dwarfed. Creatures moved in the canopy, knocking down branches and leaves, littering the paths on which the trio walked with detritus. Elongated birds with multiple wings, spun and twirled in the air above, moving more like dragonflies before soaring up through gaps to the sky above.

They had walked through the seemingly impassable foliage, over undulating ground and impossible rock formations, following the Satyr, who strode with the quiet confidence of a long-time underground commuter, his unquestioning sense of direction and purpose appearing to be the work of magic.

For a moment, Morningwood stopped and watched the women pass and walk ahead of him. Alice wore the toga he had given her as if she had been born into the loose, folded garment and her acceptance of what was happening led the Satyr to believe she thought she was still in a dream. Her calm demeanour and appearance were making her blend in well with the world that was unchanged since he had left, but it must have seemed unique and fresh to the eyes of the girl.

In strange contrast Mulberry stood out, she appeared awkward and uncomfortable. She remained naked and as was the nature of her kind she was taking on the aspects of the wild around her. Mortals had always made the mistake of thinking a Nymph was locked to the element of nature in which they were discovered because their appearance mimicked their surroundings so much. In reality, the delicate Nymphs had an empathy only with water, an element that flowed within everything and changed to match its landscape, be it the ice on rocks, the life in a trees capillaries or the tumbling fresh streams spilling down a hillside. Like water, the Nymphs would take on elements of the world around them, more so if their anxiety levels rose until it acted like an inbuilt camouflage. A truly uncomfortable

Morningwood

Nymph could become a fish in the water or a shrub in the forest if they so desired.

Morningwood was watching his companion change before his eyes, the artistic markings on her skin, the delicate blue swirls of the water had turned amber as she flowed with the sap of the forest. Her outer extremities had darkened to a warm chestnut brown and her hair had become curled, wild and as autumnal in colour as the leaves. Her more sensual curls were soft and green like moss and tendrils had sprouted from her veins and twisted about her contours, wrapping her legs in spiralling coils and tiny leaves that sank down into the ground, plucking free with each step before diving back into the soft earth, anchoring her every time her feet were placed flat upon the soil.

Morningwood walked slowly back to her side, "Your roots are showing," he said in a low voice to Mulberry, as Alice distractedly ran her hands over a tree's rough bark.

Mulberry sighed, "I'm struggling, she's so delicious I can taste her on the air, I just want to consume her." She gave the Satyr a shamed look.

Morningwood raised his eyebrows and shrugged, "You're doing better than you think." But he could see from her expression Mulberry wasn't liking this aspect of herself.

"You say that now, but I feel the desire just gathering like storm waters behind a dam." She leant her forehead on Morningwood's chest.

He thought for a moment, watching Alice bonding with a tree, unaware how much danger she was in, every second she was on this plane,

"Right! Get dressed," said Morningwood, pushing the Nymph gently from him.

"First you tell me my roots are showing now you want me to put my clothes on; you really know how to make a girl feel special!" She frowned.

"The clothes will ground you more with the mortal world and give you something to concentrate on, rather than our innocent. You don't have to wear the dress." He passed her the striped knickers and delicate vest she had worn under her clothes, from his satchel.

Mulberry realised the sense of the Satyr's words. Whilst masquerading as a human she had a genuine connection to the humans, or else who knows what would have happened the first time some well-meaning mother had handed her a baby to hold. She slipped the delicate clothes on and the mix of manmade fibres against her skin were like a soothing ointment on a burn. The problem remained, but the heat had gone.

She posed for Morningwood, hips thrust to one side, arms wide and palms to the sky, "I look like a good time girl!" She grinned.

"As long as you don't look like a Venus flytrap, besides you're the least of our worries, right now."

And as if on cue Alice let out a high-pitched shriek. It wasn't enough for panic from the duo, but they both turned. Alice was sucking her finger a pained look on her face.

"Are you okay?" Morningwood asked, already well aware she was.

"Something bit me," she said examining her finger, before shaking it about, "I didn't think dreams hurt," she said, sucking her wounded digit again, her statement confirming Morningwood's suspicions.

She believed she was in a dream and he wondered how long the self-deception would last before they started to have a bigger problem on their hands than something taking a crafty nip.

"A lot of things are going to want to bite you around here," said Mulberry and for a second Alice gave Morningwood an appraising look.

The Nymph followed her gaze then chuckled, "Not likely, as much as you might want it."

Both women laughed until Mulberry noticed Morningwood wasn't paying them any attention but was instead looking back through the parts of the forest they had already travelled. He was pulled up to his full height, chest out and neck stretched, looking every part of the wilderness spirit he had become. He turned back to them, his face serious.

"We need to move faster," he said and taking hold of Alice's arm he started off along the track.

Mulberry followed behind, now casting her own gaze back along their path. She didn't have the Satyr's senses – the keen nose for upcoming trouble – but she knew he wouldn't have quickened their pace without reason.

"Stop!" Commanded Alice, "This is my dream and I get to decide whether we move fast or stroll and enjoy it."

She was grateful her words had had an initial impact, but now she realised her self-appointed guards were looking above her and paying her no attention at all. Alice glanced up and drifting down from the

Morningwood

canopy was a host of lights; close on a dozen. Alice's eyes opened wide with wonder, they were gorgeous. She marvelled as the lights sank slowly down past her vision until they settled, hovering about her in what appeared to be a graceful spinning dance. At first she thought them to be glowing hummingbirds but as she turned her head to perceive the shapes through the bright light, she realised they were more like tiny females with heavy breasts and wide hips.

"Be very still," whispered Morningwood, holding up his palms to face Alice in the way one does when they have seen what they perceive to be a poisonous spider climbing your leg and are trying their hardest to calm you before you see it, but in the process make you more fearful of the unseen.

Alice froze, maybe the fairy lights were also here to save her from whatever creepy crawly was on her, but that naive image was soon gone when Mulberry stepped forward and quick as a flash batted two of the lights to the floor and they instantly dimmed. Several of the smaller lights levitated quickly back to the canopy, but the remaining lights dived toward the toga-covered girl and she felt sharp bites on her flesh and she screamed in pain.

Morningwood threw his arms back, bowed down and rose his head in a glorious deep animal bellow. The lights left Alice and shot along the path at speed, like rabbits running from a hound. Only one remained, the largest light, but it didn't flee it drifted curiously towards and around the Satyr, who stood and held out a hand for it to land on.

Both of the women looked on silently, although Alice rubbed at her skin as if she had wandered into a nettle patch.

"I mean you no harm Victorian, but the innocent is in my protection," he said with purpose, the light pulsed and changed colour as if responding.

Then it lifted from his hand and drifted gracefully around the Satyr as if appraising. He stood still, despite the intimacy of some of the exploration, following it with only slow movements of his head. Appearing satisfied, the light moved back up into the leaves.

Alice bent down and picked one of the shapes up from the ground. The light had gone out and she clearly saw she held a diminutive winged figure within her grasp, barely big enough to fill her palm, laid in a nest of its own blue hair. It had large eyes, closed tight; a small, simple mouth and what at first appeared to be freckles but on closer inspection were revealed to be many small black eyes, that reflected back the girl's face in their bright surfaces. Its skin was pale and corpse-like, but colourful patterns decorated its surface. Superficially it appeared dead, but she could see its full bosom moved with each tiny breath.

"I'd put it back down if I were you, it might wake up and attack," said Mulberry helpfully, but Alice reacted with a squeal, dropping it back to the ground with an audible fwlomp.

"We still need to move," said Morningwood, sensing the urgency wasn't seeping through to his companions.

"This isn't a dream is it?" Asked Alice.

Mulberry, her appearance returned mostly to human form, placed a comforting arm around the girl's shoulders, "I'm afraid not," the Nymph said, "But if it helps, the things that just bit you are," Alice looked almost more frightened and gave Mulberry a questioning look.

Mulberry looked at Morningwood but realised from his raised eyebrows he saw this more as her field of work than his.

Mulberry took a deep breath, thought quickly and linking arms with Alice followed the Satyr, "The men you met in the nightclub drugged you… Quite badly, in fact, and right now what you're going through is a really bad trip."

"Worst trip ever," added Morningwood with a sing-song voice, causing Mulberry to give his back a long hard stare, before continuing. "We're actually investigators, it's our job to get you through this and back to your father. You're experiencing a lot of things happening around you that aren't really there at all. If you look harder at your surroundings, you may see recognisable landmarks, a tree that looks like a building or a familiar public clock face on the side of a rock outcrop, maybe even a stretch of waterway that feels like one you know but just somehow in the wrong setting. Imagine your dreams smashed together with reality. Well, you're in reality but you're walking through dreams. Stuff will hurt you because it might well be a car, a flame or an angry dog, but it will look different, maybe even harmless. The people will look different and the language they use may be foreign to you, but they are just ordinary people and they're talking a language you know. Is this making any sense?"

Alice nodded, Mulberry's words made perfect sense. The visions around her had been a collection of the fantastically organic and yet had the structured workings of a sentient eye, she had already seen a cliff face that looked like a row of terrace houses and the large brightly coloured animals that snuffled in front of them could easily have been cars. The fact she was talking to a girl in her underwear who had kissed her earlier, appearing as a mermaid before becoming a tree was certainly further evidence. Of course, it also made sense she had cast as a Satyr, the handsome male she had found herself instantly attracted to. A creature she knew to be the god of lust and parties. Yes, the woman's words were an obvious explanation.

"There's more though isn't there?" She asked of Mulberry, "There has to be, or I'd be safe in a hospital – not walking it off where I might get into danger."

Alice knew she was right because the Satyr looked back over his shoulder as if she had stumbled on something they weren't saying.

In all honesty, Morningwood was simply thinking, 'Talk your way out of that question, Nymph.'

Mulberry prepared to have a go. The girl seemed quite accepting of her version of events so far, "You're a very clever girl Alice. This involves your father and his job."

Alice shrugged as if she had always expected this day to come, allowing Mulberry to continue, "We need to get you to a safe base, reunite you with your father and it's not going to be easy as there are a lot of people who are going to want to stop us and hurt you." Mulberry gave Alice the most comforting look she could muster, "So you're going to have to accept everything we say without question… Do you think you can do that?"

Alice nodded and in front Morningwood gave Mulberry an inner round of applause.

"This isn't going to work," he said aloud, looking nervously about.

The forest was too wild. Although to the untrained eye they seemed hidden, Morningwood couldn't help but feel they were out in the open.

"Do people here want to hurt me?" Alice asked, her voice wavering, looking at the powerful form of the Satyr before her.

"Possibly," Mulberry made her tone gentle, hoping to make up for Morningwood's lack of tact, "But I think what my colleague is saying, is we need to find a safe house nearby, that we can wait in whilst he finds a way of breaking you from your trance, getting you back to normality."

The words seemed to relax Alice and she nodded that she understood.

Mulberry turned to Morningwood her eyes pleading. She was at an honest loss as to what to do. The Victorians, as Morningwood had called them were like an early warning system to the dangers Alice was in. They had acted like a canary in a mine and both the immortals knew it. The Victorians weren't really of this land – they were Echoes, like the echoes of mortal architecture that sculpted the trees and landscape. Humans had a big effect on the below, the essence of just one innocent could take any of the residents back to their most primal form and a desire to feed. The Victorians however, were echoes of the fevered dreams of drug addiction. They went hand in hand with artists and creative genius. The opium dens and mass asylums of Victorian London had seen their first real encroachment into The Below, hence the name. As history changed with the artists and popular recreational drug use, so the creatures they hallucinated had changed also, from the delicate fairy host on gossamer wings, to the psychedelic dreams of hippies. Unfortunately, they were drawn faster to humans than anything else Below and the fact they had found Alice already, suggested the feeding frenzy was about to begin.

"I have somewhere we can go, if there's one around. We used to use them when we went hunting," Morningwood took Alice's arms, "Come on little lady, we'll get you somewhere safe."

They hurried for a bit with Mulberry looking back over her shoulder most of the way. She had known Morningwood for a long time and she could feel he was spooked, although he was trying not to show it. There was very little in the endless forests of the other world that a Satyr couldn't deal with, so the fact he seemed to feel there was reason for speed and hiding was worrying her and distracting her gaze.

She only turned the way they were heading when she heard Alice gasp.

Revealed in its own clearing, under a vast, domed roof of branches high above, grew a magnificent tree, possibly several judging by size, and all were tangled together with one gnarly trunk. Many thick branches stood out from the central trunks like perfect walkways, wide, flat, horizontal and all of them ended in naturally occurring, circular platforms of interlocked smaller branches and leaves. The gasp had come because the tree was doing what it did naturally in the fading light of the day. It was glowing. Not all over, but from inside wooden, pear-like protrusions that hung down from many of the branches. Night-time insects had already started to be attracted by the orange light of the lantern tree and it buzzed softly with their presence.

"We've found our safe house," said Morningwood, happily pointing at the spectacle before them.

Alice giggled as they approached, "If only you could see what I can see," she said, causing Mulberry to smile, wondering what mundane-looking building the girl obviously thought the Nymph and Satyr had as their view.

They climbed up the trunk and walked out along a thick branch to the vast platform at its tip. The moment they had all moved onto its surface, the interlocking branches creaked slowly and folded up until they were like a dense cage around them, a naturally occurring spherical tree house. At first Alice panicked, but seeing the calm of her companions she believed it was part of her hallucination and the closing branches might be something as mundane as locking a hotel room door and she calmed herself. It had been a good idea of Morningwood's, the tree was by nature carnivorous but would not harm them in a one-night stay, hunters would often use the branches to rest, protected from the elements in the tree's embrace. Of course protection was not the true purpose of the trees attributes, the glowing gourds attracted insects, they would in turn attract smaller creatures onto the platforms and those would be encased in living baskets. Not strong enough to push through the branches to escape they would be trapped forever, until their death. Their decomposition feeding the tree, like compost. The cleverly adapted, dense leafy cage also had a beautiful citrus like smell that calmed the trapped beast and effectively masked any escaping vapour of death that might warn other potential meals away.

The whole set up was perfect to hide Alice from the Underworld as it got hungrier. The Satyr's plan was basically being eaten to prevent them from being eaten.

"You'll be safe in here," Morningwood said pushing against the branches, checking them for strength, "This is a good sized space. Maybe a little snug but it's better than the alternative."

He took Mulberry's hand, then smiled at Alice, "You get comfortable. We'll be back," and he pushed and squeezed through the cage pulling Mulberry with him.

Outside on the branch, he brushed himself down, straightening his tunic.

"They're tougher to get through than I remember," He said, noticing he'd been scratched quite a bit.

Mulberry, on the other hand, had more lithely passed through and had even taken on some of the tree's aspects, her skin gave off a delicate citrus perfume and her hair had curled with a green tint.

"Are you going to be okay alone with her?" He asked passing across the satchel he had carried since his arrival Below.

He smiled, reassured at Mulberry's nod. If she thought she could control herself, he believed her, "I can cover a lot more ground without you both, especially at night. I'll find a portal. I remember a few in the area, but who knows what is lurking around them. I'll look for a quiet one and then we can get this girl home and stop whatever it is they want her father to do."

"And what if you don't come back? I know you think there is something waiting for us out there," Mulberry expressed her concerns in a whisper so as not to be overheard by Alice.

Morningwood raised an eyebrow, "I thought you'd know something was waiting for us when we got here?"

"Yes, but you don't think it's a random feeder, you think something is after just us. I saw it in your eyes when you were looking back through the forest." She hoped she could break the Satyr's cool exterior with her insight.

She was upset when he just chuckled, "If something really is waiting for us it's going to have to work hard to get to your Alice before everything else does."

He paused, "Look, the quicker we're out of here, the better. I'm going to head towards London, I know there are portals that way and with any luck one will have a lot less of a gauntlet to get through than the others. I recommend you get some sleep and make sure that girl doesn't get all dewy-eyed for a wander in our... Oh, so magical kingdom."

He smiled and without another word jumped from the branch and ran off through the darkening forest.

She watched him go, not entirely sure he was ready for his return

Morningwood

to the below, especially as he was plotting his course by Mortal landscapes. She hoped he would be coming back more than anything, as she pushed back through the branches to the enclosure within and looked at the pretty girl who sat up waiting patiently because Mulberry very much doubted she could finish the task without his support.

"You might as well get some sleep," said Mulberry with a smile, "I don't expect we'll see our friend until morning. I think he needs to stretch his legs."

Alice smiled softly and settled down in the warm interior of the natural cage as Mulberry slid down the sides to sit before her.

"How long do you think we'll need to wait?" Alice said with her head resting on her forearms.

Mulberry looked out through a gap in the tight twig cage, the night had truly fallen and insects buzzed around the glowing lanterns.

"No idea, I just know we need to stay put until my partner returns. Who knows what could be waiting for us out there…"

Chapter 13

From the moment they had left the base of the sandstone outcrop, the Redcaps had been as chaotic as an excited baboon troop. They ran free through the forest of their ancestral home, where at once everything had seemed both familiar and alien. More by chance than design they soon reached the pool. Its cool water had the same underlying scent as their sandstone passage and at once they knew they had found the portal through which the Satyr and his Nymph had passed.

That chance discovery had been some hours ago now and Spades sat angrily on the jutting rock above the still waters that reflected the night sky, wishing he had a pebble to toss into its perfect surface.

This wasn't at all what he had expected. They were the first generations of their species, more used to their perceived mortal form and the urban sprawl of man than they were to the immortal vision of themselves and the nature-choked world around them. Spades didn't like it, he didn't like it at all, he missed his tailored clothes and top of the line Lambretta, they were symbols of his rightful dominance over the others. He didn't like the way the females had looked at him, judging his worth by the dimensions of his naked form.

He felt the same discomfort in his brothers, who had shifted about awkwardly each time they felt appraising eyes upon them. They were a new breed not used to this world of exposure and face value. With this growing awareness, he watched his gang play around the water's edge, quietly judging each of them, measuring them up as possible challengers to his throne. Ringer had always been hidden beneath cheaper clothes that slid his worth down the rankings of the pack, but here he was exposed and proved to be bigger than Spades in many ways. Spades' unquestioned leadership hadn't ever been a concern amongst the cityscape in which they had grown. Ringer had only been seen as the clever one, a trait not prized amongst the pack, in fact, it had seemed a disadvantage. Spades lack of perceived intelligence was replaced by his quick and brutal actions, this awarded him a place of fear in his gang's hearts and by default their leadership, a ferocious appearance that could be challenged once others realised they were bigger and stronger.

Spades still had William though and William was bigger than all of them. Even in his immortal form his fondness for food was evident in his frame, his brother had been the same and they added weight to Spades' anger. Clever had never been the strong point of the two brothers, so Spades made their decisions for them and they accepted his path without question, making them loyal dogs, growling beside their master. Now that protection had weakened, Harold was dead and William seemed muted by the loss.

Spades knew there would be no threat from Zippo as he was the youngest and was still unsure what the future would bring for him. He filled a backup role within the troop and that was all that could be hoped for right now, an extra sword at the coming battle. Pippi looked after him, so to speak; although it wasn't really in the Redcap nature to care, she certainly got something from having Zippo around and she was prepared to defend him to keep that right. They were also the only couple amongst the group, as Robyn had made it clear to all the males if she was going to fish, it would be outside the shallow pool in which they swam. Having a mate wasn't something the Redcaps aspired to generally, they were solo by nature, but years amongst the humans had taught them the value of teaming up and for a moment Spades found himself appraising Pippi as a potential squeeze, after all he had acquired everything else that denoted status.

It was the change in Pippi's appearance which had alerted Spades of how their mortal aspects had affected their look in the Underworld. Her legs were striped, with natural markings similar to the knee socks she wore constantly and from which she derived her name. The patches that had once adorned her jacket now appeared as coloured spots of various regular shapes, upon her arms and back, to match the original placement mirrored by her now missing clothing. Her face was changed, you could clearly see she was more animalistic but the additional features of the human girl had remained with natural marking on her skin echoing the distinctive makeup she had worn around the streets and clubs of London.

Yes, they were different here but they were also still the same.

Spades peered into the mirror-like surface of the water below him. His left eye was milky white and a pale cross marked the skin around it where the Satyr had bludgeoned his head and reduced him to wearing a patch over the damage. A single dark stripe ran down his torso from throat to groin and he perceived it to be his assimilated tie, the knuckles of his right hand were raised and hard, with a metallic glint. He removed the blood-soaked helmet, the only item of clothing to stay with any of them and examined the dark markings on his bald head, they mimicked where he had once had hair, styled by the best hairdressers in London.

As he admired himself, coming to terms with the new features, the water erupted at its centre, sending distorting ripples across the Redcap leader's mirror and Robyn surfaced, like a great shark from the water and swam towards him on his rock. She went to pull herself out onto the outcrop but Spades put his hand on her head, holding her back. He didn't like the way the Redcap female was assuming she filled the same position as him within the pack and the action showed he was still able to keep her in her place.

"Just tell me what you found," he said, realising all eyes were now upon the scene unfolding, an almost pregnant pause as if they all expected a challenge at any moment.

Instead, Robyn pushed herself from the rock and swam to the pool's side without a word, causing Spades to stand on the outcrop like a proud king, vanquishing his foes. She walked from the water, still as shapely as she had been as a mortal and still with her long hair, all be it shaved on one side and deliberately she turned to face her leader. The action caused her muscles, wet with water, to stand out and glisten, a bold show of her potential strength. She bowed respectfully, although the barely concealed hatred on her face spoke greater volumes.

"There is nothing left in the water, my liege," she said on standing, her words dripping with venom. "They have brought the girl through." She sniffed deeply, "You can still smell her on the air, beneath the musk of the Satyr."

All the Redcaps including Spades took a breath through their noses and indeed the air was heavy with an intoxicating scent of the innocent, but to the males the smell of the Satyr blended in with the smell of the forest.

"We'll never find them. We have no idea where they're going or where to even start looking," whispered Ringer, more to Robyn than the group.

Spades had been looking for a reason to assert his leadership on the pack since they had changed and his command had been brought into question. Ringer's lack of faith in their abilities to find an enemy was all the excuse Spades needed.

He sprang from the rock and bounded through the air, swinging quickly from branches at the pool's edge and slammed into the bigger Redcap's chest with his outstretched feet, knocking them both to the ground. They stood up quickly, both realising this was only the opening to the battle, as the others gathered around, shouting excitedly at the unfolding violence. Ringer had not been ready for the fight, but mentally Spades had been preparing the moment he felt the situation was changing. Whereas Ringer stood from the ground empty-handed, Spades came up with a rock clenched in his fist. He brought it around in a great crashing blow to the insubordinate Redcap's face and felt the bone splinter beneath. An attack like this from Spades would normally have ended any wayward thoughts from the others and secured his leadership instantly. It seemed Spades had read the larger Redcap well however; Ringer had indeed been harbouring revolutionary ideas. His face broken and bloodied, he threw a punch at his leader but his arm, although no longer in a cast, was still injured and the blow not only failed to hurt Spades, it actually brought pain to Ringer. It was all Spades needed, he grabbed Ringer's wrist with his left hand and brought his rock crashing into the elbow. With an audible snap and a great bestial jabbering from the pack as the arm twisted alarmingly, Ringer fell to the floor, whimpering. His leadership challenge had been dealt with, but his ordeal was not yet over. The unscathed Spades walked slowly back to his resting point and retrieved his blade from the rock and returned to stand menacingly above the prone and bloody figure sprawled on the floor. He passed the weapon harmlessly over Ringer's throat then brutally severed the broken arm at the shoulder, before kicking the limb into the water.

As Ringer rolled in the dirt, fingers clamped to the bleeding stump. Spades went around individually hissing in the face of his pack, each one of them retreating from their leader's rage except Robyn, who hissed back but did not push for a fight.

Spades wouldn't have expected anything less and once more all was right with the world.

"We are a pack," he shouted at them, "If something does not work I will cut it off and discard it."

The Redcaps nodded as their leader's voice calmed, his blade red with their companion's blood, "We shall seek out our prey before they make it to a portal and we shall kill every one of them." Again his words were met with nodding heads. Spades turned to Robyn.

"You will deal with that and then follow us," he said pointing at Ringer, with his blade, "If it doesn't survive, kick it in with its arm," and with that, Spades bounded off into the forest, followed by William and Zippo.

Only Pippi paused and looked at Robyn for guidance, the older Redcap female nodded reassuringly at her pack sister and Pippi followed the group, leaving Robyn to care for Ringer. It was a shame. Robyn had always thought Ringer would be her second if she took over, but she was no nurse, although she often harboured desires to dress as one and sneak into a hospital to cause chaos.

She looked down at the twisting form of Ringer and couldn't help but see him as pathetic; emotion drained from her face as she placed her foot on his neck and pushed down with all her weight. Ringer's eyes shot open, pleadingly fixing the gaze of the former ally above him and on seeing no mercy in her face, his remaining hand grabbed at Robyn's ankle to remove her foot, but he was weakened and she was strong. Both the blood from his shoulder and the breath from his lungs quickly left his struggling form. Robyn continued to press down until she heard the neck snap beneath her. She had made eye contact the entire time and now looked down at his still body, she removed her foot wiped it on the grass and kicked Ringer into the water.

Robyn sat herself down against a tree and picked up her helmet to place it in the pooled blood of the dead pack mate. As she watched the deep red liquid soak into the leather and the body sink beneath the water she picked up Spades' initial rock, he had an instinctive eye for these kinds of things. She believed that with just a little more work she could make a passable weapon before following on.

She looked around and saw some of Ringer's teeth lying on the ground and without thinking picked them up, pulled a leather thong from her helmet and started to make a necklace as she whistled, as beautifully as a bird, *My Generation* by the Who.

***

Morningwood

Morningwood ran fast.

He finally had freedom, but he only had one night and lots of questions.

The feel of hooves striking the ground was the most satisfying experience he had felt in a very long time. For so many years, he had not been able to just run. The thrill of one hoof in front of the other, trees racing past on all side as his head made instinctive decisions to turn, jump and climb.

He was home.

He lost himself in the cool night of the other world feeling the fatigue of his heart fall away and the hours topple with it. It seemed almost a shame to reach his destination, but here he was the place where the other world connected with Greenwich.

It was both alien and familiar at the same time. He had never, to his knowledge, been here when he was in the other world, and if he had, it was long before the connection with the mortal realm. However, he knew it instantly as his London home, he could have found himself back at his door blindfold. He had certainly done it many times whilst blind drunk and often whilst being distracted by a pretty young thing he had picked up in one of the London clubs. Yes, this was his slice of London and he'd walked it for over a hundred year.

Of course, the Otherworld had its own unique interpretation of the landscape, its own wild vista with just echoes of Greenwich sculpted into its landscape. It had certainly done the Thames proud. The twisting lifeline of London had become vast and as Morningwood crested the hill, where he assumed the observatory must have made its mark amongst the trees. Before him lay the deep, fast-flowing blue waters of the Otherworld's river. It cascaded in shining waterfalls, broke into great stretches of white water, spun and churned in glorious sprays of life. The buildings that must have been the Admiralty and the many adored structures of the great Royal Navy were great chalk and granite islands that stood in the churning waters, home to dark-feathered birds that fished from the sculpted cliffs. Tonight they roosted in great noisy nesting grounds along the many ledges. Oh yes, this was the Greenwich of dreams as told by the sailors of England as they travelled the world in their great fleets. Beyond this shining sea lay the forest that was London and the Satyr could only wonder what great works of art the trees had become to mimic that great city above.

Time, however, was too precious to waste on sightseeing and he descended down toward the water's edge and his home. It really wasn't hard to find, the home of an immortal living in the world had a distinct impact on the area. The trees had grown up around a red sand outcrop that seemed even now to be freshly pushed from the ground; one bone white tree twisted up to the rocks summit and even from here Morningwood could see what he had come for.

Beside the natural rendition of his home was a crater, a great blast hole where even now nothing grew, except vines that stretched down into the fetid waters that had gathered in the depression. The Satyr clopped up to the edge and examined closer.

"I wouldn't if I were you," said a delicate voice and he turned to see two beautifully plump fauns behind him.

Each of them identical in every way, the slender legs of deer that made up their lower bodies were a soft dabbled grey. The skin of their naked torsos was wonderfully pale and blemish free, except for the one that stood forward of the other, who had a splash of red over her breast like a birthmark. Their faces were angelic with grey curled tresses that matched their legs in colour and both had ivory-white horns sprouting from their foreheads.

"A Wolf Frog has made its home in the water and it's always hungry," the red-stained faun continued, causing Morningwood to look briefly back at the still waters before he turned back to the fauns.

"My name is Morningwood," he said, standing back up and walking over to the twins.

"Oh, you need no introduction," the second twin said with the same delicate voice, "We feel your every move. We are the guardians of your home." She bowed her head in the most serene of ways, causing the old goat to bow back.

It was a revelation to the Satyr as he finally recognised the fauns that protected his door, statues that he had personally commissioned and had sculpted and would always hail on his return home.

"My loves… well, look at you both. Oh, how often I have wished for your movement."

The heartfelt comment actually caused the two perfect mouths to turn in a gentle smile.

Morningwood

Morningwood turned to the crater, "I wanted to check," he said thoughtfully and the fauns moved up to stand silently on either side of him.

"What caused it?" The stained faun asked eventually, her eyes on the crater.

"The acts of mortal men," the Satyr answered thoughtfully, "Bombs with so much passion behind them, the devastation in their world causes damaging echoes in ours."

He ran his hand across the faun's naked shoulders and pulled her in for a gentle embrace as if protecting her. The twin moved closer looking for comfort and he did the same for her.

"Will they drop more bombs?" The second twin asked.

"Maybe! They have developed bigger and bigger bombs for decades but who knows if they will use them. A few years back the two countries with the most bombs pushed each other to fight and we all thought a third world war was coming, but it seemed even these two great countries were scared of the effect of their new toys and so we thought the inevitable was avoided." Morningwood watched bubbles on the water's surface and two big amphibian eyes looked out from the murk, "It would need a truly broken mind to use that much destructive power to win a battle."

The Wolf Frog raised its ugly head from the water.

"It's unfortunate for everyone that many immortals possess such minds."

The beast's tongue shot forth, but the Satyr and fauns were not quite in its reach so it dived back beneath the fetid waters.

"Wolf Frog," said Morningwood to himself, before turning to the fauns, "As much as I would love to stay and get to know you both better, I have to go. I have a madman to stop and an innocent to save."

The fauns smiled, "You always return to us Early Morningwood," they said together, causing him to grin happily.

"Then until I return my beauties…" And he ran off back into the woods, his questions uncomfortably answered.

***

The run back was certainly a lot harder going than the run to

Greenwich, his mind was too active and he didn't relax into his instinctive nature. Morningwood had wanted his questions answered and he doubted whether the Nymph could or even would answer them. He didn't trust the FAE. He had realised early on that the other immortals had little interest in the actual lives of the mortals, even if they chose to live amongst them and offer protection. It felt like they were playing a game and the moment Alice was back, he knew the whole case would be closed, a job well done and he wouldn't have a good enough reason to continue. However, he had just seen with his own eyes that mortal damage was strong enough to damage both planes. An explosion wasn't just physical, it was imagined also. Papers carried news in print around the country and into the world until thousands of active minds started to picture the damage.He remembered during the war hearing an explosion and having the man beside him say, with steely conviction, 'Well that's Bellamy Street gone.' He had no way of knowing, but a sea of faces huddled quietly in the dark nodded, it was almost as if mortal thought guided the bomb. It just took the right words, the wrong, broken mind and you had catastrophe.

Camp Barrie, as he was now known, was going to destroy the reactor at Dounreay and that damage would most certainly go through the veil to the Otherworld and destroy the Unseelie Court. What effect this would have, was still lost to the Satyr, but he was pretty sure he should find out and quickly. First had to find Mulberry and Alice and it wasn't as easy as he'd hoped to trace his steps. It would be morning before he returned.

Morningwood

Chapter 14

Mulberry awoke. The time spent so close to the lantern tree had certainly taken hold. The swirls in her skin were now more orange than amber and gave off enough light to be bathing the inside of the wicker sphere with projected patterns. Her hair was a mass of tight-knit, dark green curls and framed her head like an Afro. Somehow whilst she had slept, she had removed the mortal clothes and lain down beside Alice. They had not only embraced, but tendrils had sprouted from the Nymph's skin and were now encircling the sleeping girl's limbs and torso, working beneath the toga to touch her soft, supple skin. Mulberry had become as carnivorous as the lantern tree and her back arched, a passionate gasp escaping her lips as her body reacted further. Alice woke sleepily, disturbed by the sounds, but the tightening tendrils panicked her and she was soon pulling them from her body and pulling away from the Nymph.

Brought to her senses, even Mulberry started to pull away from the girl and as the last of her was pulled or slipped from the intoxicating skin, they exploded apart and both girls scampered backwards from each other until they were back against opposite sides of their cage. Alice was flustered and rubbing at herself as if removing every sensation of another's touch, her eyes wide and frightened and staring at the agent sent to protect her.

Mulberry was hot, flushed and uncomfortable. She tried to keep her eyes off the girl before her, frightened what they might be giving away of her feelings and intent.

Alice was the first to speak, "You… you were…" she stammered, then she went quiet trying to find the words to say what she knew was happening, "I'm not that kind of girl. I haven't even been with a man yet. I'm traditional… I just think I should… before experimenting," she burbled quickly.

At first Mulberry was confused, she had been discovered trying to eat her own charge, the very thing she was supposed to be protecting her from. She was just lucky it had been done in the unconscious form of a slow constricting tree. Then the words sank in and she realised the girl had rationalised Mulberry's actions to the only sensible ones left to her. Alice believed she had…

"Oh god no, I wasn't…" she blurted.

"Then what were you doing?" Alice said her eyes opening wide and eyebrows going high as if to say the next answer should be a damn good one to be believed.

Mulberry almost said, 'I was trying to eat you.' But realised those words didn't help her case in either way. She plumped for, "I was trying to keep us both warm."

The moment she said it she realised it was a lame excuse and she felt Alice's eyes move over her suspiciously naked form. However, whether it was out of embarrassment for herself or to save Mulberry further humiliation, Alice took the lie as gospel, despite them both being fully aware it was not.

"I think warmth comes with clothes," she said instead and hooking her foot in the discarded stripped knickers she kicked them over to the suitably chastised Nymph.

Mulberry dressed quickly.

"When is the man coming back?" Alice said as if to take conversation from the act of dressing.

"The man?" Asked Mulberry, embarrassment clouding her thought process.

"The man, your colleague." Alice suddenly felt the morning might have gone a lot less awkward if she had woken with him naked beside her, hands wandering. The morning would, in fact, have gone awesome.

"Early Morningwood?" Mulberry absently checked, for confirmation, causing Alice to blush alarmingly.

"I'm sorry what?" She burbled, flustered again.

"My colleague, Professor Morningwood?" She asked, hoping Alice wasn't expecting another man and realising they had possibly not used Morningwood's name in front of her, as no informal introductions had been made.

"His name is Early Morningwood? His parents must have had a sense of humour then, or were they hippies without a grasp of the ironic?" Alice smiled, pleased to find Mulberry was also pulling on her dress, all be it a short, clinging one.

Mulberry laughed, "It's an old family name that has gained, shall we say, other meanings. I think he's quite happy with both images it conjures up to be honest. I'm led to believe he has other names but refuses to use them," She smiled at Alice and was pleased the moment of shared laughter had lightened the mood.

Alice looked at the beams of morning light shining through interlaced branches catching the dust like glitter in their beam, "Can we go outside and stretch our legs please, get away from this lemon smell, it's starting to make me crave gin and tonic," She said hopefully.

Mulberry nodded. She had a way with plants, even old trees like this and with a little cajoling she made a sizable gap to the outside world and they both stepped through to walk along the branch.

The morning sun was warming and already birds were awake and singing and chirping in the treetops.

"Hello, pretties. I did so enjoy your cuddle," The voice was rasping and caused them both to turn.

On top of the wooden sphere that had been their home sat Spades, legs crossed like an evil gnome. He jumped down onto the branch behind them blocking the way back into the protective cage. He was seeping more into his Immortal Redcap form, now no more than five foot in height, his skin greyer and the mottling more precise, it really looked like he was wearing a tie. He was certainly wearing a leather helmet, shining moistly with the blood of the recently dead and around his waist he had a poorly butchered pelt of some luckless animal. His arms seemed thin, but his hands were large and gnarled, clasped in one of them was the evil looking blade he carried so happily. He smiled the incredibly wide smile and flashed the impossible rows of sharp teeth that ran in circles all the way back to his gullet, a sharp black tongue darting over them restlessly.

Alice screamed.

"Run!" Shouted Mulberry.

They turned from the threatening Redcap and ran the length of the branch, but climbing up onto it and ending their escape route, came Pippi and Zippo. The female stood in front of the younger Redcap male, proud in all her Redcap glory. She still wore the leather helmet and like Spades' it was wet and glistening with fresh blood. Her body was paler than the males and her markings stood out prominently. The stripes of her thigh-length socks, the patches and makeup all gave her a camouflaged look. Like a slender predatory cat she approached, grinning along the branch. Her face was less primal than Zippo's and larger eyes gave her a more alarming countenance than the smaller male behind her, who had fewer markings and yet still had the same twisted features as Spades with small red, bead-like eyes and rows of pin-like teeth.

The girls stopped dead in their tracks and looked behind them. Spades was still approaching, the curved, heavy blade in hand. Mulberry looked down. The jump may have been easy for Morningwood, but it would have broken the girl, they were well and truly trapped.

"Hold onto me," whispered Mulberry, watching the Redcaps approach, "It's not going to be painless, but it's an escape."

Alice looked at the girl, decided she trusted her more than the creatures approaching so threw her arms around the Nymph's neck.

Mulberry turned sideways keeping the Redcaps either side of her, put her arms above her head and jumped backwards off the branch. Alice screamed again as she suddenly found herself launched into the air; a dizzying drop down to the hard ground.

The Redcaps gasped, they had certainly not been comfortable so high up, with the constant fear of falling and they had assumed all would feel the same, so their quarry was to be an easy target.

Mulberry also feared the height but she feared the Redcaps more. She caught a handful of the vines growing along the branch as she dropped past, feeling the sudden pull on her shoulders as she took the weight. As she had guessed, the vines wouldn't hold their combined weight and they snapped away from the bark, extending down as they broke and pulled free from the grip of the lantern tree. The distance to the ground shrunk and the speed slowed. But not enough. Mulberry pulled hard on the vines, her understanding of growth meant the strong tendrils snapped easily between her two skilful hands. She let go of the vines attached to the trunk and grabbed the other which grew out to the platform with both hands, the fall quickened rapidly, building as fast in speed as Alice's scream grew in noise.

Then the vines reached their length and they went from a fall to a swing. Like Jane of the Jungle, Mulberry swung with Alice clinging tightly to her chest. That was until just before they reached their lowest point and with no apology Mulberry pushed her off.

Alice was so shocked her scream actually stopped for the first time, she hit the ground hard and span backwards heels over head, stopping face down and winded on the ground.

Morningwood

Mulberry would have to let go on the next pass if the vines held, unfortunately, they did not. A sudden breaking from the tree and the whole knot of tendrils came free. She knew it was likely to happen as she had chosen the less anchored side on purpose, the other direction headed towards the trunk and neither Alice nor Mulberry would have been thankful of that sudden stop. She dropped and flew through the air, at a far greater height than her companion and crashed through the branches of a lower bush, rolling down through the breaking branches like a ball in a bagatelle machine. The whole escape had happened in moments, with the Redcaps watching motionless from the branch above.

Alice didn't move for a few seconds, she knew she was grazed and she did a mental check for broken bones too, before attempting to push herself up. Footfalls were rapidly approaching from the undergrowth and she knew they had to move before the Redcaps came down from the tree above, although she doubted they would use Mulberry's faster way after their little demonstration. She pushed herself unsteadily up, to be faced by William. Spades' thug was bigger built than the other Redcaps and still had huge dark clumps of residual human hair on his body, great clumps on his shoulders that merged into the many dark shapes that had come from his mortal clothes. His face was still almost human and his tail-adorned helmet lacked the fresh application of blood seen on the headgear of Spades and Pippi.

He looked from the blonde girl on the floor up to the branches above and his companions he had been too frightened to follow.

"Hit her!" Shouted Spades, and without a second thought, William looked back to Alice and swung his gnarled fist into her face. The poor girl didn't stand a chance, the blow knocked her sideways, sending lights dancing across her vision and sharp electric pain through her jaw. She was not knocked out but she was crying and dazed. William didn't like the sound so he kicked her hard in the stomach.

"Shut up," He bellowed, his whole countenance changing until nothing human remained – until he looked like the twisted love child of a toad and shark.

Alice went quiet, which was a shame for Mulberry as the warning shouts of the Redcaps in the tree and her running feet could now be heard by the thuggish Redcap she had hoped to reach unnoticed.

William turned to be faced by the Nymph, who looked every bit as human as she did on the streets of London. Her dark bobbed hair had returned and she was dressed appropriately although her clothes were soiled and torn. In her hands, she held a heavy twisted root and she swung it at the Redcap, who stepped and ducked from each thrust and swipe. She jabbed forward and William grabbed her makeshift weapon and tore it from her hands, swinging it hard into the off-balanced Nymph – sending her to the hard ground. The Nymph had known they couldn't tussle with Redcaps and win, but she was glad in her last moments she had given it a go.

Morningwood seemed to come from nowhere; even the Redcaps with their higher ground had not noticed his approach. He leapt as he entered the clearing and brought his great horns crashing hard into the face of the brutish Redcap as it stepped in to crush the Nymph. The blow splintered bone and sent splashes of rich crimson across the forest floor, driving the Redcap backwards a few feet.

William couldn't see, his vision was blurred, stained red and misty. His helmet was robbing him of hearing and he removed it to hear the shouts of his companions, high above. They seemed to be shouting to keep his helmet on. He wiped his eyes to clear his vision just enough to see the anger in the Satyrs eyes that stood before him.

Morningwood's neck muscles flexed and sent his head forward like a whip, shattering William's cranium and breaking his neck severely enough to drive his head down between his shoulders. The Redcap collapsed in an ungainly heap.

The pack above hollered like an angry chimpanzee troop and Morningwood bellowed his wilding call up at them. He stooped and picked up William's helmet, dipping it in the fallen Redcaps pooling blood, before hurling it high into the tree. The anger sent it soaring upwards, the force at its pinnacle was negligent but it held menace and Pippi and Zippo retreated. Spades didn't. He grabbed Pippi's arm to halt her retreat, making her face the threat. If only he could have done the same with the younger Zippo. The young Redcap stepped back too far, his footing found only air and for a second he was aware nothing stood between him and death.

"Pippi," he said sadly and the female Redcap turned to see Zippo plunge from view.

Morningwood

Spades and Morningwood saw the falling Redcap at the same time, when he impacted with the hard ground a second after William's helmet.

The Satyr didn't even look at the obvious corpse; he simply raised his palm up to Spades and extended two fingers to count the deaths, before turning his hand around like the British archers at Agincourt and smiling.

Mulberry had been conscious for the whole of Morningwood's return and had crawled to Alice, sliding the girl to safety and hiding. Alice was now hugging her tightly and crying softly into the comforting Nymph's embrace.

Morningwood had seen them go and could hear them close, but he needed to get them further to safety. He had gained surprise and luck on the death of the two Redcaps, but he could tell that even if the two remaining Redcaps got to the ground, they would give him a fight he could not win. He had only one real advantage over their brutal ferocity and that was tactics and planning and for that he needed time. He saw the female go for the trunk of the tree so he scooped up a flint and threw it hard.

It missed her but hit the tree to her side, sending up stone splinters and loud reverberating crack against the wood, sending her scampering back to the protective branch.

Morningwood had suspected the Redcaps of following the day before, he didn't know how they could have breached the Otherworld at first, but during his journey he realised the individual nature of the Redcap's exile and quickly worked out the rest. The Redcaps could track them easily, their sense of smell here would be legendary and he knew the lantern tree would be of no protection against their ability to track. The Redcaps would simply follow Alice's scent right up to the cage. He just hoped to have been back before they found her. Now that chance had passed, he could keep them trapped in the tree for a while but he really needed to keep Alice moving whilst masking her smell and he had just the way to do it.

Spades rage was absolute, but he couldn't see the sense in giving chase if it meant death. Why had he gone into the tree? They could have waited on the ground, been a force to reckon with. He watched the Satyr go into the undergrowth, where he had seen the Nymph take their prey.

They must be running. Spades dived for the trunk, but a flint flew from the bush and sent him back to safety. Now he was pinned and couldn't even see his foe, the Redcap hollered in rasping anger at the trees, he was outmanoeuvred and it angered him. He had only one hope left, that somewhere nearby, Robyn was sneaking.

Morningwood
Chapter 15

Morningwood could run even with a girl in his embrace. He had Alice cradled, her arms around his neck, face buried in his chest. Mulberry tried to keep up. She was fast but not as fast as the Satyr. She couldn't have kept up at all if he wasn't laden down, but as she too was hurt she had slowed considerably herself and was still struggling.

"We need to stop," she shouted as the Satyr gained even more ground.

Mulberry wasn't sure if he had heard or was choosing not to, as he kept running. She set off after him again. Around the next few trees he came back into view, stopped by a pond, looking into the waters and putting Alice gently down onto her feet beside it. Mulberry stumbled up, her lungs bursting her throat on fire. She glanced briefly at the pool as she leant back on a trunk and caught her breath.

"Stagnant water… Doesn't work… Neither of you could hold your breath that long anyway." She gasped a little more, thinking Morningwood was suggesting the pool as a portal for the Nymph.

Alice was stood facing Mulberry, concern on her face, back to the fetid pool of water. Even the Satyr had turned his head to face the breathless spirit.

Mulberry gasped, "You're going to have to find somewhere better… the moment I've caught my breath." She put her hands on her knees, "I hope you have other options."

As Mulberry stood, Alice screamed and disappeared backwards into the pool at speed. Mulberry rushed forward, visions of Redcaps dancing through her head and almost jumped as Morningwood triumphantly punched the air with a loud, "Ha!"

Confused, she watched the Satyr bend down and unhook a heavy vine from a jutting root. It disappeared into the water and hand-over-hand he pulled until the water became agitated and a great Wolf Frog was hauled from the rank slime with a loop around one of its powerful back legs; that it struggled against fretfully. The giant carnivorous amphibians settled in stagnant pools around the forests and caught anything that stumbled too close. They were a dark, striped green, helping with camouflage, and had skin nodules that hung down like hair around their flanks and gave them the name; Wolf. The mortal world had similar frogs but the Wolf Frog of the Otherworld was about the size of a small horse and could easily swallow something human-sized. Morningwood was looking pleased with himself as he hauled the catch in.

"What have you done?" Mulberry asked panic struck.

Morningwood gave the Nymph a hurt look as if he was hoping for his plan to be instantly seen and recognised as brilliant.

He countered her distress with a lecturing tone, pointing at the captured creature, "It takes six hours for the gases in the Wolf Frog to subdue and calm its meal. When fully unconscious, and only then, it introduces a mild gastric juice that breaks down its meal slowly over a week. Of all the predators in this forest, it is the most favourable to be eaten by and as most of those want to eat your Alice, I thought I'd get the drop on them and have her eaten by something we can trust."

Mulberry was speechless; It was the solution of a sociopath.

Morningwood continued, "I've also worked out a portal we can safely use and you now have a ride." He pointed at the frog that was trying to get back to the water, causing the Nymph to suddenly see it in a different light. It was true her species certainly had a way with creatures that shared their environment's and she had ridden both fish and frogs in the past.

Mulberry approached the frog and it pulled away from her, like a skittish horse. She looked at Morningwood confused, he simply waved a finger in front of her like a wand causing her to look down at her distinctly mortal appearance and dress. With a happy sigh, she slipped from the torn dress, and chemise vest beneath stuffing them in the satchel, standing suddenly like a proud Amazon warrior, all be it in stripy knickers. This time, her approach was more accepted as her immortal form started to show through. The Wolf Frog even turned towards her. With a delicate leap, she was astride the creature, bent low and stroking its head, whispering softly to it. Morningwood felt the pull on the vines lessen so he bent and undid the capturing loop. By the time he stood back up, Mulberry sat confidently astride her mount, her skin already becoming a paler striped green, the swirls on her skin pulsing red as if filled with blood. Her hair remained dark but had extended down like muddy dreadlocks. She looked at the Satyr, her teeth shining white with a happy grin between full, red lips.

Morningwood

"You should have just told us your plan. I thought you'd gone mad," she beamed.

"And you think Alice would have agreed to being swallowed by a giant frog that will start digesting her in a few hours?" He asked curiously, raising an eyebrow.

Mulberry pouted and shook her head, "Let's go!" She shouted and the Wolf Frog sprung off through the woods.

Morningwood laughed and ran alongside, "Possibly best if you follow me," He said and the two immortals disappeared through the trees.

***

Spades wasn't prepared to wait any longer. He ran along the branch and seizing onto the easily-climbable trunk he crawled around it like a squirrel, putting it in between him and the bush from which the flints had flown, descending as quickly as he dared.

Pippi saw the result of the action and did the same until both Redcaps were firmly on the floor. Running at the bush as a pair, they slashed and tore at the leaves and branches and found it to be empty.

As Spades raged, annoyed at being tricked, Pippi walked slowly back to the bodies of her comrades. William was heavily blooded but had come to rest in the standard position of the recently dead. She then stopped to gaze at the twisted body of Zippo. His bones broken and protruding from his flesh, blood bubbled on his chest and the Redcap realised Zippo was still alive. She approached and bent beside the broken form and looked into the eyes of her dying friend. He gurgled through the broken jaw and she could see he had bitten off his tongue in the fall.

"You have a choice," the female Redcap whispered, "You can pass on or you can stay." She looked at the body deformed by the fall, "Not in this vessel of broken substance, but you can become Sluagh."

Zippo's eyes rolled slightly at the words, prompting Pippi to continue, "You need to make the choice before it is made for you." The Redcaps knew all too well of the other option open to them, to become the restless dead.

Their boss, Camp Barrie, was, in fact, one of the Sluagh and he did alright with it. The option was – when you knew you were about to die – to move from your body and take what you were out of the living vessel. Not to become a ghost, but to be an incorporeal version of yourself. You could always decide to move into another living vessel at a later date if you could cause the current resident to move on. A prospect that would have halted the new-agers from inducing out of body experiences if they only knew there might be someone looking to move in. Of course, if your body died completely with you still in it, the options were limited to just the traditional one.

Zippo's body moved slightly, the bubbling blood oozed in dark rivers over the contours created by his flesh and then fell still. Pippi waited, the blood was still coming, dark, like oil and thick, it steamed with its own heat making a coloured mist that drifted upwards. The blood was coming fast now as if escaping from the body, it now boiled as if above a fire and the mist became smoke, a smoke that was taking form.

The spectacle had even stopped Spades who walked over, twisting to see past Pippi but not stepping out from behind her protection.

A form of Zippo hovered in the air. Not the Redcap form that should have been his essence but instead the scooter boy. His features were thin and drawn and his limbs long. His hair was cropped short as it always had been on the streets of London and his eyes were sunken and pale, appearing sightless but surrounded by dark circles as if he had needed sleep for centuries. The dark smoke pulled across his naked corpse-coloured skin, taking on the shape of his preferred mortal clothes. He drifted cross-legged on the air for a moment before unfolding and placing his bare feet on the ground.

"And now we are three," said Spades, stepping from behind Pippi. He walked past the female Redcap and slapped Zippo on the shoulder, making a solid if hollow contact with the Sluagh.

He crouched by the now lifeless body and grabbed the broken leg bone that protruded through the skin and with a ripping noise tore it free from the hip.

"Waste not, want not," he grinned and passed the gory club to Pippi. She hesitated a moment before taking it from her leader's hands. Zippo reached forward silently and ran his fingers over the broken end as if surprised to be caressing his own scaffolding. When his fingers left the shattered end, the bone had elongated into a fused point. Zippo seemed as surprised as Pippi, who broke into a smile, punched Zippo on the shoulder as a thank you and span it like a deadly baton.

"You'll have to fight them in different ways," Spades said looking Zippo critically up and down, "You're different now." He ran off towards the bush, "They went this way, I can still smell the girl."

Pippi took one last look at Zippo's broken corpse and then the silent Sluagh, before running off after Spades, with Zippo drifting silently through the air behind as if being pulled along like a kite.

***

The thrill of journeying through the woods together, in a style more traditional to the Underworld, without the slow progress of a mortal in tow, was exhilarating and soon the fear of what was sure to be after them was lost. Mulberry laughed with each giant leap her mount took as Morningwood weaved through the trees in front. The trees had become paler in colour now and soon the ground had a thick frost and snow piled up in great drifts around the paths. The Wolf Frog didn't like the colder climate and started to slow. Even Mulberry was starting to feel the cold seeping into her skin, making it feel tingly. Soon her flesh glistened and sparkled, going a far paler green than it had in the lush forest. Her hair grew, becoming wilder and spilling over her shoulders like a white fur wrap. The red swirls of her skin darkened until they were almost black in colour.

"I think we are going to have to stop," shouted the Nymph and was glad to see the Satyr turn and halt, up on the path before them.

"It's really not long now and if you stop that Frog here, it will hibernate," Morningwood looked at the winter landscape, "We're in Unseelie territory. Not really your area I'm guessing. It's going to be hard going for you but the moment the Redcaps get here they will pick up speed and if they get this far from the pond were not exactly being subtle in our escape," Morningwood pointed back at the deep tracks they had left in the snow behind them.

"What about you?" Asked Mulberry. "Can't you feel the cold?"

Morningwood shrugged, "I've felt equally at home and

unwelcome, the whole time I've been here to be honest. Sure the Seelie court could once make a small claim to the loyalties of the Satyr, but the moment we fought them and pushed them back below, I think that bridge burnt."

He shrugged, "I guess I've been out in it so long I no longer feel the cold of the Underworld." He smiled, "Come on. Not long now then we can rest."

With these words, he set off. It took a few seconds to convince the Frog to hop again, like a car starting on a cold day, but soon she was following.

***

The Redcaps had found the water hole and the end of the intoxicating smell of Alice.

"Where's that bloody Robyn?" ranted Spades, looking at the swirling water with a strange oily film floating on the top, making him pine for home and the petrol rainbows swirling in the gutters. He turned on Pippi, "Right your turn. Swim down and see where it comes out."

The Female Redcap leant at a slight angle and looked at her leader, confused, "Robyn is the swimmer, it's not a natural girl thing you know."

Spades held up his blade, causing the girl to spit at her feet, before begrudgingly wading into the water. She kept hold of her bone club but threw her helmet on the bank, uncovering a bright orange fringe of hair that fell across her face, although the rest of her head was shaved bald. She slipped beneath the murky water, with barely a ripple.

Moments later she burst above the surface again, coughing and wiping her eyes, "It's just a pond, it only goes down a few feet," she spluttered, before Spades could force her under again.

Spades turned on Zippo, who was perched quietly on the lowest branch of a tree. The freshly conceived Sluagh pointed at marks beside the pond where the Wolf Frog had come on the bank and the footprints of mulberry and hooves of Morningwood.

"You reckon something ate them?" Asked Spades, examining the tracks as a mud covered Pippi slipped and slid out of the pool, before

Morningwood

sniffing her skin and recoiling.

Zippo jumped down and picked up the heavy vine tied into a noose, prompting Spades to snatch it and re-examine the tracks.

"Looks like our Satyr friend has got the girls a ride," he sniffed the rope, "The smell could possibly cover hers," he said almost to himself.

Pippi shook her head, trying to wash the worst of the mud off before putting her helmet back on, "Could you follow the tracks, Zippo?" Pippi asked of the former Redcap, who had now jumped up into the branches and was looking intently at the ground. He looked back and nodded.

"Then we follow the ghost," said Spades, dismissively.

Pippi walked past her leader and held the hip joint under her leaders chin threateningly, "He's not a ghost."

Spades hit the bone away with his blade and a growl, "I don't care what he is. I just want him to show us the way."

Pippi was getting as out of control as Robyn before her, wherever she was. Spades would have made an example of Pippi but technically it just seemed to be him and her left and he liked having someone to boss around.

Pippi didn't want to stand up to Spades, she knew he would kill her without a second thought and only the alien nature of the world they were in seemed to stay his hand. She just wanted to protect Zippo and she realised there were many who would drive him away.

Zippo personally had lost many of his thoughts. He drifted slowly down the path following the impacts, footprints and splashes easily seen from his elevated position, while the two Redcaps followed below.

Chapter 16

Morningwood and Mulberry sat quietly at the base of a large tree, the Wolf Frog slumbering behind them in the cold, eyes rolling, belly full. Looking down into the snow softened clearing below, the duo noticed the abnormality in the undergrowth. The trees on the far side were curled in a perfect tunnel, branches looping around, joining top and bottom in a naturally beautiful cylinder.

The light should have faded to black in the disappearing darkness but instead a pulsing glow shone from the depths. The Satyr gave Mulberry a cheeky sideways smile, "Our portal home," He whispered.

Something moved beneath the snow in the clearing, disturbed by his quiet words, and a noise above them in the branches made them look up to the dark canopy. Morningwood knew that the portals attracted predators… well, in essence, they attracted everything. However, it was just the predators that remained after a while and then not just your basic hungry vulpine, but nasty twisted beasts that had found themselves, by superior evolutionary traits and animal cunning, at the top of a very unique food chain. Clearly this particular portal had picked up two. Divided by preferred terrain, something was in the trees and that meant they had to be able to fly, for a climbing predator would touch the ground and the ground was clearly alive with something big.

"Any ideas?" whispered the Nymph as Morningwood placed his back on the tree and closed his eyes in thought.

"Give me time," he whispered back, without opening his eyes.

Mulberry checked the portal again. It was a long dash and the branches above were a no go.

"Do we have time?" She asked quietly, "You only asked Alice's father for three days and by my count we are currently at two." Her voice had an air of concern.

Still eyes closed, Morningwood spoke softly, "We're in the below, time moves slower than above." He said as if stating a school playground fact and Mulberry nodded at the wisdom.

"So when we emerge you think we may still have about two days left rather than one?" Mulberry asked still curious.

Morningwood opened his eyes and looked at the Nymph, "Well, I've not done the maths but yes about that. I suggest we check a paper when we arrive however, to stop a Phileas Fogg moment."

"A what?" Said Mulberry, thinking this was another cleverest man in the room test.

"For God's sake girl read a book or two; you're Immortal! It's not like it's wasting any of your time," Morningwood said annoyed, closing his eyes again.

Mulberry rolled her eyes, she was very well read but kept away from the fictions that Morningwood was obviously enjoying. She was about to flick his ear when the Satyr opened his eyes again and turned, sniffing the tree behind him, before curiously peeling off a large piece of the bark that he instantly threw at the Wolf Frog. Instinctively the sleepy creature snatched it from the air.

Mulberry looked at the Satyr confused, "Is that a ladder so she can climb out?" She asked sarcastically.

"Give it a moment," Morningwood said, as he once again went back to leaning on the tree, eyes closed.

The Wolf Frog suddenly seemed more active, its eyes opened wide and it pawed at its own muzzle for a while with a strong back leg, then it vomited. The bark, a yellow cloud of foul smelling mist and Alice, spilled out into the cold air and onto the snow. The Frog shivered and settled back down in the snow. Alice gasped at the cold, and coughed uncontrollably, vomiting, like the Frog, onto the snow.

"You're a real class act, Early," said Mulberry derisively, walking over to the girl, to comfort her and hold back her hair.

Morningwood ignored the comments and span to watch the clearing. The snow was moving and rolling about, "We need to move. Get her up," he stated with urgency.

Alice was dragged to her feet. She looked confused but turned to her guardians for direction. Morningwood ran to the Frog and pushed it hard towards the clearing, the Frog jumped away from the irritant; it was sleepy, sick and now hungry. It landed in the snow of the clearing.

"Alice, run for the tunnel," shouted Morningwood and without question the girl spotted the interwoven branches and started to run.

As she entered the clearing, a great mouth burst free from the snow and snatched up the Frog. Alice screamed but kept running. From the trees, a great cloud of small birds erupted heading for the fleeing girl.

The Satyr leapt into the air and struck out at the flock, landing behind the feeding snow beast then ran back towards Mulberry and the trees. The birds followed.

With all the predators distracted by food, Alice arrived at the tunnel unscathed and was through, heading towards the light.

Mulberry on seeing the birds, a great flight of dark feathers and razor sharp beaks, turned to run back up the path. The Satyr could outrun her if he so wanted, making her the first target and these avian predators wanted blood. Something else was running towards them from the other direction and the Nymph realised it was the two remaining Redcaps from the tree and what appeared to be a Sluagh guide. She stopped dead and felt the arm of Morningwood around her waist as she was pushed face down into the snow.

***

The Redcaps had been gaining ground since leaving the fetid pool. Zippo was turning out to be the perfect guide, his ability to drift as if caught on the wind meant he could look down on the path from up high. Several times the Redcaps below realised they would have become lost without his silent gliding vigil.

Then the snow came. At first it had just been a hint of chill to the wind and the ground hardened underfoot before everything had drifted through translucent blues to heavy folds of white.

Spades started to see the tracks of their prey unfolding before them, but left the guidance to their silent companion. His desire for battle had quickened his pace and by the time they came to a fairly straight concourse through the trees they were stooped and running.

The forest had been quiet, deadened by the blanket of snow, but then a commotion broke out before them and shouts to run and sounds of combat filled the air. The Redcaps surged forward, to find two of their intended victims running at speed towards them, a great swirling cloud behind them. Then the victims disappeared but the flock of birds continued.

***

Morningwood

Morningwood had remembered the name of the birds the moment they had swarmed from the canopy. Scarlings! The creatures had become feared not as individuals, as they were tiny in size, but as flocks. Great murmurations of the winged predators would circle above the battlefields of the Unseelie, diving disloyally on both courts, their talons small and sharp, like the scratching claws of a cat, their beaks slicing like the finest blades. All those unfortunate enough to be caught in their spinning clouds would suffer a myriad of tiny cuts and scratches, sometimes to the point of bleeding out and becoming carrion for the flock.

As Morningwood lay on the ground, his back scratched by the few that dipped low enough, – a warm draught of air breaking over him with their passing – he thought only of the portal. He couldn't be sure, but as Alice had run to safety he had the impression she was followed. A trick of the light, a shadow given elongated movements or simply a mistake of his eye, distracted by the Scarlings. Morningwood couldn't be sure, but he wasn't prepared to leave the girl alone longer than he had to.

He heard the shouts of the Redcaps as the Scarlings met them face on and he pulled himself tighter over the Nymph below, protecting her with his body.

To Mulberry the sensation was strange, she had been saved, that she was sure of, but now she was in a muffled cave of protection. Beneath her, the cold, clean-smelling snow pushed against her naked flesh, embracing her contours and chilling her deeply. Above her the heat and musk of her companion and lover, holding her tighter than any act of lovemaking; and she felt cherished for possibly the first time in her life.

***

To Spades, the flock was merely an oncoming storm and he met it face on. His blade drawn back to attack, mouth wide to scream his battle cry and to snap every foe straight from the air. A more defensive stance was found in Pippi's form. She crouched low, spinning her leg bone club as she stooped, but it was Zippo the Scarlings reached first. They broke over him like a wave hitting the prow of a ship, dividing and surging past in agitated twisted clumps. Not one scratch or plunging beak found his cold flesh. Then the flock reformed and hit the waiting Redcaps.

Spades sliced angrily through the air, severing wings, feet and heads. Biting down hard and spitting until his mouth was full of dark choking feathers and the ground around him was littered with tiny bodies of the dead and dying.

Pippi was also striking out, her blows more structured and less savage than her leaders. She swung hard at dark patches of the swarm where the numbers massed together, breaking bodies, guiding the relentless advance aside as birds twisted and span past. They were not as fortunate as Zippo however. The birds found their unprotected grey flesh, talons snagging, tearing across the skin, leaving scratches that beaded with blood. The beaks, like cutthroat razors, sliced clean, red lines through the organic canvas of their bodies, left deep holes in muscles, grooves in bone and disfiguring damage in ears.

As quickly as it had started, the birds were passed, depleted greatly in number from the actions of the angry minions of Conand.

They rolled up into the tree line moving like a dark sheet tossed by an unseen wind, folding in on themselves like the play of a shadow in a pulsing neon light.

Morningwood pulled Mulberry to her feet, his back on fire with the myriad of tiny cuts and turned her towards the portal, forcing her to run whilst he glanced back over his shoulder.

The trio behind them recovered quickly. Zippo merely floated unharmed, but the Redcaps charged. They were a mess of open wounds, Spades' skin was a virtual tapestry of the many violent strokes of the tiny birds. Pippi less so, but still bleeding from many nasty cuts that opened further as she moved, revealing fresh pink flesh beneath her grey skin.

Mulberry started to look back but once again found herself pitched forward into the cold snow, the protective cover of the Satyr above her. Spades hollered triumphantly as he closed the gap on his fallen enemies then Pippi turned to see the Scarlings exploding around Zippo as if he were some necrotic sorcerer summoning a host of dark winged demons from the depths of hell. She too dived into the snow, staining it red with her spilt blood.

Spades took no evasive action at all; he was too intent on sliding his blade through the back of the Satyr into the Nymph below. The Scarlings hit him unhindered in his unprotected back, many of them sticking into the soft flesh and bunched muscles beneath like darts. The impact lifted him into the air and his blade fell to the snow. The birds lifted him high, pecking hard and swarming across his body, a flurry of cuts opening on his flesh and spraying crimson across the pure white below. He bit and tore, more out of animal anger than a desire to free himself, snapping at the air like a rabid hound his lips flecked with blood red foam. A beak found his one good eye and popped it like an infected spot with a simple sharp jab. Then as easily as he was lifted, he was dropped to the ground with a crunch.

The Scarlings were much depleted in number, only a few birds remained but the flock turned and they dived once more. As they surged, Zippo surged too, his clothes becoming like smoke and every tiny creature that passed through the haze fell lifeless from the sky.

"Run," shouted Morningwood pulling Mulberry back to her feet and they dashed, but the Nymph halted at the clearing's edge, "The beast?" she said panicked.

"It will be dead or feasting, the Wolf Frog flesh is poisonous to most," The Satyr reassured her, but he saw the fear still evident in her eyes, "I'll go first you follow quickly after." Trusting the truth of his own words he ran across the clearing and into the wicker portal, he still had an innocent to protect and couldn't pause to pamper an unfounded fear.

Mulberry watched him go, her eyes on the snow, searching for any sign of movement, then her fears moved behind her. The Redcaps were all still there, the Sluagh hovering unheard above them. Mulberry was alone with them all. Her head turned but they were not advancing, they lay still in the snow. They could even be dead, surrounded by a landscape of motionless black corpses on the crisp white blanket, like a night time sky in negative. Mulberry moved forward towards the edge of the clearing and tried to steady her nerves before bolting to the portal.

***

The portal saw a lot of action that night. Alice had run blindly towards the light until it enveloped her. For a moment, she felt the light become solid and it was like pushing through treacle. Then she was out in the darkness, the air was cool but not cold and the snow she had briefly been surrounded by was gone, along with the ever-present giant trees. The grass beneath her bare feet felt somehow more real than the surface she had felt beneath her soles before. The trees were in clumps around her and the distant landscape had the glow of a city's lights bleeding into the night-time sky. Behind her was the grass-covered, earthen mound of what she remembered from school as being a long barrow, a place where the Anglo-Saxons buried their dead. One end of the barrow had rough-hewn, tumbledown stones around an impression. Her disorientation made Alice believe she may have come from inside. As she looked at the hole she saw movement and for a brief moment the drug hallucinations returned, as she believed the figure that emerged from the burial ground was one of the horrific creatures who had taunted them in the tree. Then the light of the moon caught the features better and Alice could see it was a girl. Possibly a girl she had disturbed from night-time activity. The girl certainly looked the type for drug abuse or maybe even her lover was still inside the barrow, pulling on his trousers. For a brief moment, Alice believed the woman to be completely naked. The next second she was dressed, albeit as if clothes had been hastily pulled on, confirming her thoughts. The girl certainly had an element of low rent about her. Alice was pleased to see another human, it meant she'd broken the hallucinations. For a moment, she considered the figure could be the true form of Agent Mulberry, but the clothes and hair shaved on one side of her head revealing a stitched wound, drove that thought from her head and filled her with a moment of cold dread.

***

Robyn had left the pond soon after her little project was finished. She chose not to follow Spades. In fact, she had chosen at that moment to never follow Spades again. She instead followed the Satyr, her loins ached so much for the musk he gave off that she could follow him as easily as the others were following the girl. She followed him to Greenwich, then back to the pool where he had

Morningwood

captured the Wolf Frog and then onto the portal.

The moment Alice ran through she took her chance and went after her, the job they had been tasked with was a fairly simple one after all.

Robyn now walked towards the girl in the toga, happy that her own form reverted quickly back to the mortal appearance she had grown up with, including clothes; although she was aware how dishevelled she must look. She let go of the stone in her hand and as it fell, it extended the strong, flexible handle from her sleeve, which she caught, in her palm. With a simple lifting of her arm and flicking of her wrist, she cracked the girl's skull. Alice fell lifeless to the floor, a small stream of bright red blood ran through her golden hair and sank into the soil. Robyn stepped over the body, without even looking down and continued to walk off into the night towards the distant lights.

Chapter 17

Morningwood ran the length of the tunnel. The light enveloped him and he felt it pulling at his flesh, great grasping, sucking motions on his skin that felt like he was being torn apart. He kept running, despite the growing pain that lanced like lightning through his muscles and rasped his bones. He screamed with the agony of the transformation and burst free from the light into the cold early morning air of East Sussex. Suddenly, the mortal legs were alien to him, the ankle injury burned like fire and he collapsed to his knees, body dripping with sweat that washed the blood from the scratches on his back and stung as salt found the wounds. His hands went to his more human face and held it tightly waiting for the pain to die. Eventually the sensations subsided, leaving him weak and nauseous. He moved his fingers from his blurred vision and let the air caress his eyes until tears ran down his cheeks.

Then he saw her.

Alice lay on the ground a few feet away, her eyes staring at the kneeling man before her, lifeless, all light cast from them. Her legs were bent slightly beneath her as if she had collapsed at the knees, falling gracefully like the dying of a ballet swan. Her lips were parted, giving her a slightly serene, yet wanton visage and a single tear had run from her eye to meet the blood that followed her hairline to the ground. Morningwood removed his hands fully from his face and looked at the dead girl, quietly contemplating the waste of such a precious life. He leant forward and placing his hand on her face, closed her eyes sadly, smearing blood down her perfect features.

He heard the engine of a car and then he was bathed in headlights, the harsh electric beams draining all romance from the tragic scene. He did not turn, even upon hearing the doors opening behind him.

"Professor Morningwood, place your hands slowly on your head," came a familiar voice behind him.

He was too weak not to do as directed, he knew what this must look like. He placed both his hands on the back of his head and listened to the approaching footsteps. The cold metal of a handcuff bracelet was clipped tightly around his right wrist before his hand was moved to the small of his back pulled by the manacle. He didn't

Morningwood

resist. Then his other hand was moved down from his head and clipped behind him so he was bound. The moment the second bracelet was in place, another man – a man in uniform – walked around to Alice, leant over and checked for a pulse. The young officer turned to whoever was behind Morningwood and shook his head.

Morningwood was pulled roughly up by the handcuffs, the familiar voice behind him talking as he did so.

"Professor Morningwood. I'm placing you under arrest for the murder of Alice Moore and the suspected murders of the Rothborn family and Agent Gale Mulberry."

The last name was slightly unfamiliar to Morningwood, as he had only ever known her as Mulberry, but he got the gist of what was being said, though any second Mulberry could burst out onto the scene and spoil the accusation. He was turned to face Inspector Burkmar.

"You have got a lot of explaining to do. Luckily this time I'm not expected to deal with you all by myself." The angry officer of the law dragged Morningwood towards the cars and he realised there were two, the standard police car with its doors open and a larger, silver-grey Daimler Majestic Major.

As they approached the bigger car, its back door was opened and Morningwood was bundled inside to sit next to a clean-shaven, dark-suited man in a trilby. All the occupants of the car wore trilbies, the driver and the upfront passenger. Inspector Burkmar closed the door and tapped on the roof. Without hesitation, its engine already running, the Daimler pulled away from the crime scene.

For a while, they bumped over uneven ground, leaving the field and getting back onto a track that led to the road. They eventually turned onto tarmac and the smooth engine sound purred as they picked up speed. The front seat passenger reached up and turned on the interior light, then turned in his chair to look back at the bloodied toga wearing man, head bowed in the back seat, arms handcuffed. The trilby-wearing man was the only unshaven face. He had sharp features and a regimental-looking moustache. When he spoke, he had the bearing of a highly educated member of the British upper class.

"Well Morningwood, seems you've been a bit of a naughty boy. Not only have you slaughtered a respected family and killed the daughter of a committed government employee. It also would appear you've murdered one of my agents."

The final words broke through his reverie and Morningwood looked up into the face of the suited man, "Kokabiel!" Morningwood said, instantly recognising the man before him, despite some of the recent human additions to his features.

"You're showing your age Morningwood," the man said with a smile, "I tend to go by the name Deputy Kochab, now."

"You're FAE," said Morningwood looking at the other people in the car, whom he now had every suspicion were constructs, men made from animated human parts and easily able to deal with a Satyr in human form if he got out of hand.

"Oh, we're all FAE, but we few have the heightened positions of Agents of the FAE," Deputy Kochab said with an almost teasing smirk as if he loved a good acronym. Morningwood's eyes went back to the speaker before him in the car, "Do you have any idea what trouble you are in, Morningwood?" Kochab continued.

The Satyr said nothing.

"Then I shall enlighten you. We, at the Fellowship of Amalgamated Empires, take it upon ourselves to make sure the two planes don't do anything unlawful and immoral to each other. In this instance, you have stepped over the lines of both the law of this plane and the morals of ours."

Kochab took the moment for another quiet smirk, "I do believe it was even your kind that enforced those morals when you felt my kind, were taking liberties. Oh, how the tide has turned."

The car turned onto a main road and the lights and traffic outside were suddenly a lot greater, although a sense of upcoming dawn was tingeing the night sky blue.

Kochab turned to look out of the front windscreen but continued to speak, "What have you done with Agent Mulberry's body, by the way?"

It was a simple question asked with no emotion. If the Deputy truly believed his agent dead, he wasn't showing signs of missing her. Morningwood didn't say a word. He knew situations like this had a way of snowballing and he would rather the man before him spoke and gave away his intentions, rather than adding a storyline of his own.

"She wasn't one of our best, but she certainly wasn't one of our worst either. Simple job really, go get a girl back that a misguided Sluagh sent to the Underworld. She should have been very good at it, but she made a schoolgirl error," he turned and looked at Morningwood's resolute face, "She involved you."

The words were designed to rile up the Satyr but he wasn't going to bite, it was what Kochab wanted. Morningwood had known the Seelie court member when he had walked the world, offering up arcane knowledge for riches, sex and the bigger taboo of consumption. He had even sired some of the giant mutated creatures they had needed to drive through portals, to another planet that could support them better than Earth. He knew Kochab well because he had personally faced him on the field of battle and won. So it was going to take a lot more to rile this Satyr to anger. Morningwood looked silently out the window.

"Oh you don't think you're a problem...? You don't think you're a danger to society?" Kochab grinned nastily, as if he was ready for the silence of the appointed protector of innocents, "So the fact we have several witnesses that will testify, in a human court, to seeing you killing youths on scooters, doesn't worry you at all. We also have a police inspector who has signed a statement to say you beat up a man in police custody. A man who is now dead, alongside his entire family, with the car you were seen driving off in, parked outside his house. There's a lot of blood on both seats. Blood I'm sure tests will prove is Agent Mulberry's... Then, of course, the same inspector, an independent officer, and three agents, saw you crouched alone over the body of a recently murdered girl. A girl you were asking questions about."

Kochab turned back to the windscreen, "No, I think we all know what you are Morningwood. We don't even need to find the body of Agent Mulberry to convict you. We just need enough witnesses to ensure the correct punishment is administered. It's the hangman's noose for you Morningwood, and then oh how the mighty hero will fall," Kochab even jerked his head as if acting out a death by hanging, before he chuckled.

Morningwood ignored the jibes and continued to run the recent events through his head. There was every possibility he had been set up by a bitter Seelie to settle a very old score. Could Kochab be behind all the events that had happened, it was certainly a lot more his style than Camp Barrie… In his mind's eye, he could see Mulberry joining the FAE and falling under Kochab's command. The information coming out of her link with his old enemy and his formulation of a plan. How difficult would it be to get Camp Barrie to kidnap a girl with a bigger picture story and then send in an inexperienced agent to break the case? Mulberry was trying to get in the Court's good books so it wouldn't take a lot for her to think of going to an expert, outside source for help. The most obvious expert would be her ex-lover, the well-known protector of innocents. Then Kochab could just stand back and watch a Satyr at work. Notching up the human and court crimes he breaks. Kill off the agent who got his help and the girl he was supposed to save and you have a crime of both worlds. It was simple enough to be true but complicated enough to not seem planned. Suddenly Morningwood was worrying about Mulberry, if he was right, then Kochab had killed Alice and believed Mulberry to be dead as well, which either meant she was or she was going to be. His thoughts were interrupted.

"We're here," the driver said as the car indicated and they drove off the main road into a courtyard of an official-looking building.

***

Morningwood was walked from the car. The sun was up and the early dawn light was reflecting off the windows of the old, red, brick building. He was flanked by the two silent heavies of Deputy Kochab, who walked in front of his prisoner like a hunter leading a captured man-eating lion through the streets and villages, to show his worth as a hero.

As they went through the front door, people were clearly turning up for the early shift and many eyes were upon the strangely attired man. Ears listened as Kochab booked in his prisoner, loudly requesting a cell for 'Early Morningwood, multiple murderer.'

Head still bowed, Morningwood was lead through the tiled corridors. A uniformed officer, although not police, wearing the uniform of a guard, opened up heavy doors before them with a big bunch of keys. He was lead down flights of stone steps, all cold on his feet until he reached another desk. A ruddy-faced bruiser of a warden sat behind it and looked up from a ledger. He moved his tea cup off the desk onto a low concealed shelf and brought out a flat wooden tray.

"Name?" He asked.

"Early Morningwood," the Satyr replied, causing the desk guard to look up his pen.

"I can confirm that name," added Kochab, and with a questioning tilt of the head the man added the name to his ledger.

"Any personal items?" The guard asked and Morningwood shook his head. The guard looked him up and down, "We'll need that sash," he said, pointing at the belt around Morningwood's waist. Kochab removed it and put the sash in the tray as the guard added a note to his ledger, before filling out a ticket he slipped into the front of the tray.

"Cell 3," he announced as he put the tray back beneath the desk, and the guard with the keys unlocked a door that led them to a corridor of other doors. Each had a number, painted large at eye level. Murmurs came from the other cells as the incarcerated woke.

Cell 3 was already stood with its door wide open. It had no window at all, just a high grate, through which cold air flowed. A metal bed with a rough grey blanket and white pillow was bolted to one wall, with a bucket beneath. Morningwood walked inside and Kochab removed his cuffs, before quickly stepping back. The Satyr turned in the middle of the room and faced the two men in the corridor. The guard, without another word, closed the door as Kochab smiled, behind him. The key turned and several hidden bolts shot across.

Morningwood was alone, for the first time since leaving the Otherworld.

What the hell had gone wrong? The girl was dead and the FAE and the police had been almost instantly on the scene. Something really wasn't right. He hoped not mentioning Mulberry was still alive meant he had an ally on the outside or at the very least protected her from the worst. But he had left her alone with the Redcaps and although they had slaughtered the Rothborn's to get them through to the Otherworld, maybe they were in Kochab's employ.

Then a real sickening feeling rose up in the Satyr, maybe Mulberry was in Kochab's employ. He hadn't seen her in decades and she could easily have had an axe to grind.

He assumed that whatever was happening, they would be telling

Alice's father that they had found his daughter's body by now, surely that would stop his plans for the nuclear plant? Then the thought hit him; maybe he was wrong about Kochab setting him up? Perhaps all that had happened was really the work of Camp Barrie and it had been seen that the loss of one innocent life would protect many. Maybe Kochab had simply been lucky stumbling on his old enemy and had found a Scapegoat, literally.

Morningwood's head was swimming. He was too tired to think, he had been without sleep for many hours now. He climbed onto the bed and lay down, looking up at the ceiling. His eyes felt heavy, so he closed them.

Chapter 18

Spades scrambled to his feet, he felt feathery corpses beneath his hand as he pushed himself upright. The snow beneath him compressing as he shifted his weight, making his movements wobbly and unstable. Zippo sat silently in the tree, his head cocked to one side like a curious bird, watching Spades' struggle. It was like observing a baby deer trying to stand for the first time. Spades never once glanced up at the strange figure above him, one eye was white, the other a gaping round hole through which sticky blood trickled like a tear. The leader of the Redcaps was blind. Zippo's focus drifted, as he watched Pippi pick the metal blade up from the snow. She walked purposefully up to their leader, her feet crunching as she approached through the frozen crust. Spades stopped moving, listening intently to the approaching feet.

"If you're going to do it Pippi, you best do it quickly," he taunted and turned his sightless eyes on the female Redcap. She stopped in her tracks, actually fearful of her blind leader.

"That's what I thought," he said, his voice dripping with menace, "Now give me my blade." He hissed, "Handle first or I'll gut you."

The female Redcap spun the sword so the pommel faced Spades and slowly approached him, he held out his hand straight and flat and she placed the handle across his palm, his fingers closed around it like a bear trap. Spades darted forward grabbing Pippi forcefully around the neck as if he could see her, as clearly as she saw him. His blade came up sharply, with the point a hair's breadth away from her eye.

"In the kingdom of the blind…" Spades whispered. Zippo moved in the tree, but Pippi raised a hand and stopped him. The movement made the blind Redcap turn his head, listening for some tell of the Sluagh.

"He's your silent protector now, is he?" Spades giggled, turning his head in jerking movements hoping to get a bead on Zippo, but when he couldn't find him his attention went back to Pippi, "I could just pop them out." He almost sighed at the gloriousness of the threat, then let her go, gasping for air and rubbing her neck, "Where are the protectors?" Spades shouted to the trees.

Pippi approached the clearing, to check for tracks and to put distance between her and Spades. A gigantic dead creature lay half concealed in the snow. It was flat like a fluke worm, pale yellow in colour with irregular grey markings. Its mouth was badly torn and bleeding and parts of its body bubbled and hissed, with expanding, mucus-like foam. The ground was so badly churned the dark soil was exposed above the snow.

"They went through," said Pippi looking at the portal and moving forward, but Zippo jumped silently down in front of her, blocking the path. The silent figure pointed at the tracks of bare feet that ran up to the dead creature but indicated they didn't continue further and follow the straight line of hoof prints into the portal.

"What is it?" Asked Spades, his voice commanding, not liking the silence.

"The Satyr went through, but the Nymph was eaten," Pippi imparted to her blind leader, but the Sluagh started waving his hands frantically in front of her and shaking his head.

"Hang on," she added to her last statement.

The Sluagh held one palm flat and put two fingers from his other hand to resemble a running figure then he made the fingers jump. Content that the message had been understood, he pointed to a further set of tracks, the large imprints of webbed feet and a speckling of blood on the ground. Pippi checked with her own eyes and looked back at Zippo, who nodded, smiling.

"The Nymph went to follow the Satyr across but seems instead to have taken the Frog and headed North… It appears they split up," Pippi amended with Zippo nodding in agreement.

"Then go find her," Spades shouted frustrated, "She hasn't got a warrior anymore. I will follow the Satyr."

For a moment Pippi hesitated, "But you're blind?" She said confused. Then on seeing the look that crossed Spades face she continued, "I'm sure you'll find a way. We will follow the Nymph as far as we can," And Pippi tapped Zippo on the shoulder and they were off.

Spades listened to the sound of Pippi departing through the snow, as instructed before he stopped and suddenly started swinging his blade about himself to test the Sluagh was not still hovering about. Satisfied he was alone and his commands were being met, he walked into the portal.

Morningwood
***

The journey through was no easier for Spades than it had been for Morningwood, his body was torn apart and reformed. The moment he felt the air change, as the distant familiar smell of pollution reached his nose, Spades fell against the hard earth wall of the long barrow tunnel. He patted at his body enjoying the feel of his tailored clothes beneath his fingers, although they felt ragged and torn. He moved his hand into his trousers and tugged free the animal skin he had wrapped himself in, throwing it onto the floor in disgust. Then carefully he reached up to his ruined face and felt the medical pad stuck over his eye. Spades peeled it free and blinked, his vision was blurry but he could make out the walls of the tunnel he was in. He stuck the bandage over the empty hole where his good eye had been plucked out. The Redcap could see again, albeit it forever impaired.

Looking towards the tunnel mouth, he could see blue flashes and believed it was the work of the portal but then he remembered where he actually was and the familiar flash of police lights were not far away. He tucked his blade into his jacket and ruffled his clothes before stumbling out. The policeman who looked towards him first was taken aback.

Then he stood and rushed forward, shouting to his fellow officers, "We've got another Victim!"

And inwardly Spades smiled.

***

Morningwood opened his eyes, it was difficult to say how long he'd been asleep, but he was good at recuperating, so he felt refreshed even after an hour. A cloud of smoke drifted over his head and he turned on the bed, to see the source. Sat in a simple wooden chair, was a man who looked all the world like Father Christmas. He was wearing a blue suit and a dark grey trilby with a red band rested on his lap. He puffed happily on a pipe with a warm smelling tobacco, his blue eyes fixed on Morningwood. The Satyr sat up and peered at the friendly face for a moment, discerning a man with younger features and blond Viking hair.

"Dagda?" He finally said, and the smoking man grinned, "You

look healthy," said Morningwood, which he always thought of as man code for; 'You've put on weight.' It was obvious the man before him knew the code, as he tapped his belly, nicely contained beneath a tailored waistcoat.

"I've done well for myself, it has to be said," the man chuckled. "Which is more than I can say for you, my friend. Seems I always find you in prison."

For a moment, the man looked awkward. He searched for a place to knock out his pipe and Morningwood helpfully passed forward the bucket from under the bed. The large man emptied the pipe, and placed it into his pocket, "I'm here on official FAE business."

"Got yourself a new club then?" Morningwood said with a smile, causing the bigger man to raise an eyebrow.

"Very droll," Dagda continued, ignoring the joke, before removing a second pipe from a different pocket, a leather tobacco wallet, and a small metal tool, for tamping the tobacco down. "Not sure if contraband is allowed but here, just in case you fancy a smoke, it's my spare." He passed the gift to Morningwood, who took it, although he hadn't smoked a pipe in a while.

"I also brought you some clothes, can't have a man walking about in a toga now can we," He pointed to a pile of folded up clothes on the very bottom of the bed, "The coat's yours, it's got your glasses in the pocket. They found it in the Mini at the stately home. The other clothes I picked out myself. I think I remember your size. I brought you a hat too, I seem to recall you'd decided to stop wearing one, like that Kennedy chap, but I think sartorial eloquence is sometimes all we have left. Shouldn't wonder if that's what got him shot, so much easier to spot a chap without a hat… Anyway, listen to me going on like a mother hen." Dagda dabbed at his brow with a spotted handkerchief, "So did you do it?" He asked almost out of the blue.

"I said nothing to your colleague and I'll say nothing to you. Despite our past," Morningwood said curtly.

Dagda looked hurt, almost at himself for having asked the question, "Kochab isn't my colleague. Same organisation, but he's more home office to my foreign office. We are so different it's inevitable we'll end up keeping an eye on each other, at least if we weren't so tied up with all the others," he stood to go, "Well I hope it all works out my friend," he said almost sadly.

Morningwood

"You had some official FAE business?" Morningwood asked. Surprised the man was about to leave and not really wanting to see him go.

"Did I? Well, that's long forgotten, that's the problem Early, I forget a lot at the moment. It's age you know. Parked my car in Duke Street two blocks over and I've been saying it over and over again so I don't forget," he shook his head, "But knowing me, I will anyway, and still end up walking." He started to move out of the cell, "Bloody lax guards here. Didn't sign me in or anything… Well, I doubt you'd be wandering about. You're locked up and these doors are pretty big. Anyway, my friend, I hope to see you soon, stay lucky old bean." And with a slam, the door was closed again.

Morningwood looked at it for a while.

Dagda was slipping, he'd once been a great warrior. They'd fought together and on the same side too. Morningwood shuddered, if that's how mortal bodies changed you, maybe it was a good thing he'd soon be dancing at the end of a rope.

He looked at the clothes and checked the labels. Finding they were the right size, he stripped off. Pulling on the comfortable underwear and neatly pressed shirt, he slid into the suit Dagda had brought him, wondering if the familiar design was FAE issue, before laughing at the thought of wearing the hat in the cell, in the interests of 'sartorial elegance'. Although he did have to admit he looked rather fine in a dark, tailored suit. It was indeed his coat, although he couldn't remember having put the glasses in the pocket, he thought they'd been left in the glove box of the Mini. Morningwood reached inside and took out the glasses he had stolen from Nigel and slipped them on, they did help. He felt something else in the pocket too. Pulling it out, he found a neatly folded map, a circle around a small airfield; the name 'Jess' written above it and 'Scotland, 4:00 pm' written below.

Morningwood looked at it, then down at his suit, hat and coat. The door was closed with no way out. He couldn't remember the bolts going across but there was no handle on the inside and it fit the doorway snugly, you'd need a screwdriver or blade to lever it open and Morningwood hadn't thought to bring one. He turned to the pipe and the tamping tool laid out on the bed. One end a little metal disc for pushing your tobacco down, the other end a blade for cleaning out your bowl. Morningwood could have laughed out loud. He opened the tobacco wallet; it had a small amount of folded money and an unopened tobacco pouch inside. Putting on the coat and hat and pushing the tobacco wallet in his pocket, Morningwood levered open the unbolted door with the pipe tool, pulling it closed behind him. He slipped the pipe between his lips and walked up the corridor and through the end door. A different guard now manned the desk.

"Goodnight," Morningwood said confidently.

"Goodnight sir," chimed back the desk guard, not really looking up from his ledger.

Morningwood tried not to go bounding up the stairs, although his heart was beating fast. God bless old Dagda, not such a fool after all, he thought. He was heading out of the main door when he stopped and walked back into the building, despite his desire to flee. He had been right, he had passed by an office, it's door slightly open. Inside sat Deputy Kochab, smug as ever. Morningwood didn't want to dally too long but the other man sat with his back to the open door had waves of white hair. The delay could get him caught, but eventually the figure turned just enough and Morningwood's suspicions were confirmed; Kochab was talking to Camp Barrie.

The Satyr left the building as quickly as he could. So there was indeed a conspiracy afoot. The two men had looked at ease in each other's company, friends even. He almost concluded his theory had been correct, he'd just been set up, but then the face of Dagda drifted back into his mind. His old friend had practically told him they didn't trust Kochab and would be watching him if they could. That wouldn't necessarily stop Kochab framing an old Satyr. The FAE officer was an immortal with a broken mind and a hatred of the Unseelie Court and no real love for the mortals. Dagda needed Morningwood to tie up the last pieces of the puzzle, that's why he had an escape plan and directions to an airport.

Okay, he had to get to that airport by four. He looked at a clock, it was just past two, a lot later than he had thought, he would never make it, he needed a car. Then he grinned. Of course, he had one; it was in Duke Street, two blocks over.

***

Morningwood

Morningwood stood beside the only car on Duke Street, a faded red Ford Cortina Mk1. He looked up and down the street again but certainly no Daimler as he had hoped. He tried the door and when it opened, he got in. Dagda had been forgetful after all, there were no keys in the ignition.

After a moment's thought, Morningwood leant across to the glove box and opened it. He reached inside and retrieved the keys, before pulling forth a small revolver. He clicked open the chamber to find five bullets loaded and an empty chamber for safety. The FAE obviously believed something dangerous enough was happening to include a gun as part of his getaway equipment. Morningwood hadn't held a gun for a few years now, but instantly the weight felt familiar in his hands. He could hear the zing of bullets as they whizzed by, the smell of gun smoke thick on the air and the rallying cries of his fellow soldiers. As each old memory worked through his conscious, his legs started to throb and without taking his mind off the firearm he rubbed them with his free hand. It had been a big sacrifice but so many more had made far bigger sacrifices. War had changed and the Satyr had changed with it. He placed the gun in his jacket pocket, wiped a tear from beneath his glasses and put the keys in the ignition. The engine growled but failed to start, it growled again but still nothing. Morningwood slapped his hand on the steering wheel and the horn sounded making him jump.

He took a deep breath.

'Calm down,' he said to himself, 'You've done all these things before, you can do them again… Time to stop hiding.' He pulled out the choke, applied some throttle and turned the key. The engine fired and purred roughly. He smiled and pulled away from the kerb.

***

Morningwood arrived at Biggin Hill Airport around three. It was certainly small, but busy. He pulled into the car park and stopped the car, sitting for a while watching the coming and going of planes before getting out and walking to the main doors. A friendly-looking man looked up at Morningwood's approach and the smile felt warming to the Satyr, who realised he hadn't seen a genuine smile in days, they had all been tinged with an air of sadness or confidence building. The smile was infectious and Morningwood beamed back.

"I've got a four o'clock flight," he said confidently.

"Commercial or Private sir?" The man asked with a slight Home Counties twang to his words.

"Private, I believe."

With a nod of his head, the clerk went to one of the two ledgers open on the desk in front of him. Without looking up, he asked, "Pilot's name?"

Morningwood pulled the map from his pocket and read the scribbles, "Jess?" he said as if questioning himself.

"Ah yes, sir. If you go through the door over there, your plane and pilot will be getting ready. You're not due to fly for a bit, so we have a lounge you can use if you'd prefer to stay warm?" The clerk pointed out the places he mentioned as he talked.

Morningwood looked from the door out into cold and then over to the warm lounge, with its comfortable seating and a middle-aged woman, complete with tea trolley and cakes. He was suddenly aware he hadn't eaten in a while but concluded a stale Eccles cake possibly wasn't the best thing to fill the hole.

"I'll go out and meet my pilot," he said and the clerk smiled with a cheery;

"Have a good flight Sir!"

With no bags to carry, Morningwood went straight out through the door and headed towards the hangers and light aircraft. The windsock was blowing hard to the West and the air was chill, causing him to shiver as he walked. Maybe the lounge would have been better after all, he thought, but then his eyes rested on a shapely woman moving around the plane. It was nice to see even in private flights there was the chance of a stewardess.

"I'm looking for Jess," Morningwood announced. His voice raised over the sound of a taxiing plane.

"That's me," said the woman, holding out her gloved hand to Morningwood, which he promptly took in his and shook, "You're a friend of my father's I'm led to understand. He wants me to fly you to Scotland, correct?"

Morningwood was a bit shaken at the thought that Dagda would have children, but then again, it stood to reason, he had always liked the ladies and unlike the Satyr, Dagda wasn't sterile. He kept his composure however, as if all the information was well known to him.

"Is that all he told you," Morningwood asked, hoping there might be a bit more information.

Jess chuckled, "He told me not to sleep with you."

The openness of the last comment was disarming but it made Morningwood laugh appraisingly too, "And do you always do what your Father says?" He asked with a grin.

"Nope," She replied with a twinkle to her eyes and a smile playing across her unmade-up lips.

Chapter 19

Mulberry had watched the Redcaps. When she saw they weren't moving she'd started to follow Morningwood, but the moment she had gone to step foot on the clearing The Beast had reared up in an explosion of mud and snow. It was thrashing about, its body already foaming with a strange chemical reaction. Then it collapsed and in a few seconds the Wolf Frog crawled from its bloodied mouth. It seemed the frog had more than one life to give. It was disorientated and looked a bit like a dog's chew toy, but all in all, it was fairly unharmed. Morningwood had been right, they were poisonous to most creatures that tried to eat them and amongst its other defensive methods it had actually pierced its own flesh on its toes, forcing the bones through like tiny claws, using them to grip the soft mouth of the predator and prevent itself from being swallowed. It may not have been a top predator itself, but it certainly wasn't prey either.

Mulberry approached full of concern for her mount and gently patted its neck. It was surprisingly calm despite the ordeal. She looked back at the Redcaps now getting to their feet and made a decision. She knew they would follow someone, but if she and Morningwood went different ways, the Redcaps would need to decide which to pursue, maybe even split up themselves. She didn't have time to think it over and decide if it was a good plan or not, so remounting her Frog, she bounded off towards London.

She could already hear the Redcaps squabbling as she went. She might not get enough of a lead on them and without access to this Portal she would have to find another way out. If the Redcaps pursued Alice out of the portal, she knew the human girl would be protected by Morningwood, but she also needed a plan if they chose to chase her through the Otherworld. She would have to avoid where major cities and the Otherworld merged, as the landscape became too twisted and chaotic. Maybe if she went North, she could make it to the Unseelie Court that Morningwood believed was under threat.

She knew she could possibly find allies to help her journey, the Redcaps had been exiled as enemies of The Court, but then so had she and she very much doubted her punishment would be merely exile if she were found here. Working as an Agent of FAE had seemed like the first step to her redemption and possibly her ticket back home. It

Morningwood

wasn't that she didn't like her life amongst the mortals, but as a convicted exile, their world had always been a prison to her. Morningwood was fine, he had chosen to exile himself, so as much as he didn't feel welcome here, there was no reason other than his own feelings that kept him away. Mulberry's crime, the one that had led to her exile, had been Consumption. The most heinous of all the crimes an Immortal could commit against a mortal, for once you had succumbed to their flesh it was an addiction. The punishment was a cruel and unusual one that often created greater monsters than it cured. It was decreed that you should live amongst your addictions without further offence. If an immortal continued to consume mortals, becoming a monster of human legend, then it was a monster that the humans hunted down and killed, and if that was to be your fate, then so be it.

Consumption as a crime was a tricky subject and open to much debate amongst the courts. It was the way of things that a mortal would sometimes stumble into the Underworld and many, unsurprisingly, didn't survive the dangers of a land where you are the greatest of narcotics, but that was seen as a natural event, something you couldn't be held accountable for.

Mulberry hadn't however stumbled on some poor mortal in the Otherworld, hers was not a lost child that had fallen through the cracks of their own dreams; no she had lured her victim to his death. She had journeyed into the world of mortals and seduced a young man until he accompanied her of his own volition back to the Underworld and during the act of love-making she had killed and eaten him…

It was the greatest of crimes. She had been found guilty by members of the Seelie Court and banished without trial. Knowledge of her crime being seated into the minds of every individual of the Underworld, even Morningwood's, though he chose never to mention it. If she was ever to return, she had first to make amends. Live amongst the delicious mortals she so craved without further harm to them at her hands. She had been given a sentence of a decade and one day for each year of life the consumed had lived. That had been one hundred and twenty long years ago and she still had eighty years and a handful of days left to serve.

Working for the FAE had been her chance to lose some of that sentence, but now she was back below, where if she were to be caught she would start her sentence again, and she was loving being home too much to just give up.

No, she couldn't find allies. She had to do this herself. She had been sentenced by the Seelie court. Maybe if she could warn the Unseelie Court of matters unfolding, they would take her beneath their wing and she could return home.

She leant in close to the Frog and whispered gently, placing her hands either side of the great head. Yes, this was the life for Mulberry and she needed it back at all costs.

***

Spades had been taken straight to a hospital, the talkative officers filling him on all the details he might have missed. So, the Alice girl was dead and they were blaming the Satyr for it, even had him locked up in some prison awaiting sentence and by all accounts he had been caught bang to rights. They were even pinning the Rothborn massacre on him, saying it all linked together. Spades could hardly contain his glee.

The morning was turning out to be a good one. They had treated his eye and multiple wounds; he was well bandaged beneath the hospital robe. The Redcaps had completed their mission, even if it was by luck. That the protector of innocents, who had done so much damage to their plans, was actually taking the fall for their crimes was a bonus, and Spades was sat in a hospital bed being looked after in a private room like royalty. Yes, it was a perfect day. Although he would have to give a statement to the police, so he was trying to think up a good one when the nurse came in. Spades lecherously took in the uniform as the nurse read his clipboard. Highly polished shoes, dark black stockings, pale blue dress, pulled in at the waist with a wide belt – showing off her figure – and finished with the curious watch pinned to her bosom.

"So, will I make it nurse?" He asked.

"Oh, I do hope so, or else Barrie will have to choose a new leader," the nurse lowered the clipboard to reveal Robyn, a big grin on her face, looking surprisingly good in a nurse's uniform and glasses.

Morningwood

"Where the bloody hell did you go?" hissed Spades.

Robyn laughed coyly, "Well while you were playing with budgies, I went off and killed little Alice so I did." She did a little curtsey. Suddenly every psychotic detail about her seemed magnified. Spades felt vulnerable in the hospital gown and bed.

"Where's Ringer?" He asked curiously.

"I killed him too. He was broken… like you," she said her face becoming serious, Spades looked for his jacket and Robyn also glanced around the room, following Spades' gaze.

"Oh sweetheart, are you looking for your knife? The police have that. Found it in your jacket while you were in theatre. The nurses were all talking about it. I kept your rock though," Robyn lifted her skirt and pulled the simple club out from its hiding place, held in position by the tension of the wide belt.

Spades sprang forward, but Robyn caught him with her free hand and forced him back through the air and down onto the hospital bed, with a crunch, knocking the fight out of him.

"I'm not going to kill you silly," she whispered. "I'm here to get you past the police."

Spades lay still. He was indeed broken, in this body his wounds were just too great to offer much fight against the female Redcap and she knew it.

***

The policeman on the door of the private room smiled as the nurse exited again, this time with the young man in a wheelchair.

"Right I'll just get him down to theatre. We'll be about half an hour if you wanted to get a cuppa at the nurse's station, sure the girls would love to see a man in uniform for a change," She flirted.

"I'm a married man!" The policeman laughed, although he was quite happy to be getting some attention.

"They're only going to be looking officer; they don't bite – unless you ask nicely," And she wiggled past, winking back at the policeman, who thought for a minute and then left his post for a drink.

"You're certainly sure of yourself," said Spades, as he was wheeled out of earshot.

"Well, I need to be, don't I? I have a gang to lead." The last words were said with no playful edge and Spades spun around to look at Robyn, "Like you didn't see it coming. Now close your mouth, you look like an idiot," she said coldly.

The thing was, he had seen it coming and the events of the Otherworld had been enough to give Robyn the boost she needed, damaging him enough that he would never be strong enough to fight her again. None of the others would have had this strength. He thought she would have needed Ringer to take over the pack but all she really needed was for Spades to not have William and Harold. Right now, however, it was just the two of them and even if he had been in peak health, he realised the girl would have given a better fight than most of the men he had ever met. Unlike Spades, she also had cunning and that meant she could win before the first blade was even drawn.

They exited the hospital and a scooter was waiting for them in the loading bay; a fishtailed parka and two of their trademark leather helmets on the saddle.

"It's a Vespa," said Spades, with a tinge of disappointment to his voice, "I'm a Lambretta guy. And there's also only one of them."

Robyn handed him the parka and one of the helmets, "Stop complaining. You're driving, I want to snuggle," she put on the other helmet.

For some reason this didn't fill Spades with confidence as he mounted the scooter, Robyn climbed on behind him and wrapped her arms around his waist.

"Who's scooter is this?" He asked out of curiosity. He wasn't upset about riding stolen equipment but he wanted to be pre-warned if the police flagged them down.

Robyn smiled, "Well there's the thing. I got it the same place I got the uniform. Pretty little thing she was. I'm sure the papers will have a field day when they find her."

Spades was starting to worry about how easy Robyn was killing. It was random enough to not leave a trail but Spades knew too much blood always had a way of leaving marks.

"We've got a train to catch. Take us to Euston Station," said Robyn suddenly, causing Spades to look at her.

"Shouldn't we see Camp Barrie?" He asked, thinking he still

Morningwood
wasn't quite ready to follow Robyn blindly.

"Already have done sweetie, who do you think gave me the tickets?" She held up five train tickets to Scotland.

"The others aren't coming," said Spades, wondering what the new leader would do with that information as she was clearly unaware of how many had died and how depleted her new pack was.

"Well, maybe we'll get a refund then," replied Robyn with little thought to the reason behind the lack of a gang, "I'm sure we can do the next bit on our own."

The scooter drove off and Robyn snuggled into Spades back, today was going to be a good day.

***

Jonathon sat quietly in his car, a shadow of his former self, sunken-eyed and chain smoking. His daughter was still not returned to him and he now believed that the agents had not succeeded in getting her back from the kidnappers. He reasoned the only way he would ever see his beloved Alice again, was to carry out the original plan, as laid down by the well-spoken man in the trilby. He had to tamper with the safety procedures of the reactor and set it to meltdown.

He looked up, before his car stood the great sphere of the Dounreay Nuclear Power Station, like a vast featureless globe dominating this stretch of Scottish coastline. He had often marvelled at how beautiful it was on the drive towards it, but today it just resembled a bomb.

He had driven in through the security gates and parked up early that morning, but couldn't bring himself to leave his car. It was an action that could have raised suspicion in others, but often he would sit in the comfort of his own vehicle, going through his paperwork and listening to the radio. Today the radio was silent, but he was still in his car as shifts changed and the skeleton crew of the night made way for the greater number of workers, who came in from outlying villages or just walked in from the cabins and the hotel reserved for workers who were normally further afield. A real family community in this distant location.

Jonathon was a familiar face around the site, despite being an irregular visitor here to go around and check all safety measures were being strictly adhered to. Recalibrating settings to make sure any problems were noticed the moment they happened. Such a familiar face in fact that many people who walked past his car, stopped and waved. He hated that more than anything. Their friendly faces would haunt him for evermore when he set the reactor to explode and took them with it if they hadn't made it far enough away or to safety bunkers around the site. He was a father though and that came with greater responsibility. He had to save his daughter whatever the costs. It wasn't his job to save everyone else.

He had a full day to prepare the meltdown. So many safety precautions to negate, so many distractions needed to stop his work from being spotted and if he did things right, he would give everyone enough time for an evacuation. He might be caught, of course, even jailed, but he would cross that bridge when he came to it. Alice was the only reason to continue now.

He stubbed out his cigarette in the already full ashtray and stepped from his car. The next few hours were crucial.

Morningwood
Chapter 20

Morningwood couldn't remember the last time he had been in a light aircraft. Jess was a very confident pilot and the flight was pleasant, taking them up into a clear cold sky that allowed fantastic views across the English countryside. Jess watched Morningwood study her instruments and look excitedly at the structure of the plane as the wings were buffeted by crosswinds and moisture formed along them.

Eventually, she asked if the Satyr would like a go at the controls and he took over with a boyish glee, listening carefully to her clear instruction and asking questions about why certain things had to be done and what problems he could face. Steadily, the winds became stronger and he reluctantly handed back control of the aircraft to the more competent pilot. He liked her calm nature very much.

He had taken the hour before their departure to get to know Jess better and not in the way that was expected of his kind. He had made her tea from a great silver urn and stopped his gnawing hunger by helping himself to her sandwiches, as she checked the plane over and readied for takeoff.

Jess was indeed the child of two Immortals and had therefore avoided the curse of the Titan mutation. She had chosen never to leave the mortal world and so had no idea of her Immortal form and whether it favoured her Father's or Mother's aspects, or even if she had taken on an image of her own. It had been an upset to her parents who felt she was somehow missing out on a wonder that few would ever see, but they respected her decision and felt it was better for her to find her own path than follow theirs. She had been obsessed with flying from an early age and both her parents had encouraged it, it may not be the Underworld, but she still got to see a world very few others experienced every time she took to the skies. Her father, the ever-lovely and resourceful Dagda, had made sure she was always fuelled and ready to fly, for her own enjoyment mainly, but also as an important aid to his work. With no connections to the Fellowship of Amalgamated Empires, if he chose to act outside the confines of his agency, he could do so with impunity and with not much more than a moment's notice. Of course, Dagda had spoken to his daughter in great lengths about exactly what it was he was asking her to be involved with and warned her of the dangers of this secretive life. She had lived a mortal existence (albeit a privileged one), but both her mother and father had made her fully aware of the Otherworld until she understood that nothing was what it seemed, there was no black and white amongst the Immortals. They had explained that someone may become a criminal of the Underworld simply because their actions went against the politics of the courts; the crimes of the Immortals rarely had anything to do with the morals adhered to by mankind. The rules were made by courts populated by statesmen and women elevated to the position by birthright, as opposed to ability and these courts would often be serving their own agenda before they represented the agenda of the people. When things were done for self-gain, anyone who stood against you was a threat and Jess had her eyes and mind wide open to the dangers if she was to act against their rulings. She had accepted this responsibility without question.

She was the perfect person to be flying the Satyr upcountry, she had no agenda other than to pilot her plane and she knew the immortal world only as a history rather than an interaction. Morningwood could relax as he would around any mortal and soon the conversation drifted away from all the troubles he had seen and all the hardships he was about to face, to the everyday small talk of two people getting to know each other better. She was a wicked flirt; her conversation was ribald and funny. Morningwood felt the pressure lifting from him with each mile and soon he found himself enjoying the flight and the landscape that passed beneath him until he found himself as interested with the view as he had found initially with the workings of the plane.

"We're just about to go over the ruins of Scarborough Castle," informed Jess happily, whilst checking her map. "Isn't that the seat of one of your courts?"

Morningwood watched the castle pass beneath them, he knew the echoes of the Underworld would sometimes reflect on the mortal landscape, though never as prevalent as they did the other way around. He always put this down to the shorter lives of the human race. The living landscape of the Underworld would emulate the beautiful creations of man, especially those with a greater relevance and impact because they had time to grow and change, unhindered by the natives. In contrast, for the Underworld to make an impression on the world above, a mortal would have to be inspired by the echoes in his short lifetime. Then for that inspiration to find form, it would have needed to happen to a mortal with the ability or money to build. It was rarer still for the natural landscape to mimic the echoes of the Underworld because Man was so destructive and controlling of the natural world around him. No tree really had the chance to mimic before it was cut down for firewood or building materials. Because of all this Morningwood didn't really keep up with the human structures that emulated echoes, beyond the very ancient burial places that acted as portals. The structures went up too infrequently and fell into ruin too quickly to recognise. He'd had some pointed out to him over the years and often just took the teller's word for it, but this was an important structure and pointed out to him by the daughter of a man whose job it was to be in the know. The Seelie had been forced back into the Underworld by the actions of the Satyrs and they would have needed to set up new courts, traditionally one on each land mass. Morningwood knew exactly where the Unseelie Court was as it had been there for aeons, but he had no idea where the Seelie had ended up on their return.

"You sure?" He queried, more out of confirmation than out of doubt.

"Positive. It's where Mum and Dad go to get back through to the Underworld, there's an FAE Headquarters on-site too."

Morningwood watched the buildings on the headland as they flew out over the water, taking careful note of its positioning and layout.

"I often wish I'd kept up more on the politics of home. It must be nice getting all the information from your father so easily?" He asked hoping to sound flippant.

Jess looked over at the Satyr with a chuckle, "Is that your best questioning technique, aren't you supposed to seduce answers out of me? You didn't even try it with a shirt button undone,"

Morningwood laughed himself. Jess was a lot more used to this spy world than him; he was just an old world warrior, a bit out of his depths.

"Not very James Bond am I?" He chuckled.

"Aw, you're doing okay. You look the part and you've certainly got me hot under the collar," she grinned.

Morningwood looked down at his suit, "If only the clothes were mine."

"Feel free to take them off and pop them in the back, if you're uncomfortable," Jess joked.

They chuckled for a while longer.

"You really don't know do you?" Jess said with an air of disbelief.

She had flown a lot of immortals over the last couple of years and conversation, although guarded, was always knowledgeable of the politics of the Underworld. It was refreshing to know that not everyone was up on the latest scandal or political power play.

"Not really, I'm more of a casual observer," Morningwood said looking across at his pilot, "I made the decision very early on to not let my kind take liberties, and with that achieved it seemed foolish to be constantly looking back."

Jess took an audible breath as if she was about to break her own code and needed to steady herself, "Well it's a fairly simple thing really, according to Dad. It all started when the Redcaps and Fomorii began to cause damage amongst the mortals. The Redcaps were very much solo at first so it wasn't a problem, but then Fomorii renegades started to use them like little armies."

"I remember all that," said Morningwood, "It was around that time I started finding their nests and... well, you get the idea. I even did a few little hunts with your father. It doesn't explain an agency."

"Well that's the thing, it does," continued Jess, "It wasn't just you having a pop at the Immortals who had settled here. Everyone had a go, and not just other Immortals. The British really got their act together when it came to eradicating non-humans; they just managed to keep it out of the history books."

Morningwood sighed, "I'm fully aware of that time; I used to act as a consultant, seemed only fair to teach them how to look after themselves from the likes of us. It also meant I didn't get any wake-up calls at the end of a revolver."

Jess looked over at the Satyr, it was a revelation to her, how involved he had been over the years and yet somehow outside the loop. "Well, with all that going on, the Redcaps went to ground, took on full mortal guises, along with Fomorii and any other immortal that wanted to slip by unnoticed. Quite apart from the fact the Underworld was still exiling people here, like a dumping ground for the dangerous. Trouble was, they were putting lions amongst the antelopes and as everyone knew from the Seelie Court moving here, that wouldn't end well, they needed keepers on hand. So the Seelie stepped up, using the selling point 'it takes one to know one' and they formed the FAE. Stupid name, Dad hates it."

Morningwood laughed, "I'm in full agreement with Dagda on that one."

Jess smiled before she continued, she liked the fact Morningwood was her dad's friend and not just someone he knew, "So, at first it worked pretty well. The FAE were policing the immortals here on Earth. The thing is, it's become more than that. The stalemate in the Underworld has become a bubbling cauldron, with no obvious solution. When things hit walls, some people try to work out how the walls can be knocked down."

Jess went quiet and looked across at Morningwood, who was looking at her intensely, listening to her history lesson unfold.

"So your Father's worried the fight down there is going to spill out up here?" Morningwood confirmed.

"It's already breaking out up here," she said looking concerned.

"Well let's try to make sure this incident isn't one of the turning points then," Morningwood smiled at Jess and was pleased when she smiled back.

"There you go," she said happily, "You are James Bond."

***

The next couple of hours passed with little conversation, the buffeting winds above the sea were taking Jess's concentration fully to the art of flying, leaving Morningwood alone with his thoughts. He had to assume his mission to Scotland was to stop a man from destroying a nuclear power station, with the knock-on effect of destroying the seat of the Unseelie Court. His chief way to do that was to tell him his daughter was dead and give the man no reason to commit the heinous act, having nothing to gain from it. Of course, it also meant the revelation gave the man nothing to lose either, in which case the Satyr would have to find another way to stop him. With that thought, he could feel the heavy weight of the revolver in his pocket, both physically and spiritually. He had never been a father himself, but he was a son and he knew how protective a parent could become of its children. His father was the last of a species, the great Silenus. Ancient and addle-brained, his father had bedded the teasing female fauns just to bring himself heirs, but the many resulting offspring were as sterile as mules. Nature breeds by design, a continuing circle of life. Parents have children that become parents. The Satyrs stood outside that circle, the first and last of their kind and that was why, without exception, they had chosen to protect the human innocents from the twisted morals of the immortals. Humanity had become their children and like protective fathers they stood beside them.

The question itself was simple, could Morningwood get the attention of Jonathon Moore and with no evidence, convince him of the death of his daughter, causing him to stop the meltdown. If the answer was no, could he snuff out that one mortal life and possibly save the immortal lives of hundreds? It would seem to most, an easy decision to make, but to Morningwood it was the difference between a light bulb and a candle. He could walk from a room and turn off a hundred light bulbs, by a single switch, without a second thought, extinguishing the constant glow. The cool unfaltering light gone. The world plunged into darkness. The candle, however, was a different matter; he had to concentrate to blow out just one flame. The closer you got, the more alive it became. A dancing fluctuating array of colours, affected by all around it, rising up in brilliance or dying down in near defeat and in return giving back, light and heat.

When it was gone there would be the same darkness but Morningwood never missed the steady glow of the bulb but he always missed the dancing flame. It was never about what you produced in life it was about the way you went about producing it. He knew he wasn't alone in this thought, only the blowing out of candles felt like enough of a sacrifice to earn a wish. It was why humans were so like a narcotic to the immortals, their flesh was still only flesh, but its consumption released the giddy feel of destroying something beautiful.

He turned and looked at Jess, carefully reading her instruments, fighting the elements. So beautiful and so alluring because she chose humanity over immortality, choosing to experience certain finality rather than an endless horizon, to be the flame, not just the light.

He would try to convince Jonathon, but if he failed he would burn with him. He reached into his pocket and removed the revolver, opened the small triangular window that flooded the plane with cold and threw it out into the sea far below.

"Something you want to tell me?" Asked Jess as Morningwood closed the window.

"Just making sure I didn't have any temptations," he said giving his pilot a smile.

Jess assumed it was some kind of weird Satyr thing and let it go without further question. They were starting to see Scotland below them and soon she would be flying into Wick.

***

The train journey had started whilst Morningwood still nestled asleep in his cell, but it had been a blast from beginning to end. Robyn and Spades had stowed the scooter in the guard's van and then gone to their carriage. A slim corridor led them to a compartment, one long, blue, upholstered seat, facing another, wire luggage racks above. The couple sat down and soon a businessman entered the carriage, bowler-hatted and struggling with a leather suitcase and umbrella. He nodded at the couple and lifted his case onto the rack before sitting down, removing his hat and unfolding a copy of The Times he had expertly managed to keep clasped beneath his arm. He smiled at the couple and then took in their attire. Spades was clearly sat in a hospital gown, barefoot and wearing a khaki parker jacket, his head heavily bandaged. Robyn was dressed as a nurse, although she had folded up the hem of the sensible dress to ride the scooter until it was almost indecent in length and showed off her stockings. The man realised he was staring when he felt both their eyes upon him.

"Off to a party?" He asked, hoping to break the awkward silence.

"A reunion," added Robyn helpfully, with a disarming smile.

The man nodded, as the train pulled from the station, "Very nice. Fancy dress obviously?"

"Obviously," said Robyn with a grin, whilst Spades looked out of the window, watching London drift past, still not happy with the change of command.

"I do like dressing up," said the man, a wistful faraway look on his face, picturing the fun of past parties.

"It's a lovely suit," complimented Robyn, causing the man to smile.

"It's from my Saville Row tailor. I do feel if you're going to wear something regularly it should be quality," he said happily before leaning forward as if to say something conspiratorial, Robyn leant in too, enjoying the game of conversation, "I have another two in my suitcase." He continued, "They say manners maketh the man, but I don't think they took into consideration the importance of a good suit." They both leant back laughing.

The door opened and stopped the laughter, as a serious, ashen-faced ticket inspector leant in. Tickets were checked and the compartment fell silent again.

It was some time later when Robyn asked the man if he knew how much longer the journey was. He had been doing the crossword and everyone had been left with their thoughts.

Spades was thinking about how far they kept moving away from his beloved London and Robyn had been thinking through a series of grizzly unfolding plans, whilst the gentleman had been trying his hardest to distract his attention from the very short-skirted girl directly in front of him. Being brought back into conversation with her didn't help.

"This is the longest stretch, young lady. Acres of wonderful countryside, but you'll soon be seeing the northern towns again," the man replied helpfully, before stopping and glancing on the seat beside Robyn, happy to have somewhere else to direct his eyes.

"I didn't notice that before, is it aboriginal?" The man said hoping to impress the saucy young girl with his knowledge of the world; to point out to her he wasn't just a city suit.

"This? No, it's just a rock on a stick. I made it myself," she grinned and the man was aware of the slim pale scars that ran from the corners of her mouth, following the cheekbones.

***

Jess smiled at the Satyr from within the warmth of the plane's

Morningwood

hanger. They had landed almost an hour beforehand and settled down to plan Morningwood's next move.

"I'm going to be here until tomorrow if you need a flight back," she said, watching Morningwood studying the map her father had given him. He didn't look up so she continued, "I'll be staying at The Mackays Hotel, in the town, if you need a warm bed for the night." She went quiet, having a sip of her tea, "Of course I'll be in it… naked."

"What?" Said Morningwood looking up from the map distracted by something, but not sure what.

Jess laughed happily, leant across and kissed him passionately. The Satyr instinctively kissed back, her lips warm and soft, the pleasant sensation causing just the right amount of increased heartbeat and interest before she broke away and Morningwood raised an eyebrow.

"It's a girl meets Satyr kind of thing," she said with a breathless smile, "In case I don't see you again. I would have been annoyed at myself." She stood up, straightened her clothes in a slightly fidgety way, her cheeks flushed, "Now this war isn't going to prevent itself. You need to get going," she said with her voice wavering.

Morningwood stood up himself. "Thanks for the flight," he said, and Jess pointed at the door as if his instructions had been given and the Satyr walked out into the night.

Jess fell against a wall biting her knuckles, 'Damn. Just from a kiss!' She thought.

***

Morningwood left the airport and looked to find a taxi. He hoped he could still do this kind of stuff on his own. He wasn't truly convinced it was his fight, but the more he thought about it, the more he realised it had always been his fight, it's just now the rules had changed. He wished he'd waited for Mulberry now and hoped whatever she was doing, it felt more structured than his plan.

Chapter 21

Of course, Mulberry's structure was completely out of step with the mortal world. She hoped she had worked out the time difference correctly and would be in the right place if needed. The Journey through the Underland had been more fraught than Mulberry would have liked and time was becoming a premium. Not because of the obstacles she met, but rather the places she had to avoid.

The Wolf Frog was a good companion and as they passed through the warmer lands of the Seelie Court. The heat had started to warm its blood and the abundant food gave it energy. The creature's speed increased until the wind rushed through her hair with every bound.

Soon the world, however, turned back to the cold winds of the Unseelie and the snow banks grew in size. Mulberry's mount slowed as the temperature lowered and the strain of the journey played heavily on its limbs until it stopped and refused to move any further despite her gentle urging. The Nymph dismounted quickly, her aspect had changed to accommodate the landscape and she realised she could move faster without her sluggish ride. With a brisk pat, she was gone. The Frog eyed her as she moved away; they had been almost one for a very long time, the Nymph's words at the heart of its simple mind, driving it on. Now it was free, but still it hesitated like a loyal hound and although it did not follow, it chose to wait in case she returned, like the seasons.

It had always been the way that the years were divided like seasons. The Seelie brought life and sunshine, the Unseelie brought the cold and darkness. When the Seelie left for the land above, the Underworld froze, a blanket of snow spreading across the land. The Underworld became of one court and although the time was brief, it had been welcomed like a golden age. Then without warning the Seelie had returned, fresh from war and needing to know there would be warmth and new blooms. The Unseelie did not see why they should relinquish a world that had been handed to them. The Unseelie knew darkness in all its forms but the Seelie were now bathed in blood and with their return came war.

It raged in great clashing battles until areas were won or lost, kingdoms became bathed in an eternal winter or an endless summer.

Morningwood

Nature suffered, calling out for the order of seasons to be restored, but by now both courts believed that to relinquish their control would mean they would never find power again.

They had met an impasse; the battles had ended but a true cold war began.

It was this divide that Mulberry was banking on, she practically skimmed over the surface of the snow to reach her destination and soon she broke through the frozen forest to the ice plain beyond. The Unseelie Court stood on the coastline, a great glacier of a building. Morningwood had been right, it looked like a sprawling version of the ruined castle from the postcard when it had been in its heyday. Sat close to the Unseelie Court, a great patch of unfrozen land circled a giant lantern tree. Devoid of leaves and grown so quickly it had brought up huge rocks in its branches, it formed just one great sphere and from between the latticework cage of wood and rock shone the most vibrant of light. Despite the cold Mulberry could feel it's heat from where she stood a good distance away.

***

Pippi and Zippo had lost the trail several times over the last couple of days. It was certainly more luck than judgement that found them on the edge of the tree line watching the disappearing figure of Mulberry.

"She's going to get away!" Pippi shouted at her silent companion, and without thinking she broke from the safety of the tree line to give chase.

The words echoed across the ice field and Mulberry turned to see her pursuers. She was still a far greater distance from the Court than she was from the trees and fear gripped her heart. She had to outrun the pursuers or her mission would be over.

Pippi saw the surge forward and realised the chase was on. She pressed forward until she was at a sprint. The shape of the bone baton she held felt good in her hand and she played with the option of throwing it to slow her prey, but she was faster and the gap was closing quickly, she would be close enough to strike far quicker than Mulberry could escape.

Zippo was tired, he had carried Pippi most of the way, with her dangling beneath him like a bird of prey with a catch returning to the nest. The going had been a lot faster and she worked well as a spotter of tracks but now the Sluagh had nothing left to give, even without his carried load. He simply watched her stored energy come into play as she went after the Nymph they had sought for many hours. As he hovered, Zippo saw the Frog break from the trees. It had rested, growing colder before it came to the realisation that food had always been plentiful with its rider around, and so followed her once more.

It needed energy if it was to survive, and on seeing the form of Mulberry it went after her and was pleased to see she had found food too. Despite the speed of the Redcap, it was faster and in just as much hurry to reach its target.

Zippo could not call out a warning but force of habit caused him to bellow out a silent shout of danger and to his surprise Pippi turned.

The Frog struck with its sticky projectile and the Redcap was snared, caught by surprise. The tongue hit her in the chest and stuck solid but Pippi was not prepared to be a meal.

She spun the baton in her hand, brought the point to the fore and drove it through the fleshy tube, pinning it to the ground and digging in her own feet to make a secure anchor. The Frog, rather than reeling her in, was being pulled along by its retracting tongue. Its strength was great and Pippi felt her feet move and the bone weapon started to pull free from the soil.

Then all things went at once, the pin wrenched from the ground and the Redcap lost her footing, flying towards the open gullet of the Wolf Frog.

She was prepared this time and stretching out into the shape of a star, grabbed the lips of the giant amphibian and halted her progress. Zippo had now arrived and from the sky he landed heavily on the creature's back, his clothes breaking off into the deathly black smoke finding the Frog's nostrils and open mouth, disappearing quickly inside with the first intake of breath. It bucked once, its eyes rolled alarmingly, then collapsed on the snow, dead, curls of smoke exiting its open mouth.

Pippi was cursing loudly as she peeled the tongue from her skin and retrieved the bone baton. A look behind her proved the Nymph had escaped and was safe in the embrace of the Unseelie Court. She struck the corpse with the club end of her weapon and helped Zippo slide from the already crystallising back, his smoke clothes returning, but gossamer light in their look as if they were being used up by the kills.

"She's gone," spat the Redcap, "We should return, tell Spades the news."

Pippi's words were met with an agreeing nod from Zippo and they set off back to the woods to find a portal.

They had passed many in the last couple of miles, Scotland was truly a place of tunnels between worlds and it was easy to see why the Unseelie had held onto it so strongly. With so many to choose from, the pair found it easy to find a portal that had attracted no predators. The landscape was so bleak and the portals so numerous, they did not have the same prey luring advantage as they did in the South.

Although they didn't have the knowledge of experience, the journey through was smoother than those in the South too and soon Pippi was stood on a rise in the Scottish Highlands looking down at a winding tarmac road. She sat awhile on a rock, adjusting to the feel of clothes back on her skin, the less wiry limbs giving her shape. She had never considered herself vain, it was difficult to enjoy your own appearance when your pack sister was the gorgeous Robyn, so she had certainly revelled in the freedom of the bestial features she came to sport in the Underworld.

At first she waited for Zippo to appear, but when she realised the consequences of the death in the Underworld, she called for him. The loose dirt of the hillside span in front of her, lifting up briefly in the simplest of shapes before falling heavily to the ground. Pippi stood with the weak sun at her back casting a greyish shadow across the ground. For a moment, it looked only as remarkable as her own outline but then it moved, manipulated by another hand and although Pippi stood with her back to the sun it was the image of Zippo that lay across the floor.

"You made it through!" She said happily, although the true loss of her companion was evident. The shadow nodded, before pointing off towards the road. "Yes, we need to choose a way and follow it. Find a phone box and call Camp Barrie," she concluded.

The shadow almost humorously sculpted itself into the image of a telegraph pole and Pippi turned and saw the line of poles following the road.

"Of course, the telegraph poles will lead to a phone," she said confirming she had understood the instruction, as she turned back to the shadow of Zippo, "You always were the clever one."

The shadow shrugged.

***

Mulberry had not made it to safety, but she had seen the intervention of her old mount. Taking the chance to hide rather than run, she had simply dived beneath the snow whilst her pursuers were distracted. She had no illusions the Wolf Frog could win the battle and felt sorry for it if it managed to get a psychotically-fighting Redcap into its slow-digesting belly, but it's death was mercifully quick in the end. For a moment, she mourned her mount's passing, before watching the Redcap and the Sluagh fall for her deception of safety.

When she felt she was finally alone, she shook herself free of the snow. Enclosed in its watery element, her skin had become almost as translucent as ice. She walked back the short distance to the Frog and placed her hand upon it as if draining its remaining life force. Her body shifted to the rich green patterned skin, her fingers webbed and the dreadlocks returned, whilst the Frog shifted to the frozen corpse it was, all colour draining. It was the greatest homage the Nymph could offer her fallen ride.

Thus attired she turned and approached the Court.

It could easily be mistaken for a building from a distance and certainly had been sculpted in places to show images of figures and creatures. Defensive positions had been fortified and enclosed, but up close it had the same structure and design of a glacier. Ice so thick and old it appeared as strong and unchanging as rock. The colours of it were myriad, from the subtlest translucent blue through the soft virginal white of snow to the hard grey of ancient ice. Great seams of black volcanic rock marred its many layers and ran down through the impossibly high edifice. It wasn't a solid, unmoving block however, the warmth of the lantern tree had caused the surface to warm and steam rose to become clouds around its more chill surfaces. Waterfalls carved grooves and bubbled and splashed into vast clear pools and mountain lakes in which creatures played.

In fact, if you looked, the glacier was alive with moving figures, many frozen into its surface and forming the decorative architecture. Once she realised this, the Nymph realised the Court was watching her every move and the building was alive. There was no real entrance to the Court, but a natural bridge over a channel of churning water led to a greater fissure in the face of the Glacier and crows spiralled above. The carrion bird was a natural denizen of the Underworld that had settled unquestioned into the world of man. They were the eyes of the Unseelie Court on Earth and by their presence Mulberry knew her entrance was observed, the knowledge of her crimes already known. If she were not halted at this point, then she would be expected to continue onward; permission would be silently given.

If she were not welcome, then the terror of the Unseelie would descend upon her.

The Barghest were the guardians of any dark court, great monstrous hounds with an appetite as much for destruction as they had for filling their bellies. Under the noisy croaking of the restless crows, she could hear their uncomfortable, deep throated growls deep within the Court and could picture their dark black shaggy coats and burning red eyes as they pulled at their restraining chains.

She walked on until the great walls of ice rose up either side of her. And the true chill of the Court seeped into her bones. Her presence had not gone unnoticed by other creatures either. An Ice Nymph somehow moved within the wall beside her. Mulberry concluded the structure must have been like a vast aquarium, liquid on the inside, possibly leading up to one of the great pools on the glaciers surface. The Ice Nymph had sadness in her eyes and a shape that would have only been considered pleasing to the monstrous angler fish that lived in the ocean's depths. If it had not been for the phosphorus lighting that played beneath her skin, she would have been truly ugly to behold.

Eventually she swam away, leaving Mulberry to look at her own reflection in the ice wall and breath a sigh of relief that she too was not of the creature's aspect. Her body had returned fully to the spilling tangles of muddied dreadlocks, her skin still the rich green of her homage to the Wolf Frog, striped limbs and dark red swirls.

She jumped when the Ice Nymph returned and slammed against the inner surface of the wall. She had brought with her another creature of the water – a mermaid – dark in aspect, but still beautiful and made more so by the closeness of the Ice Nymph. The two followed silently along beside her, a silent swimming honour guard. The mermaid kicking its powerful, smooth tail to propel it onwards, the horrific Ice Nymph following along the wall, hand over hand like a mime trying to escape an invisible box. It was unnerving to have them with her but at the same time it gave her comfort to not be alone. They were, after all, of the same breed as her, despite their appearance and they distracted her long enough that she forgot the sound of the hounds. Soon she was walking into a great chamber, and her silent watery companions were left behind as she entered the courtyard of ice.

It was to all purposes a throne room. The space was empty apart from a ziggurat that rose up from the floor, upon its uppermost surface the Lord of the Unseelie sat in a great outcrop of rock and ice. Mulberry glanced back to face the wall upon which he looked and a host of silent faces stared back at her like the statues of twisted saints on the walls of a great cathedral, honouring the macabre. These statues were the Court and their silence was because their Lord was to attend to a matter and that matter was Mulberry.

She walked up the great ice steps to the throne. Glad to have the faces of the Court behind her, although she could feel every intense gaze.

The Lord was magnificent.

Half frozen into his natural throne he looked as if he had grown out of the very ground itself. Although sat, she could tell he was close on nine feet tall if he had stood up from the structure to which he was frozen. His head was sculpted and had the look of an octopus trying to impersonate the noble head of an elephant. Eight thick, smooth tentacles ended the face of the Unseelie Lord. The middle four twisted together like a strong, manipulative trunk. The outer four, two each side, curled in great arcs, held bone rigid, giving him the countenance of four powerful tusks. His eyes, of which he had four, were dark and full of wisdom. They watched her climb slowly towards him. His body was heavy and scarred, like a great white whale and obscenely male in its nakedness.

Morningwood

As she reached him, she realised she had no understanding of how to behave. He sat like a man. No, she corrected herself, he sat like a king, his muscular arms resting on his throne. His great hands ended in three thick digits like a pachyderm foot become as dexterous as an ape. His great feet were planted firmly on the ground, which circled up around them until he was indiscernible from the rock upon which he sat, in both texture and colour. The whole image made it clear, that if you wished to depose the Lord of the Unseelie you needed to unseat the very land itself.

Mulberry stopped before him and sank to her knees, head bowed, hair spilling across the floor exposing the nape of her neck, so she looked more like a willing sacrifice than a loyal subject.

The silence went on for an age. She desperately wanted to raise her head and look upon the Lord again, but she could hear the growls of the Bhargest in the distance.

"What brings you to my court, White Mulberry of the Gales?" The Lord spoke, his voice resonate and deep like the powerful sea rolling in a cave. She knew he would know who she was, but to hear him say her name made her blood run chill.

"I bring warning Lord," she said, her voice not much more than a whisper and she almost felt the Court behind her crane forward to hear her words.

"You bring warning to me. An exiled Nymph brings warning to a High Lord," his voice was neither questioning nor mocking but she knew if her next words were not chosen carefully then she could end her life on the spot.

"There are plots in the above to harm the Court," she said, not raising her head. She chose not to suggest the Court was in danger or could be destroyed, as they were inflammatory statements that could only hurt her case.

"To harm us you say?"

Mulberry was pleased her choice of words had not angered the Lord before her.

"And I am to assume that knowing this knowledge, the harm is preventable?" It was the first real question and Mulberry hoped it might be a breakthrough as a question usually means you are being spoken with, not spoken at.

"Yes, Lord," she said, knowing not to ramble in the presence of a power that could snuff her life in a thought.

"And for this knowledge you expect what in return?" The Behemoth Lord asked of the creature before him.

"Forgiveness," she whispered.

Morningwood
Chapter 22

Just outside Edinburgh, the new ticket inspector boarded the train and, as was procedure, proceeded to recheck tickets along the train. It was often a thankless task as weary passengers searched again for tickets they would frustratingly explain had already been checked. So each new compartment was just another unwarranted intrusion. He opened the door to a carriage with its blinds drawn, expecting the worst kind of reception. It was always a worry you'd walk in on a private discussion or sleeping passenger you would have to wake up. Luckily the occupants were a trendy young couple, he assumed were from London. The young man was asleep in a nice fitting suit but appeared to have a tie around his face, covering one eye. It certainly matched his suit nicely, but he still looked strange to the more conservative man who had grown up in a small mining town, before taking to the railways, to avoid long days down the pit. The lady was also dressed in a tailored suit and wore a bowler hat at a rakish angle. She was awake and smoking a slim cigarette that filled the compartment with a bluish smoke. The moment he entered she coughed and held up already punched tickets without saying a word, but the inspector took them and punched them again to show he was doing his job.

"Lairg," he said absently, "You'll need to change at Inverness."

"Thank you," the woman said with a sweet smile.

"Do you need a hand putting that suitcase up on the luggage rack?" He enquired looking at a bulky old suitcase on the floor.

"It's very heavy," said the woman, "And a bit sticky, I wouldn't want you to hurt your back or get your uniform mucky," she said again with a winning smile.

"As you wish," he said, smiled and left the carriage pulling the door closed behind him to give the couple privacy again, thinking to himself; what a nice young lady if only they were all like that his day would go much better.

***

It was night-time before they arrived at the distant Scottish train stop and quickly unloaded the scooter from the guard's van. The station car park was well lit but the station house was closed and as the train pulled away it gave the feeling of being stranded in the middle of nowhere. Two lads were loitering beneath the light as if it was the only place to hang out and between them stood a battered old moped. The sudden arrival of real mods and a scooter was the best thing that had happened in years.

The boys gathered around them excitedly, asking questions:

"How fast did it go?"

"Why were they in Lairg?"

"What was the rock on the stick for?"

***

Robyn and Spades headed towards the site at Dounreay. They had to make sure the complete mission was carried out. At any time, the police could contact the girl's father although Robyn had been assured by Camp Barrie this was an issue that had been dealt with. They just needed to know he was going to go ahead with the task, even if they had to force him.

They were surprised when out on this lonely Scottish road what appeared to be a hitchhiker showed up in their headlight beams. She started waving the moment she could be seen, and soon the scooters slowed. It was Pippi, and she knew straight away something had changed. Robyn rode a Lambretta whilst Spades followed slightly behind on a moped, the type of bike ridden by delivery boys, that sounded like it was powered by an elastic band. The couple also appeared to be wearing matching suits. The biggest surprise to Pippi was that Spades could see to drive.

"How the hell?" Said Robyn jumping from the scooter and embracing her pack sister, the moment she worked out who it was who stood beside the road.

"I phoned Camp Barrie, he told me you'd be coming in on the train and I should walk this road 'cos it was the only one you'd be able to take and we should get back together," she pushed herself from Robyn's embrace.

"He told me about Ringer," Pippi said giving Robyn a look, "I assume you killed him?"

"It was the only thing to do. All part of the great circle, Pippi.

Morningwood

Girls on top now," Robyn looked back at Spades, who almost growled at her but thought better of it. Power was driving Robyn into a killing frenzy and now wasn't the time.

"Where's Zippo?" The female Redcap leader enquired.

Pippi pointed at the shadow that was cast by the scooter's headlamp and it bowed towards Robyn.

The lead Redcap bowed back, "Charmed I'm sure," she said with an affected posh accent.

"Another one who would still be with us if you hadn't just gone swanning off," said Pippi with annoyance in her voice.

"He is still with us," said Robyn pointing at the shadow, "And the moment we can find him a body we will."

"Trust me there's a lot of those coming up," added Spades, "Your new leader seems to think it's the end of days, all of a sudden."

Robyn turned on Spades, her face full of joy, warning Spades even more effectively than a growl would have, "Would you prefer you were still in charge? What was the body count again? How many have we lost whilst under your command? Four by my count, five if we take Zippo as a casualty."

"Which we do," added Pippi.

Spades bristled, "You killed Ringer, with your own hands," he shouted angrily.

"It was with my foot actually, and only after you chopped his arm off. He wasn't going to last much longer. If anything my actions were out of mercy," said Robyn lightly tipping her head coyly to one side.

"There are still four of us, despite Zippo's condition and if it works for Camp Barrie, it will work for him. Pippi here can choose what wrapping her man comes in." She fired up the scooter's engine, "Pippi, you're behind me, Zippo, you're riding with Spades."

Pippi hesitated for a moment. She was drawn to the power of Robyn, but she still blamed her for a lot of their current situation.

Then she saw Spades nod at her. It was a simple gesture as if to say; 'Come sit behind me and soon things will return to normal'. She looked at her pack sister and although less obvious than Spades' nod, a look crossed her eyes that showed how flimsy Robyn knew her grip was on the leadership.

Pippi made her choice and straddled the seat behind Robyn. As the two vehicles moved off along the dark Scottish road, Pippi hoped she had made the right one.

***

Morningwood was getting out of a taxi at the far end of that same road, many miles away. The nuclear site before him was lit up like a national monument. The great white sphere glowing with reflected light as if the powers that be had lassoed the moon and pulled it to Earth.

"Need me to wait?" The taxi driver asked, prompting Morningwood to lean back down and look through the window.

"I should be alright. I think it might be a long night," he replied with a smile.

With a friendly nod, the taxi driver pulled away, driving back off into the night, leaving the Satyr a lone figure on the road.

The gatehouse guard eyed Morningwood suspiciously as he approached the barrier. He had only started his night-time vigil a couple of hours earlier. First, he had seen off the day shift, as was normal, with the tooting of horns from the regulars wanting to be signed out with little effort and the odd, unfamiliar face coming over to sign out personally to prove they had left at the end of the day and not knocked off early – as was often the case with contractors who still had a long drive ahead of them.

The night shift were now all in the building keeping things ticking over. Usually, the gate guard would have no further duties until the shifts changed again, but here at his barrier was a bearded and suited man, turned up in a taxi as if he was planning on going to a party. For some reason the guard felt he should pick up his torch. He'd always been told if you feel threatened, take your torch. It's long and heavily weighed down with batteries. You can get a good swing at a man with the right type of torch. He stepped from his guardhouse and walked towards the man approaching.

"You alright there Sir?" He hailed, as a form of friend or foe warning, half expecting the gentleman to just be a looky loo attracted over by the spectacle of the sphere but actually with a destination elsewhere.

"I'm here to see Mr Moore," Morningwood said confidently.

The Security guard cupped his ear suddenly aware the distance

Morningwood

was too great for him to really hear properly, despite the quietness of the location. Morningwood continued the approach so when he repeated his request they were an ordinary speaking distance apart.

"I'm here to see Jonathon Moore," he said calmly, aware his appearance on site must be out of the ordinary and it was obviously upsetting the gate guard enough that he was holding his torch like a mace, the beam shone at his feet.

"The Safety Inspector?" The gate guard asked with an element of confusion on his face, "He's not due for a couple of weeks."

"Ahhh!" Said Morningwood, worried he had indeed jumped to too many conclusions and the man he sought wasn't here after all.

"I'll check the log, but it would have to be a surprise inspection if he did show up today."

With these words, the guard retreated to his hut and started looking through the signing in book, leaving the Satyr stood at the security gate.

Morningwood looked up to the clear night sky, the stars were brilliant overhead. He had missed them living so close to London. He started to whistle and realised how cold it had become when his tune came out with misty blasts of air.

"My mistake. Here he is, signed in this morning," said the guard interrupting the tune and holding up the ledger, as if his words alone were not enough to convince, "Was he expecting you?"

"Not really expecting me, but he certainly will know who I am and why I'm here," Morningwood replied. He wished the man would invite him past the barrier so he didn't look pushy and arouse suspicion.

"I'll give him a phone sir and tell him you're here." The guard disappeared inside the hut for a second before leaning back out again a bit embarrassed, "Who actually are you?"

Morningwood chuckled, "I'm Professor Morningwood. I'm here about his daughter."

"Alice isn't it?" The gate guard asked as if showing off his knowledge of employees without making it a statement and appearing big headed.

"Yes, it is," confirmed the Satyr, feeling awkward at the use of the present tense. He was pleased when the guard disappeared back inside to make the call, he was starting to get a bit chilly stood out here on a cold, clear Scottish night. It was almost as if the guard had heard his thoughts and when Morningwood next made eye contact through the window of his hut, the guard waved him over, phone pressed to his ear. He walked around the barrier, something that had always amused him about security barriers; they were only to stop cars and then only the ones that were slowing to stop anyway. They were more an honour system of security.

He walked into the guard hut and was happy to find a paraffin heater was keeping the room toasty. A black and white television was on in the corner with the sound down and through the fuzz he could see a bearded man in a tank top explaining algebra on a large blackboard.

"They're just trying to find him," said the guard, placing his hand over the mouthpiece of the phone and on seeing the television was still on and attracting attention, added, "It's the Open University on BBC2. Can't get a signal for anything else and the fella's voice keeps me company. Beats the hell out of the Shipping Forecast," and he tapped a silent radio on the desk.

Morningwood nodded and absent-mindedly straightened the antenna of the television to remove some of the fuzz.

"It's the reactor," said the guard, phone still pressed to his ear, "It plays havoc with the recep –"

The guard's voice changed as his small talk was interrupted and he went all official, trying not to let annoyance enter his voice as he saw the man in his hut pick up and start fiddling with his torch. He took it carefully out of his hands and stood it back on the side, never breaking his conversation with the other end of the phone.

"That's not a problem. I'll ask the man to come back tomorrow," he said calmly before replacing the receiver.

"Well, you heard that. I'm afraid they can't find him and if he's doing an inspection, he might be in parts of the reactor that aren't safe to get into. It's a shame you didn't come during the day; a lot more staff can root around for him." The guard sagely nodded his head and spun in his chair, "I'll take a note of your details and when I see him I'll pass them on. What hotel are you staying at?" He enquired, taking a notebook from a drawer, placing it on the desk, and wondering where the pen had gone.

"I'm sorry," said Morningwood apologetically.

Morningwood

"Don't be sorry, it's a big site but I doubt you put anybody out too much."

"No, I'm sorry," said Morningwood again and knocked the guard out with the torch.

He hadn't liked doing it. Despite all the films, the Satyr knew that a knockout blow to the head could cause serious damage. He laid the guard down on the ground before tying him up with the television and radio cables and sealing his mouth with a strip of gaffer tape pulled from a temporary patch on the chair. He slipped the guard's pass from his neck and the keys from his belt and pushed him beneath the desk. He was about to walk away when he thought differently, put the man's jacket beneath his head and turned him into the recovery position; if he had done damage he might as well try and lessen the impact. He raised the barrier and turned off the lights in the guardhouse, closing the door behind him.

Chapter 23

Morningwood walked confidently into the foyer of the power station. Another guard was on the front desk, a young man, possibly recently out of school, reading a magazine. He looked flustered as Morningwood entered and put his magazine down, closing it quickly. Morningwood held up the security pass and without checking, the desk guard nodded him through, seemingly happy to see the man move on. The Satyr chuckled to himself as he walked through the door to the corridor beyond; he wondered how long embarrassment at a natural curiosity would remain an issue amongst mortals. He had found himself pass through more than one portal in his life unchallenged, as some gatekeeper blushed in his wake.

The corridor was clinical and lined with doors, all with little windows that allowed the Satyr to examine the rooms quickly without entering. Many were in darkness, but one contained people working at desks and control panels. They had a glass window before them that overlooked the interior of the reactor, with its metal walkways and stairs.

Eventually, all the rooms were in darkness, however many corners Morningwood turned, and the place began to feel very empty.

His way was finally barred by double doors, securely locked with an access card. He tried the hole punched card he had taken from the security guard and was both happy and surprised when it opened. Beyond the office, corridors became gantries and walkways as seen through the control room window. The lights were protected by metal cages and signs and safety barriers were erected everywhere. On pegs, this side of the door hung big white coats and yellow safety helmets. Without thinking, Morningwood slipped them on and passed through to the industrial workspace of the operation.

It was after a few moments of searching that a moving light below attracted his attention and Morningwood descended into the darkness, turning on his own purloined torch. He heard the light below him go off with a click and saw the beam disappear, but he still carried on his descent, listening to the sound of badly stifled breathing.

On reaching the lower floor he shone his torch straight into the face of Jonathon, cowering beneath a metal stairway. The man looked

Morningwood

scared, so Morningwood shone his torch onto his own face then back at Jonathon. Recognition was playing across the haggard man's features. He was sunken, sweaty and broken as an individual.

"My Alice…" he whispered, "Do you have her, can I stop?" His eyes were already glassy with tears and he looked like one of the true Underworld denizens, despite his attire.

"You can stop," said Morningwood his voice staying as calm as he could.

The man started to cry drawing dark lines through the dust on his face, "I was so close to finishing… I could have…"

Morningwood shone his torch up, wondering what had been done to turn this source of energy into a bomb big enough to affect two worlds.

"Can you reverse it?" Morningwood asked.

"Have you seen her?" Jonathon asked, his mind on a single track, "Or are you just a messenger?"

Morningwood turned his torch back onto the man, but he did not see the pleading father; instead the silent face of the dead girl caught in the police car's headlights. He saw the faces of so many innocents who had fallen in the path of the immortals' journeys. So many times he could not be there to protect them from his own people.

"I have seen her," he added when the man's sorrowful image broke through his memories. He wanted to tell the father of the loss, but a grieving man would be no use to him. He needed a man buoyed up by joyfulness to remove whatever actions he had put in place.

"Is she well?" Jonathon asked. He was starting to doubt the words of the man before him and needed proof.

Morningwood, pointed with the torch at the workings of the great reactor, "You will need to remove what you have done and I can take you to her."

"Is she well?" Jonathon asked again, realising his basic question had been avoided. He wasn't a simple man and wouldn't be taken for one. His words were said slowly and with great care. He knew if he did not get an answer then the bearded man spoke falsely.

Morningwood knew this too; he turned and faced the father. He could not choose for him, the path of his next action had to come from the man himself.

"She is dead."

There was no way he could have softened the blow, he had seen it done so many ways and always the grief was the same. The individual would have to act on that grief how they saw fit.

Jonathon had heard these words before, spoken without an understanding of how it would tear his heart apart and the words had not been true, they were words used to manipulate his actions.

"How dare you?" Jonathon hissed, "How dare you use my Alice against me. The task is almost complete but without me the reactor will enter a catastrophe of its own design, you cannot halt it without me and I will not halt it until I see my daughter." He felt powerful for the first time in all of this, he had the might of the reactor behind him. He did not, however, count on the Satyr's actions.

Morningwood grabbed the man by the scruff of the neck and like a wayward child pulled him struggling back up the stairs. His feet slipped, his shins banged against walkways and guardrails. If he went to struggle he was pitched to the floor, its grate-like surface scraping his flesh. Then he was almost thrown through the door, his angry complaints became pleading as he realised he was coming back to the offices of the skeleton crew that manned the station during the night time hours.

Morningwood had feared the man would dig stubbornly in like a tick. Why should he not go forward with the only plan to save his daughter? If he was wrong and his daughter was dead, what did he have to lose, his life was over in his eyes. Either way it was only his daughter's life that counted.

The night watch were surprised when the door opened and a bearded man in a reactor coat and safety helmet marched a bloodied and crying inspector into their control room and forced him down into a chair. The actions showed the man was not involved in an accident but somehow was in trouble. Everyone knew Mr Moore was on-site, despite not having seen him, because a few moments earlier they had gone looking for him. The faces all turned from the man they knew, to the man they did not.

"You are about to have a catastrophe in your reactor," the stranger said with a commanding voice, his best one, learned over many military campaigns. He was not a leader of men, but he knew the exact tone to make men followers. A few of the gathered workers looked at the bank of dials and lights behind them.

Morningwood

"It's a possibility the signs won't show on your read-outs, but don't let that stop you running checks," the Satyr stated, seeing they were hanging on his words.

A few of the workers took that to mean start checking, so returned to chairs and started quickly typing on built-in keyboards to run diagnostics.

"This man has been threatened with his daughter's life to blow up the reactor and I'm sure some of you can understand how that might feel and why he would want to hide his being discovered and hide it well. He is not a bad man he is a scared man. I don't know the questions to ask him to stop this but you may. Assume you don't have long and anything I can do to help. I will."

***

Robyn hadn't known what to expect, but the great white orb leading them to the horizon had certainly not been it. They drove as fast as the moped would allow them, passing into the streets of the small town that had obviously built up around the castle long before the reactor was even here. The streets were empty, with folks already in their beds in this quiet stretch of Scotland. The local bar still had lights on but they were dimmed and obviously the last drinkers of the night were just finishing their pints, a tired landlord enquiring if they didn't have homes to go to. Despite the hour, a dog walker in overcoat and pyjamas was taking out the family pet that just wouldn't stop scratching at the door and together they watched the two noisy vehicles go by as the dog cocked its leg up the corner of a neighbour's fence.

The security barrier was up and no one came to investigate the approaching scooter and moped, they drifted through the gates without problem. Awake beneath his desk in the dark, the gate guard screamed against the tape across his mouth, hoping to alert the passing vehicles to his situation but their whining engines and his muffled voice had no way of really competing and the guard remained undiscovered, unconscious of how lucky that actually made him.

Robyn held aloft her hand and both the bikes came to a stop before the main doors and the trio dismounted, followed by the unseen form of Zippo.

In the ride Pippi had come to terms with her new leader, she hadn't wanted to at first but it all started to make sense now. Under Spades, it would always have been just him in charge and he was brutal. No other opinion mattered and although they certainly had fun causing chaos and hanging out, they only ever did it on Spades' terms – many of them held the scars that attested to this. Under Robyn, it would certainly be different. She was as mad as a bag of frogs but she knew how to let other people have a say. She knew she didn't have all the answers, she just often had the most direct ones. They had lost out on more members joining the gang in previous years because Spades was the kind of leader who felt threatened by change and his reputation often kept others away. Robyn would certainly have their numbers swelled quickly on the return to London and they would be a gang to be reckoned with, possibly even allowing more girls and non-Redcaps to join.

Yes, it had taken awhile but Pippi was happy.

They walked through the door into the foyer and the poor lad on the desk was beside himself. He had of course hidden his magazine in a drawer the moment he had heard the scooters approach, but although he had maybe expected a late addition to the night time team, as it appeared to be a busy night, he had not been expecting two young ladies and a suited pirate. They'd made it past the main gate so they were most certainly supposed to be here. Lennie hadn't worked with Mister Mackay for long, but he knew he wasn't the type to let people through his gate who were not invited. However, the trio didn't look like they truly belonged anywhere. The suited man with a tie around his head and the scruffy-looking girl in striped, knee-length socks, walked behind the prettier girl in the suit and bowler hat. They walked right up to the desk and the lead girl smiled.

"What's your name?" She asked in a flirtatious manner, throwing the young lad off guard.

"Leonard," said Lennie, before suddenly feeling very old and formal in front of people clearly his own age.

"But folks call me Lennie," he added.

The girl in the bowler nodded at him.

"Take off your hat Lennie," she practically purred and the desk guard took it off without thought. In all honesty, he felt silly wearing a hat indoors but Mr Mackay insisted on it, said it was part of the uniform and showed they were on duty. Lennie was a fairly attractive lad for his age of good height and with a mop of dark hair supposed to look like the Beatles haircut but one he couldn't help combing into a side parting out of force of habit.

Robyn turned and faced Pippi, "What do you think? Will he do?"

Pippi appraised the guard further; making Lennie feel uncomfortable and straighten his tie as if he should at least try to look his best in front of girls his age. You didn't get a lot of choice up here and the only girls his age were his twin sister and cousin.

"I like his look," Pippi said offhand, "But really it's down to Zippo."

Behind the desk guard and unseen by him, his shadow changed. Then, after a very brief moment, disappeared. Lennie wondered why the faces of the three before him had started looking curiously at him as if expecting him to say something. He went to talk but suddenly felt like he was struggling to swallow something. His throat felt blocked, his limbs got a big attack of pins and needles and he started to panic.

"Zippo's not going to be able to do this himself, Spades, would you like to give the boy a hand?"

Robyn looked at Spades as if to say the choice was still his, however. Spades couldn't believe it; he loved the violence but had wrongly assumed it would all be Robyn's domain now she was leader as he had always seen it as a privilege of position. He didn't want to appear too eager however so shrugged and walked forward as if under duress.

Lennie was struggling, he stumbled slightly and held the desk for support, but the man with the patched eye was heading forward and he hoped he knew the right way to help.

"Don't leave marks," said Pippi despite herself and Spades growled at her.

He turned and grabbed Lennie's tie, pulling him down forcefully onto the desk wrapping it around his neck several times and pulling hard, so it slipped and tighten about his throat. Lennie was beside himself with panic, he gasped and struggled, trying to get his fingers beneath the fabric, but his heavy, numbing legs weren't giving him enough leverage to fight back.

His eyes and tongue felt like they were coming out of his head and his last thought before death was how his father had insisted he wore a real tie to work and left the clip on in the drawer.

"That's enough sweetheart," said Robyn, putting her hand gently on Spades arm.

The male Redcap released his hold on the tie and moved back, the body slipped to the floor, kicking the office chair away that span across the floor, behind the desk. A moment later Lennie stood back up, his skin a bit paler but pretty much normal. He untangled and took off the tie and folded it neatly on the desktop as the other Redcaps watched.

"Zippo?" Said Pippi questioningly and Lennie went to speak but no words came, so he nodded.

"Cat still got your tongue then?" said Spades, looking at his old pack mate in his new body. Zippo nodded again, a look of disappointment on his face. Spades looked at Robyn, who was raising an eyebrow at the lack of sound.

"Bit his tongue clean off during death," added Spades helpfully.

"Right!" Said Robyn finally understanding the silence of Zippo, "Check those drawers Zippo. See if our guard had a weapon or two, failing that use the office equipment and your imagination."

***

Just down the corridor in the control room, most diagnostic tests were complete and the gathered technicians were reading the many reams of printer paper checking results, whilst Morningwood crouched beside Jonathon waiting for solutions.

"Nothing we can find," said an older man with a haggard face, checking again. He looked at the inspector sat quietly in the chair, "Please Mr Moore, help us out, if there's a meltdown it could be catastrophic." Despite the plea, Jonathon remained silent.

If being thrown up the hallway by Morningwood had taught him anything it was the definitive fact that the Satyr was the bad guy. He used violence and threats, whereas the man who had kidnapped his daughter had used only her. Of course, he saw both men as the bad guy, but only one had something he wanted and until he saw him or his daughter he was going to go ahead with the plan.

Morningwood

"Is there anyone else you can phone?" Asked Morningwood, "If you can then do it and get them up here, we may still have time."

The gathered night-time techs thought and a woman with dark waved hair and slightly European skin tones chimed up, "We can call Duncan McRae, he's certainly going to be nearby and he knows this reactor like the back of his hand."

"Then call him," said Morningwood, pointing to the phone on the command desk, "In the meantime, can someone physically go down to the reactor and check instruments. Just in case you spot something."

It was quite amusing to Morningwood that his commanding voice was gaining such respect, not one of them had asked who he was and he had walked in with one of their colleagues badly roughed up.

As two of the tech's volunteered to go check he heard the female technician get through to what must have been a sleepy specialist, "Sorry to wake you, Sir, but we have a problem at the reactor and we need your hel–." Unfortunately, the rest of the conversation was interrupted when the control room door burst open and four angry Redcaps surged in.

Chapter 24

Morningwood's reactions were still good. The technicians jumped at the sudden intrusion of shouting attackers and retreated, the phone receiver dropped to swing on its curly wire, but the Satyr was rolling. He grabbed the security guard's torch he'd been carrying and came up fast to his feet. He span to face the intruders and instantly recognised members of the pack from London, now back to their human aspects. He knew the Alpha, so picking his target carefully swung the torch upwards and caught Spades underneath the jaw, sending him up into a backwards flip, hoping to fell their leader and throw them into confusion. The action had been an overextension and his arm went high exposing his chest.

It was Pippi that spotted the opening in the warrior's defences and flew into him, diving almost unseen around the somersaulting Redcap leader of old and hitting the Satyr square in the chest with her shoulder. She had already got up speed to come through the door so she executed an almost perfect tackle, lifting the Satyr from his feet and carrying him backwards.

Morningwood retreated with the force and hit the table behind him on which the printer stood. It was a fairly low piece of office furniture and he went straight over it, Pippi pushing her charge – so she too went with him and in a chaos of arms and legs the two were airborne for a moment before the desk was no longer beneath them and they came crashing down to the floor. Morningwood's arms went up instinctively to protect his face, so he failed to land a blow on the female Redcap with the torch before they hit the solid ground. Luckily for the Satyr she was the lightest of the group so the impact of her on him wasn't enough to wind him but it did force him into a spreadeagled shape on the other side of the table.

Pippi had also been saved from a winding blow as she had landed on her victim's body, which cushioned her fall. The whole entrance had happened in almost slow motion. It had unfolded so perfectly, she seized her advantage. In her hand, she held the bone baton, removed from the corpse of the original Zippo. She pushed herself up from Morningwood's chest and brandishing her weapon in both hands, above her head, went to bring the club down hard on his face.

In a split second the Satyr knew he couldn't bring the torch back

Morningwood

up with enough force to dislodge his attacker, but in his left hand he had felt cable. He grabbed it and pulled as hard as he could. The great computer printer, a nice heavy duty one, came off the table they had flown across with speed and as Pippi was about to land her blow, it struck her hard in the back, forcing her down onto Morningwood's chest. The table also tipped and landed with its heavy side across the back of the Redcap's knees with a nasty crunch.

Robyn had entered the room just as Jonathon had leapt from his chair in front of her, instinct telling him to flee. She had her rock club in hand and with a skilful flick brought it around into his shoulder. The joint at the top of his arm shattered painfully on impact but also broke the flexible stick of the weapon, sending the rock skimming across the floor to disappear beneath the control console.

Jonathon tipped sideways onto the floor and like a scared dog he scampered into the footwell of a desk to hide and whimper. He recognised the youths as the ones that had lurked outside his home ever since the trilby man had entered his home and he knew they were sent there to guard him as the man had warned he would be watched. He had also seen them fight in the car park with the man who dragged him from the reactor, so he knew they were not together in this. He had not seen them since that incident but now they were here to see he was doing his job and he knew they still had his daughter… somewhere.

Zippo entered and appeared to have two blades, one in each hand. They had been a large pair of scissors the Sluagh had broken apart to act as weapons, not too sharp on the cutting edge after years of cutting anything that was needed at the front desk, but prised apart they would certainly pierce deeply if thrust. He ran at the technicians, who couldn't work out if their desk guard was a friend or foe until he sank one of the blades deep into the older technician's abdomen. He fell away, with a sucking noise, a bloom of red spreading across his shirt.

Morningwood tried to roll clear but the printer had pinned him as well as the prone Redcap. He was going to strike her with the torch just to make sure when Robyn's foot crunched down on his wrist until his hand popped open and the torch rolled clear.

"I do believe you and I have been here before," she smiled, running a finger over the stitches in her shaven hair, bending down she picked up the torch. "I got a kiss last time." She swung the torch hard into Morningwood's temple, breaking an arm off the stolen glasses and sending them skidding from his face. The Satyr went still.

"Tie him up!" She shouted, pulling a dazed and hobbling Pippi to her feet. She turned to check Spades was also getting to his feet, which he was, picking his dropped weapon up off the floor, the long cutting arm of a paper guillotine.

"Tie them all up," Robyn grinned, "See Spades, that's how a team does it. We've just taken over a nuclear reactor."

***

It was never nice to get a phone call in the middle of the night when you were already asleep, but it certainly became a lot worse when the phone call became a listening ear on a violent attack on some of your work colleagues. Duncan McRae listened with increasing horror, his hand firmly over his mouth as he heard shouts of anger, toppling furniture and screaming. The moment he heard the final words from an unknown voice, he hung up and rummaged in his bedside drawer for his address book. The nuclear power plant wasn't the only thing on this small far away stretch of coast. The Royal Navy had made it the home for tests on nuclear submarine engines and although their base was mainly engineers and scientists, Duncan knew they had a unit of twenty armed Royal Marines on base at all times.

He found the number and dialled quickly sat on the edge of his bed, heart racing. The phone seemed to ring forever before a stern voice answered. Of course, Duncan could only get through to the workshops so he knew the voice would be a security guard and hoped it was one of the marines directly. He explained the situation as quickly as he could and after being told to calm himself numerous times he was eventually put through to the commanding officer of the stationed unit. As much information as could be taken was eagerly given, although in hindsight that was scant little. The commanding officer took the situation with exceptional seriousness, which filled Duncan McRae's heart with a lot more confidence than he had before he made the phone call.

As he put the receiver back down, with strict instructions to phone no one else, he suddenly felt very helpless. He went downstairs to his kitchen and poured himself a large gin before opening a window. The coast was quiet at this time of night and if anything happened he would easily hear gunshots from here.

***

The naval base went into a quick and well-practiced military drill and in next to no time, one squad of ten armed marines went to check out the nuclear reactor. It felt foolish to abandon the military site in case it was a distraction technique; they could always call for reinforcements if needed, but the site might just have been occupied by protestors and to send the whole platoon of twenty troops would have been foolish. The lieutenant went with the squad, to give a powerful chain of command but he left his serjeant back at base so both units had an officer present. They weren't far along the coast at all and could easily have marched but it seemed wiser to take the lorry, just in case they needed a barrier to hide behind.

The drive out of the base and along the road felt like popping to the shops, but the open barrier and darkened guard hut was an indication of a serious security breach. The lorry slowed, its headlights picking up a prone and tied security guard in the hut's doorway. Mr Mackay had crawled from beneath the desk like a worm hoping to somehow alert a passer-by. Lieutenant Cogger jumped from the cab and ran over, whilst his troops took up defensive positions all around.

Peeling the tape from the man's face, he helped him up into a sitting position against the hut's wall. Mr Mackay started talking instantly, "It was just one. He wanted to see the safety inspector, knocked me out with my own torch," he spluttered, in an outpouring of words and gulping air.

"Calm yourself, man, we have talk of others on-site, could that be possible?" The officer of the Royal Marines enquired calmly, checking the seriousness of the guard's head wound.

"I heard other vehicles going in; by the sound of it I'd say scooters or mopeds," he added as the office untied him.

"Could you give us a description of the one you did see?" Asked the officer, more out of a desire to keep the man talking calmly than a need for information.

"Erm… Average height, wearing a dark suit and tie, a long beige Mackintosh overcoat and a trilby hat." He paused running further details through his head, "Thick glasses, the frames, not the lenses and a beard." The man added, "Although those could be a disguise." Mr Mackay rubbed at his wrists, sore from pulling at the flex bindings.

"Did he give a name at all?" Asked the officer, looking around aware they were taking a lot of time and their presence could be spotted losing them any advantage.

"He told me his name was Professor Morningwood, but on reflection, that is more than likely a comedy name," the security guard added, feeling a bit foolish as if all the elements had been there he just hadn't seen them.

"Don't worry, we'll take it from here, you go back inside, keep low and keep the light off." And with these words the Marines bundled back into the lorry and then rolled quietly up to the door, turning the truck to give as a great a defence as possible.

"Should we go in Sir?" Asked one of the Marines as his commanding officer surveyed the foyer.

"Yes. Four men into the foyer, it seems to be empty but keep your wits about you. Two of you circle the perimeter and the rest stay here with me by the truck. We'll set up a defensive position. If we encounter trouble, I want everyone to regroup back here. If you need to engage, verbal warning's first before firepower. I'm sorry to handicap you like this, men, but we have civilians here and I don't want a scandal hitting the papers. If you come under fire, aim above heads and retreat. Hopefully, it won't come to that but it's best to know what were dealing with before we get into a firefight."

The troops had practiced the manoeuvres before on their own base and a four, four, two split was standard. The four who approached the foyer did so in a structured two forward, two covering set up until all of them were inside the building.

***

The Redcaps had tied everyone except Jonathon, who cowered under the desk shivering uncontrollably and was occasionally taunted by Spades. When the Redcap bored of that, he picked up his guillotine blade and looked at Robyn.

"What exactly are we waiting for? We could slaughter everyone and be gone!" The former leader asked. Robyn didn't turn away from looking at the unconscious Satyr.

"Just until a few warning lights start going off and we can make a move, knowing the place will blow up as ordered."

Spades shrugged and walked out into the corridor. It was perfect timing, the first of the soldiers was just coming through the door to examine further.

He saw the Redcap and started to issue an order. "Get down on the ground –"

He was in the process of shouting when Spades opened his throat with a slash of the guillotine blade, near taking the soldier's head clean off and sending an arterial spray of blood arching into the room.

The Marines behind saw the attack, but following orders fired high, shattering strip lights and bringing down ceiling tiles. Spades ducked instinctively, bringing him level with the soldier's rifle. He dropped the long blade and snatched up the assault rifle. The troops were already retreating from the foyer, but the soldier by the door hesitated at the thought of leaving his companion. It was enough for Spades to fire into him, felling his second victim in less than a minute.

Outside Lieutenant Cogger recoiled at the sound of gunfire and they faced the building waiting to give assistance to their retreating troops. The radio operator, on his commander's orders, rapidly informed the naval base they were under fire and all troops should be on site fast.

Inside the room, Robyn and Pippi shot towards the door, looking at their comrade and ducking at the continued fire.

Spades was holding one assault rifle and gleefully pulling the other one into the corridor. When he turned and crouching ran back to the control room, he had two rifles in his arms like a bandit from a Mexican western.

"Yeeha!" Spades shouted triumphantly, adding to his western image, "I think we've got the attention of the locals."

Chapter 25

The Lord listened and the Lord thought.

When his words finally came, they rumbled around the room, deep and calm, like the threat of a storm announced by distant thunder.

"If we broke our code and entered the world of Mortals there would be war, but if we stay below we will be dealt a blow from which we may not recover. The problem you bring me is great, with no real solution which could end well for my Court."

Mulberry had not raised her head in the presence of the elephantine lord since she had spoken and been listened to. It was the Lord's decision on how to act, but unlike the great Lord she had taken the time to think on her journey and had thought of a possible solution to the problem. She said the only words she felt could help.

"The Wild Hunt, Lord."

The words brought a murmuring to the Court behind her and the Lord shifted in his throne, ice cracking as he leant forward.

"Do you summon them forth?" Rumbled the Lord.

The courts babbling grew with a sound of approval until all four of the Lord's eyes fell on their ranks and a hushed silence fell. The Wild Hunt had long been the Unseelie's only action amongst mortals and any member of the Court could invoke its despatch for one night until dawn and only once in a year could they ever be summoned. They would go forth and capture mortals for the Unseelie court to feast upon, a barbaric gathering but a popular one. There hadn't been a hunt for almost eighty years as the mortals now protected themselves against it and the hunt would often come back empty-handed. Of course the hunt didn't come without its drawbacks and the summoner of the hunt would be forever exiled to the land above, a fitting payment, but one that proved too high for many, despite the accolades they received from their peers.

Mulberry knew if she summoned them her exile would never end, but she was exiled now and yet she stood here in the Court of the Unseelie. Rules were there to be broken, even in nature and if being amongst mortals for the past century had taught her anything, it was to take risks.

"I summon them," she whispered, and her whisper echoed from the frozen walls to every ear.

Morningwood

***

At the Naval Base Sergeant Philips, rallied the remaining troops. It appeared this was no mere diversion, the attack on the reactor was the real thing and they had casualties. A second truck quickly filled with troops as heavy snow fell from the cold skies above. Phillips looked at the swirling flakes; it was going to be hard if they didn't finish this quickly. The Scottish weather could chill your bones and kill your will to fight and their men would be out in it, whilst the terrorist or protestors barricaded themselves in the warm. The drive was short but already the road and countryside all around was white. Lieutenant Cogger greeted the new arrival with a raised hand and the second truck joined the first, making the barrier stronger.

As Phillips and his unit set up, Cogger spoke to his fellow officer, "We have no idea how many undesirables are in there, but we know there are nine possible hostages. We have two men down and they have lost their armaments, so we know they have firearms inside, although with limited ammunition for them. The reactor has nine possible exits including the main doors. I need to despatch four units of two men, out into the field, to cover two of those exits each, it is not ideal, but I would like eight men to remain here, whilst a rota system of two floating men moves around the building on patrol. Every ten minutes I want that patrol to swap places with one of the exit units, keep everyone moving so this damn snow doesn't freeze us and slow our reactions."

"You heard the Lieutenant," Shouted Philips, in a military manner before assigning units their own exits to watch. It was a system they had drilled in the past so was easy enough to follow. Soon every exit was covered and the antagonists were sealed inside by a ring of Royal Marines.

***

Inside the reactor control room, the Redcaps were gathered. Robyn was looking out of the office through the window in the door. The body of one of the dead soldiers had wedged the double doors open and she could see into the foyer and some of the movement outside.

"Well if it's a war you wanted Spades. It's certainly a war you've got. Another lorryload of soldiers just turned up," Robyn said with some of the sparkle now removed from her voice. She was fine with the violence, but only if she knew that it was against those unable to protect themselves or one on one. She very much doubted the four of them could take on the army, even with guns.

Spades tried his hardest to not look worried. He wanted the others to see that under Robyn they were now under threat.

"Guess we just stay put then. We've got hostages. Come the morning the media will be here and we can just walk out without fear of death, maybe do time, maybe get off." The ex-leader tried to sound unfazed by the situation.

Robyn shook her head, "Fantastic plan if you don't take into account that that snivelling dog there," she pointed beneath the desk at Jonathon, "Has set this place to melt down. The best we can hope for is that on hearing the evacuation alarms, the soldiers will storm the building in a last attempt to release the hostages and we can take them out on our terms and still have enough time to get out of the blast area."

Her comments were ended by a loud sound from outside, a deep musical note that rattled windows. All the Redcap pack turned as one and Morningwood opened his eyes.

The soldiers outside also turned towards the direction of the sound, a long, resonating boom through the silent sheets of snow. The sound of an unholy trumpet blast.

The Wild Hunt came.

A great portal opened up in the hill beneath Dounreay Castle and the baying of Barghest and the great hunting horn sounded again, echoing around the landscape. The folks of Dounreay, who knew better than to investigate unearthly sounds, bolted their doors and turned out their lights and gathered protectively together.

Then they came. Four great beasts, running slavering into the snow. The Barghest were as black as pitch with great shaggy coats. Their eyes blazed red in thick, knuckle heads, wide, powerful jaws hung beneath, lined with tusk-like teeth that drool ran between, like great glistening strands of rope. As they ran, it was evident they were the size of wolfhounds with the muscular build of bulls and each one dragged with it a great iron chain, through the snow.

Morningwood

These creatures were followed by a small group of handlers made up of Shellycoats, Boggarts and Sackmen, twisted versions of humanity, dark of countenance and bestial of face. The Shellycoat's loved the cold turgid waters around the Court and dressed themselves in the flotsam of the sea. Nets weaved with kelp and decorated with rocks and shells, clinked as they ran, giving them the appearance of great turtle-like beings, who had evolved alongside man. The Boggarts were the colour of soil and great tufts of moss and grass grew from their hunched, rock-like bodies. Finally the Sackmen; ancient souls with wasted limbs and emaciated torsos. Long grey beards their only protection from the cold on their pallid, blemished skin, dragging the sacks behind them into which they would gather the kills and captured of the Hunt.

Behind them all ran Mulberry. Her form was still that of the Nymph, not the mortal because the hunt brought with it the essence of the Underworld, there would be no mortal forms amongst them now and as one they spilled down towards the reactor.

The plan was simple, to take everyone from the site, to invade, kidnap and find Jonathon if he was there, in the hope that it would stop the reactor's meltdown and save the Court.

Mulberry, still exiled to the world above, would report to the FAE and the perpetrators of this heinous plan would be sent before the Unseelie Lord and punished. She did not know if they would find anything. Morningwood could have had the whole thing sewn up back in London, but she could not take that risk. She did not know what to expect but she certainly wasn't expecting the army.

The descending group, including beasts, numbered less than thirty but they had a dark presence that brought the guns of the army to bear down on them. It was not too foolish in this situation to see them as a foe and the order was given to open fire, with extreme prejudice.

The bullets flooded forth and the four Barghest were enraged as their flesh was ripped and muscles stung, but they did not falter. A Shellycoat went down in the hail of bullets, adornments fracturing as each round struck home and two Boggarts fell to merge with the landscape. The Sackmen were tough and bullets tore bloodless holes through their skin and features as they barrelled forward, the hail of fire slowing them not one inch.

Then the armies met in a crashing of bodies. The Barghest were vicious at the best of times and fought over the kills, grabbing fleeing soldiers and savaging them on the ground, Lieutenant Cogger being the earliest of casualties as he rushed to protect his troops. A soldier from the back of the truck concentrated his fire on one spot of a great shaggy beast and it eventually fell lifeless across the body of its last kill, muscles twitching with stored energy.

Before he could shout the attack tactics to his fellow troops, the soldier was grabbed by a looming Sackman and he disappeared into the confines of the old man's bag as if he had never existed and the battle strategy vanished with him.

***

In the Corridor where Robyn had now moved she could see the approaching Hunt and knew they would be as much a target as the mortals, the Unseelie Court had been roused by the Nymph and now its wrath was upon them.

She stormed angrily into the office and pulled Jonathon screaming by his broken arm from beneath the desk, hissing her words into his face, "This place best explode or I'm killing you like I did your simpering little girl but trust me it won't be half as quick!" She stood, "Redcaps with me. Zippo guard the hostages. Kill anyone who moves."

And taking a rifle from Spades and handing it to Pippi she moved out into the corridor followed by her pack. Picking the guillotine blade up from the floor she kicked open the double doors and entered the foyer as the first Barghest smashed through the glass.

Pippi and Spades opened fire their bodies vibrating with the powerful recoil as rounds from both rifles started hitting the same vulnerable spot, just beneath the jaw, until the beast collapsed like a puppet with it strings cut. Pippi's gun ran out of ammunition first as the next hound ploughed into the room, followed by the final one hot on its tail.

The first went for Robyn who, whilst knocked to the floor, grabbed its tusk-like teeth and forced its head back, slashing at the exposed throat with the makeshift blade, whilst it raked away fragments of her suit and drew blood on her flesh.

Morningwood

The second went for Pippi but turned as Spades fired the last of his rounds into its neck. The click of his gun making him change tactics in a heartbeat and swing the weapon like a club as the creature lunged, bloodied towards him.

Pippi jumped onto its back and dug her sharp fingers into the creature's head, searching for soft eyes. The creature ignored the Redcap on its back and lunged forward towards its attacker until teeth found Spades throat and it bit down hard, tough ivory sliding around his windpipe, breaking skin and holding the Redcap in an unbreakable choke, as Sackmen and Boggarts entered the building.

Chapter 26

The lights on the control panels all lit up as a solid bank of red, as a siren started to sound through the reactor and echoed outside across the heads of the soldiers as they battled with objects of their nightmares. At the sound, the gathered technicians started to shake and some cried, they were trapped at the hands of psychopaths, surrounded by gunfire and at the mercy of a nuclear meltdown. One tried to run for it but the speed with which Zippo cut him down made the other retreat further into the corner.

Jonathon crawled over to Morningwood tears filled his eyes and ran down his face, "I'm so sorry," he whispered over and over again as he untied the Satyr, "I can stop it, I just need him gone," and he looked at the back of the Sluagh.

Morningwood stood quietly, he could taste blood in his mouth and feel the pull of the bruise tightening his face. He removed the broken glasses and placed them on the desk and walked quickly up behind Zippo.

The Sluagh made flesh saw the hope in the technician's eyes before him and turned, twin blades at the ready. The Satyr was right there and pain moved through Zippo like a wave.

Looking down he saw the Satyr's hands around his wrists, twisting his own hands back and up. The blades had entered through his security uniform, up under his ribcage and into both lungs. Blood bubbled up into his mouth and spilled over his lower lip running down his chin. The Satyr walked him back against the wall, not letting go of the blades.

"You'll not have long, longer if you leave the blades in, but you have a choice," the Satyr said calmly and let go, turning his back and walking away.

Zippo could feel his life leaving him, twice this Satyr had ended his mortal form. His anger rose, he wasn't letting him walk away unpunished. He pulled the blades free with a sickening suck and with a noise of rage spilling forth from his throat he charged.

Morningwood span on the spot, halting the charge with a powerful punch to the face. Zippo flew back, hit the wall and slid slowly down, all air gone from his blood-filled lungs. The blades fell from his open palms with a chink.

Morningwood

"That would have been my choice too," said Morningwood with a faint pang of regret.

"Right, Mr Moore," he said, his voice commanding as he turned back to Jonathon, trying to be heard over the constant siren, "Tell these good people what you did, so it can be reversed."

The night technicians edged meekly forward past the bodies of friends and foe, as Jonathon quickly explained the safety features he had bypassed. All Morningwood could really understand was that a lot of water needed to be added and quick. It had been a simple case of draining off the coolant as warning systems had been recalibrated not to notice. The Reactor had been in meltdown for over an hour and was close to going critical, but it could be reversed.

The bad news came when a technician pointed out the recalibrated dials were making it impossible to flood the system fast enough, unaffected safety systems were telling them it would overflow.

"I don't understand if it's just a simple calibrator go in and reset it," Morningwood suggested, trying to show common sense.

The technicians all looked crestfallen. One of them spoke up, "It's a manual override system, you'd need to know exactly what bits to adjust, pick the wrong one and we just cause bigger problems."

"Then Mr Moore can adjust it," he said looking at the broken man for a moment, "Or at least take one of you and show you what to adjust,"

It was Jonathon's turn to pipe up, "It's flooded with radiation, possibly enough to kill all who enter."

"What if that person was super-healthy?" Enquired Morningwood.

"Well, they may be able to shake off the effects but it's a big risk, even in radiation suits," added a technician.

"Then there's no debate. Mr Moore and I are going in, get the suits ready."

***

Pippi had her arms around the neck of the Barghest, locked in a squeezing hold. The beast was tough, but Redcaps were strong. She felt things giving inside. A Sackman approached her silent and unseen, the perfect stalkers. His wizened arm reached forward and was severed at the elbow. The hunt follower turned to be faced by the grin of Robyn. She had killed the Barghest and, soaked in its blood and dressed in rags, she had pulled herself from beneath its weight. She had killed two Boggarts to get to the Sackman closing in on Pippi.

"Hello sweetheart," she purred and cut off its head with a single blow.

With the extra time, Pippi strangled the hunting beast and it collapsed, dropping Spades lifeless body to the floor.

Both girls looked at him laid on the floor for but a second, eyes wide and blood pooling around his crushed neck, before turning on the final members of the Hunt that stepped through the door.

It seemed the soldiers were no more, but they had certainly thinned the famed Wild Hunt.

***

The radiation suits were uncomfortable to wear, all-covering rubber that instantly built up the temperature with Morningwood's trapped heat. The mask restricted vision and held his face in a tight seal that pulled at facial hair. They were baggy in the body for ease of movement, but it just helped to slow the Satyr down, causing him to waddle. Despite all this, Morningwood hurried Jonathon along the corridor knowing a battle of epic proportions must be happening behind them. He had heard the horn of the Wild Hunt and knew instantly that the Unseelie Court would be coming to clear house. He had no real idea of the reason for their timely involvement but assumed Mulberry must be somehow behind it. His backup plan had always been to warn the Court if they had not convinced Jonathon, since he had not seen his companion after his exit from the Underworld he hoped that had been her thinking too. If she wasn't behind it then the prospects were a dangerous change of circumstance, the Hunt would simply take everyone and inhabit the land to make sure it didn't happen again. That would be an occupation he doubted, even with Satyr help, the mortals could recover from, without a lot of damage to both their world and history.

Morningwood

As they passed through the double doors into the reactor area, Morningwood could feel how greatly the heat had already built up in the vast room of gantries and pipes, until a heat haze hovered above the metal walkways. Imagination could easily play tricks in the claustrophobic suit but Morningwood could feel a tingle move across his skin, the unsettling movement of hair on his body as if insects crawled upon him. He started to sweat instantly and looked across to see the sunken eyes and flushed skin of Jonathon through the eyeholes of his mask as he did the same. The noises that echoed through his suit, from the siren to the footfalls as they walked, were like listening to sounds underwater, but his own breathing was loud and real. The reactor was popping, creaking and vibrating with sound, as they descended down to stand before a great selection of sealed boxes lined up along the wall.

Jonathon moved forward and taking a special key from his belt, unlocked the boxes one after another, opening the covers to reveal valves and dials, with not one giving any clue to their importance despite the numerous signs and labels. He reached for the last cover with his broken arm and winced, grabbing at the sudden wash of pain in his shoulder that doubled him over and caused him to drop the key, which bounced across his feet and headed for a gap down the side of the walkway. Morningwood stepped down on it as it went past stopping it dead. As Jonathon straightened up from his pain, the Satyr bent over, picked the key back up with a grateful sigh and opened the last cover.

"Show me the valves, you're in no fit state to move them yourself," said Morningwood, placing his mask against the technician's so the sound travelled easier over the distracting noise of the alarm. Weakly, Jonathon pointed towards the first box. Morningwood turned and took hold of the first valve with his gloved hand and checked for a nod. As he got one, he started to turn slowly, watching the needle on the dial drop, with each twist. Jonathon squeezed his arm to tell him that was enough and Morningwood stopped. The technician nodded again.

Jonathan looked slowly along the dials, his vision blurring in and out with the building heat and the pain in his shoulder growing. He could feel his whole world pulsing, along with his vision, then without warning he saw nothing and fell to his knees, body convulsing. Morningwood went to his side, but the man held up his hand to halt him, pushing himself back to his feet. The heat was too much. He couldn't see to give instruction, so he pulled his mask off and took gulping breaths of the hot air, breathing it deep into his lungs. He felt them burn as he pointed at the next dial. Morningwood wanted to pull the mask back onto the man's exposed face but it was evidently the only way they could continue and he controlled the desire.

"This one, two turns," Jonathon said and the Satyr moved in and turned the valve until he shouted stop. Morningwood looked at him. The radiation was starting to affect the Satyr too, the levels were building and he envied the exposure Jonathon had to the cooler air. If he was thinking of removing his suit, the desire left him when Jonathon pushed back his rubber hood and clumps of hair simply slid from his head. The safety technician watched them fall and threw up, before wiping his bloodied mouth on the back of his glove. Morningwood could see an approaching end so pulled the man's focus back to the dials, tapping the next one.

"No, not that one," said Jonathon, his voice cracked and dehydrated in the heat.

Morningwood moved on and got another nod and another display of vomiting. He couldn't show compassion now, the man before him was dead already, just too stubborn to lay down yet and they had to carry on and save others. He turned the valve and watched the dial drop.

Behind him Jonathon collapsed.

Morningwood turned and forcefully dragged the man back up and pushed him against the boxes holding him up with one hand.

Turning his head slowly, Jonathon checked the dial and nodded, his eyes closing.

"Just one more," shouted Morningwood inside his suit, manhandling the dying man to the next box, Jonathon's skin was now flush and sweating, eyes watering and most of his exposed skin was hairless and blotchy. "Stay with me," continued Morningwood as he shook him awake.

Jonathon tapped a dial but the action seemed clumsy to the Satyr so he queried it. The man looked again and nodded, he went to talk but his mouth was dry and lips broken, no sound escaped them. He instead mimed a sign to turn the valve three times. Morningwood complied and the job was done, he let the technician slide down the wall as he pushed the covers closed.

His own head was muzzy now and his legs felt as rubber as the suit, but he still bent down and picked up the fallen man, swinging him across his broad shoulders like a fireman would carry a victim from a blaze. Then getting as stable in his footing as possible, he started to walk back up the stairs, surprisingly stumbling only a couple of times. He felt Jonathon convulsing on his shoulders and heard him vomit more. Morningwood was pleased he couldn't smell anything in the confines of the tight rubber mask, as his own stomach was churning. He was sure the smell alone would take him the last few steps closer.

He steadied himself on the handrail and tried to focus on the signs, despite the swirling red warning lights that turned the world crimson and the constant throbbing siren. His moment of pause helped and he started to clear his head. One sign with a clear arrow pointed towards the decontamination showers and he turned that way, taking his load clumsily with him.

The doors opened and he placed Jonathon on the floor and turned them on.

As the liquids hit the suit he felt instantly cooler and for a moment he closed his eyes and thought of fresh spring showers as the water thudded rhythmically off the rubber, he shook himself from the relaxing vision and slowly turned to face the technician. He lay propped against the wall like a rag doll and was perfectly still, despite the action of the chemical shower on his exposed skin, staring eyes and open mouth. Morningwood leant forward and closed the man's eyelids with his gloved hand. He had known he was dying, the moment he took off the hood but to see him there, a pawn in a game played by Immortals, angered the Satyr more than he could say.

The water slowed and stopped, the suds washing away down the long drains and a green light filled the room, on locating its source, Morningwood read a sign beneath that simply said, 'Clean.'

He removed his own mask and slid down the wall beside the body of Jonathon.

***

Two Sackmen, a Shellycoat and a Boggart stood before the Redcap girls. Mulberry watched from outside the door, she had seen too much of the fighting skills of the vicious Redcaps to feel even slightly protected by the spear that had been given to her. A red light span above their heads, filling the corpse-strewn room with crimson shades and making it look like the embodiment of hell.

Robyn stood like a warrior of old, her body upright and ready for action, the vicious, stolen blade held at a right angle to her hip. Her clothes hung off her, revealing glimpses of the tight muscular body beneath and the bowler hat she wore pushed down almost over one eye, dripped in the blood of her kills. It was only her eyes and manic grin that shone out through the sea of red that proved how much she still wanted to battle. The glistening of sweat on her skin and heaving rise of her chest a testament to how much she had already fought.

Pippi by contrast had hunkered down, her position more akin to a cat that was waiting to pounce. She didn't seem to move or even breathe, her eyes fixed on the Hunt before her. The only indication she was ready at all was the heavy chain she held across her, that span in her left hand like a deadly propeller, the lead of the dead Barghest, still attached to the corpse, but with enough give to be used in battle.

At first nobody moved. The Hunt was fully aware it had free range to kill and despite their losses they saw it as only two more defenders to get through. The Shellycoat moved first, his heavy irregular rock flail, embedded with shards of metal ore, dropped heavily to the floor, the chain still held in the hunter's hand and the fight was on.

Pippi loosed her chain towards the Shellycoat, who sidestepped and ran forward as the makeshift weapon flew harmlessly past his head. His charge was met by Robyn, who took three quickening steps forward and launched herself into the air like a spinning wheel, passing him upside down to strike across his back, landing in a crouching roll to spring up beside a Sackman.

The ancient Huntsman had already had a sizable amount of damage and resembled dry leather rags stretched over a bone frame. The Redcap punched her hand into a hole in the ruined chest, grabbed and pulled forth the desiccated dry organs from within and brought her head crashing into his, leaving a vivid blood impact on the old grey face, causing the Sackman to crumble before her.

Pippi's action had not missed at all. She would have expected any warrior worth his salt to have evaded the obvious attack, but her true purpose was made clear when she pulled her chain back with a twisting of her hands. It arched in the air, the flicked movement travelling its length like a wave as it recoiled. The Shellycoat had reacted to Robyn's passing blow and was stretched tall from the sharp impact, the returning chain found his neck and with its speed snagged and spun around the softer flesh like a noose. Pippi tugged and the ocean denizen was pulled forward heavily on his face and as he fell she let the chain drop from her hands and jumped forward, seized the Unseelie hunter by the ears and lifting his head began driving it repeatedly onto the concrete floor of the foyer.

Mulberry realised if her Huntsmen all died she'd be alone with the Redcaps. She used the fear to inspire action and sprang from the shadow, spear poised catching Robyn in the shoulder, the well-crafted but delicate point slid effortlessly through and brought pain to the Redcap leader that came out in an ear-shattering scream.

The noise and shock of the impact paused Mulberry too long to press her advantage and Robyn firmly grabbed the shaft that disappeared into her soft flesh so no more damage could be inflicted and the girls became united at opposite ends of the pole. Robyn was stronger by far and, using herself as a pivot, she span Mulberry against the only remaining window of the foyer, hoping to shake her free.

The Nymph knew the danger of being weaponless and held on tightly to her spear despite the pain as the window shattered with the impact. Mulberry knew she had to hang on whatever the torment or she would be just another Redcap victim. She pulled the spear back towards her, hoping to free it but the flayed points of the deadly tip dug into the Redcap's shoulder, preventing it from pulling further but causing enough pain for Robyn to rage. The Redcap leader needed an end to the pain, so grabbing the shaft in both hands she leant back and lifted Mulberry from the floor, with the applied lever action of the embedded weapon and spun.

The shock of losing her footing alone was too much and Mulberry flew through the air hitting the side wall hard and disappearing behind the desk, under a cascade of billboards and corporate art.

As Pippi felt the Shellycoats skull crack, she was grabbed from behind, in the vice-like grip of a Boggart. She kicked and struggled as she was lifted from the ground, but it was like fighting the rocks themselves. The final Sackman loomed silently before her and she saw him open his bag with its dark bottomless interior.

Robyn hit the back of the restraining Boggart, jamming the spear handle in the jutting hard shapes of its back and move swiftly forward pushing the shaft painfully all the way through her body until weight sent it clattering against the floor. The impact turned the Boggart around, turning him from the Sackman and protecting Pippi briefly from capture. Robyn picked up the spear from the ground and with a painful throw pinned the Sackman to the wall.

The Boggart laughed a rumbling laugh at the bloodied girl before him and started to squeeze Pippi until she had no air in her lungs and her mouth opened in silent horror.

Robyn wasn't prepared for anyone to hurt her pack sister and brought her booted foot up fast and although she was sure she felt a toe break, the Boggart dropped Pippi gasping to the floor, before he too fell on his knees beside her. Robyn surveyed the battle's imminent conclusion and stepped from the Foyer, Pippi thought she'd been abandoned once again, but Robyn reappeared a moment later with a loaded assault rifle.

The Sackman was struggling along the handle of the spear pinning him, so she shot him first until he hung like a skewered Hoover bag in need of emptying and then the rest she unloaded into the Boggart, sparks flying as the bullets struck the rock-like skin, but even the Boggart fell down dead to its side.

Pippi stood up with the help of Robyn. From the pain in her chest she knew ribs had broken and she wanted to rest, but her Leader seemed anxious to move.

"We need to go," said Robyn looking into the eyes of her pack sister and indicating the warning lights, "We can't have much time."

And she ran across the bodies back to the broken door.

"We need Zippo," said Pippi and went back through the opposing doors to the control room, leaving Robyn to shake her head at the strange weakness her pack sister had for the male as she ran for the scooter. It was on its side from the battle, corpses cooling all around, but it was quickly righted and started first time.

***

Pippi entered the control room and technicians who were sat at desks gasped at her sudden appearance stood quickly up and moved away. As they parted, she saw the lifeless form of Zippo against the wall and a space where the Satyr and father were missing. She turned, nervously expecting Morningwood to be behind her but on seeing the empty corridor instead chose to run.

The technicians looked at each other and took back up their stations, keeping a wary eye on the door.

***

Pippi jumped on the back of the scooter.

"Where's Zippo?" Asked Robyn.

"He's not coming," Pippi replied with a shrug and with the siren still going behind them, Robyn weaved between the bodies of soldiers and immortals and drove as fast as she could for the hills.

Chapter 27

Morningwood opened his eyes in the Decontamination Room and listened intently to the silence, before pulling off the hood that still covered his ears and breathing the disinfectant smelling air; his thoughts confirmed: the sirens had stopped.

He stood slowly with legs as wobbly as a newborn deer and vomited until his sides hurt. The radiation had taken its toll and he would need medical assistance soon, but he was alive and the sirens had stopped as a result of his and Jonathon's action. Actions that had cost the father his life.

Morningwood walked out into the hallways and leaning against the wall for support, slid back to the control room, his rubber suit squeaking in a way that set his teeth on edge. His timely entrance was met by a sea of smiling faces, rows of green lights lit up the control panels and attention had moved to caring for the dead.

***

Mulberry regained consciousness behind the desk, a rapid blinking of eyes followed by a shooting pain in her back and neck. The room was deathly silent with no coloured light but in the distance she could hear what sounded like screaming. She pulled herself painfully up and looked over the desk, using it for support.

Outside the sky was lightening as dawn approached and the bodies of the Hunt and corpses of the Barghest grew paler until they no longer existed, although the ground was far from free as it still remained peppered with dead soldiers and the lifeless body of Spades.

Mulberry herself was in her mortal form again, uninfluenced by the power of the Hunt. Naked, her skin pale and human, her hair short and dark, she opened the satchel she had kept around her shoulders and dressed quickly and somewhat painfully over her bruised body. On gaining her feet, she pushed opened the double doors that lead further into the base. It wasn't screaming, it was a cheer, a happy, excited cheer that just kept coming. She followed it along the corridor stepping respectfully over the decapitated soldier to an important-looking room and saw a group of six technicians gathered around a seated man in a baggy rubber suit.

Morningwood

Even from the back she recognised Morningwood and entered. Faces turned to appraise the lady in the doorway, gauging if she was a threat, until the Satyr turned and smiled, he looked flushed and weak, with a swollen black eye.

"We won," she said simply, and the whole room cheered again, except Morningwood, who simply nodded with a half-turned smile – she had never seen him look so tired.

***

It turned out that the gate guard, Mr Mackay and the Chief Technician; Duncan McRae, had both felt great concern at the continued gunfire and then its sudden stop with no all-clear, so had phoned through for more help. It had come quickly in the shape of Naval Helicopters and more troops and although police had set up a cordon around the area, a lot of other services had turned up and were on hand if needed.

The troops secured the reactor and ambulances were called in to see if they could deal with the dead. By the end of the day, twenty-four body bags lined the tiled floor of the foyer along with a sealed temporary coffin, complete with a radiation warning symbol and the stencilled words, 'Hazardous Material.'

Morningwood had been flown from the reactor almost immediately, to be treated in an isolation wing, leaving Mulberry behind, where she now stood quietly beside the coffin of Jonathon Moore and thought about how tragic and preventable his loss was.

***

It was days before news started to filter out about the reactor. Names were kept out of the press and numbers of dead, but it was certainly the headline of national papers for a couple of days, although none could quite agree on what had happened and the powers that be certainly weren't saying. Speculation of a preventable nuclear accident seemed to be winning popularity as a reason over the less threatening, foiled terrorist action. It seemed the British public certainly liked a failure over a win.

Morningwood read them all with interest from his hospital bed, happy to see the mortals were still hiding the actions of another world and he actually wondered if they even consciously covered it up any more. He had been quarantined and only certain people could come in and see him. Special blood had been couriered in for his blood transfusion, apparently sourced by the official who had been working on the case alongside him. Yes, it seemed Morningwood had been excused of his supposed crimes and was actually being held aloft as a hero; but one who had to remain anonymous, for reasons of national security. After all the excitement, Morningwood was glad of the rest. He could have done without the plastic sheeting that hung like curtains around his bed, but at least it was clear and let the light of the window shine through. He enjoyed the comings and goings of the distorted shapes outside the curtain, it was like he was in a fishbowl but was looking comfortably out rather than being disturbed by those who looked in. It was on the first day of the second week that he felt he could talk to one of the shapes outside the barrier.

"You're not a real nurse?" He stated and the rippling shape turned towards the screen listening, "It's an English uniform and we're currently in a Scottish Hospital."

The curtain parted and Robyn stepped into the room, a smile playing across her lips, "You're very perceptive," she said with an impressed nod.

"So has Conand sent you to kill me?" Morningwood asked coolly, causing Robyn to raise a questioning eyebrow.

"Camp Barrie," Morningwood corrected.

"Oh! No, we've gone freelance, Pippi and I, see if we can get some work of our own. In fact, that police detective who had it in for you found our old boss's corpse bled out in his office, after a call for his arrest with regards to the Rothborn killings," she said with disengaged nonchalance, before continuing, "You did kill a lot of my gang however and… well, I'm sure you realise I can't let that just go," she said, with a shrug and cheeky smile.

"Of course not," said Morningwood sitting up in his bed. Conand had escaped justice again. Bled out just meant he had disposed of the body he was inhabiting and was either in spirit floating around or already the proud owner of a new form. Whatever the case, he too would have debts to settle.

Morningwood

Robyn approached until she was just inches away from the Satyr then kissed him passionately, her fingers wrapping in his hair, her other hand on his chest, feeling the rising beat of his heart. Then she broke away with a breathy sigh and theatrically fanned her face.

"But not today," she whispered, "I think you've got too many guests coming."

Then without another word she walked to the door, opening it on a large figure that stood there. The Nurse passed him by and the figure entered the room. It was Dagda who pushed through the curtains, grinning hugely.

"You dirty old Dog. Can't help yourself can you? I know an English nurse uniform when I see one. Have you been ordering in, playing dangerous?" The big man asked with a chuckle.

"You've no idea," laughed Morningwood.

The big man picked up the clipboard from the end of the bed and read quickly. "You're making a fast recovery and got the blood I sent you. The experts seem to think you got a lesser dose than Mister Moore. They told me no one could have recovered from his exposure or even close…" he tailed off as if thinking.

Morningwood chose not to interrupt, they both knew it was his Satyr constitution that had coped with the radiation and the timely arrival of Dagda's gift, not a lesser dose.

Dagda continued, "…We could certainly use skills like yours in the FAE," he said, putting the clipboard back.

"Not a chance," said the Satyr with a serious tone, "We're here because we are all exiled. It worries me that an agency has been set up to watch over the actions of Mortal and Immortal affairs, but only the Immortals get to join, it's like having a prison patrolled by prisoners. When it comes down to it, Dagda, all the time I know you are watching the mortals and acting as police against our own kind, I will be watching you."

"Can we consult with you?" The big man asked running fingers through his beard.

"Whenever you need to my friend. In fact, I insist upon it," the Satyr said with a smile.

"We're not all like Kochab, you know," Dagda countered with a cough, "In fact we're clearing house as we speak."

Kochab's Daimler pulled in through the gates of the London scrapyard and watched as his constructed heavy slowly closed the gates behind them. They were sealed in and to Kochab that meant no disturbance as he went about his business. He would have been happy to do the meeting alone, as he knew he could handle the would-be whistle-blower and her humorous demands by himself, but he was even happier to be doing it with his backup as he got to watch without getting his hands dirty. Over the last few days, he had done a lot of watching as his constructs worked their magic.

The car came to a stop and the gate-closing heavy opened Kochab's door. The Deputy of the FAE stepped out, his polished shoes going instantly into an oil-streaked puddle and he raised his eyebrows and gave his henchman a withering glance at the lack of a warning. Together they were joined by his driver and securely flanked by muscle, Kochab walked around the stacks of broken cars and household appliances until Mulberry stood before them.

She was dressed appropriately for the mortal world her hair dark and bobbed, a long trench coat and sensibly knee-high patent leather boots. The Nymph said nothing and the Deputy had to laugh at her supposed power.

"So you have come to say goodbye then," Kochab sneered, "I heard you summoned the Wild Hunt up in Scotland and I'm sure you understand we can't have you continuing to act as an agent in the light of this revelation."

Mulberry nodded, "It's a shame you feel like that Deputy Kochab. You see it's been brought to my attention you planned the whole reactor meltdown alongside Conand. How long do you think you will survive as Deputy if that get's out?"

Kochab laughed heartily, turning to his straight-faced heavies and being disappointed to once again see not a flicker of mirth on their faces.

"Information that is only known by a Satyr and some Redcaps, if they still live. Oh yes and you a doubly-disgraced Nymph."

"You're forgetting Conand," said Mulberry with a smile, playing her trump card.

"Everyone will be forgetting Conand soon. Seems he took his

own life this morning when he found out his boyfriend was shot dead in an ally. My boys were there to see it all. Make sure it all happened properly," Kochab said with a twisted smile, enjoying the look on Mulberry's face as the news sank in.

Mulberry looked crestfallen, "You've already tied up the loose end?"

"What did you expect? I planned to destroy the entire Unseelie Court. I'm hardly going to let that get noticed by a few stragglers. Camp Barrie is dead, his Redcaps have been manipulated and right now one of them should be placing a pillow over your Satyr's sleeping head and by my reckoning that only leaves you."

As his words finished the two heavies moved forward, big feet splashing in the many puddles of the yard. Mulberry had nowhere to run, but she made no attempt to even move… because she didn't need to.

A crack of ice sounded beneath one of the approaching thug's feet. It was a fairly normal sound and he ignored it at first, but then, all the puddles were frozen. The ice crystals spiralled up the metal stacks of cars and cookers. The ground became hard as the breath of Kochab became clouds in the air before him. He wrapped his coat around himself. Kochab's thugs had no breath, and they also had little warmth of their own. The bodies froze quickly, ice crystals forming on their skin and eyes. Their movements slowing as they approached. Until they stopped entirely.

Mulberry pulled on gloves and picked up a metal bar leant beside her.

Kochab watched as she approached his constructed henchmen, evil intent on her face. One strike to each with the bar and they shattered.

"Thought I'd even the odds," said the Nymph with a smile.

The Deputy sighed, bored of the little games, reached into his pocket and pulled out a snub-nosed revolver, pointing it at the Nymph, "Clever trick. Expensive trick for both of us but I can make more. You, however, only have one life to give. Seems like such shame to cut your extended exile short, but no hard feelings."

"I don't have an extended exile," she said calmly, ignoring the gun, "I did a trade, with the Unseelie."

"And what trade could they possibly want from an insignificant sprite like you?" He asked chuckling,

"They just wanted you and a confession," Mulberry added coldly.

Kochab finally understood the importance of the change in weather and the ice now spoke volumes. He could feel a greater chill at his back and it wasn't just from the air.

He turned slowly, his revolver dropping to his side, the crystals in the air behind him had opened to reveal the majestic throne of the Unseelie, sat upon it the great Dark Lord himself, frozen in place. His four wisdom-filled eyes fixed on Kochab and the Immortal felt the cold build in his heart, rooting him to the spot. The great Lord's trunk untwisted and the tusks became supple until all eight pale tentacles writhed before the impassive face, turning the Lord from an ancient pachyderm full of courtly advice to a great vengeful kraken of the seas.

The appendages moved so slowly forward, seeming to stretch from beyond their realm, feeling over the cold metal and frozen ground of the mortal scrapyard, until the tendril tips played across the form of the mesmerised Deputy, who had planned them such harm. They slowly caressed his skin, and moved across his clothes, exploring, searching... tasting.

Then in a flash, the tentacles ensnared their prey and recoiled. The portal closed with a clap like thunder, that rolled around the stacks of detritus and toppled piles of rusting cars into the dirt.

Then everything fell silent.

Kochab had been judged.

Mulberry had to admit Dagda had been right, the Unseelie Court had a dark style.

As she walked forward she kicked something metallic, where Kochab had stood and looking down she picked up a bunch of keys, some belonged to a house but a couple belonged to a car. She smiled as she looked across at the Daimler sat waiting patiently by the gates; maybe the rest of her exile wouldn't be so bad after all.

***

Morningwood left the hospital, as always an unsung hero. He knew the FAE would have sewn up all the loose ends, made the problems go away. The world had remained unaware of the Immortals

Morningwood

now for so long. With their brief lives, it was so easy to let the Immortals drift out of history and into legend, but now he knew that the Immortals were back and messing with them, using them freely like pawns, where pieces could be easily sacrificed to topple the kings; he couldn't allow that. This meltdown had been too close and too many innocents had died in their Immortal game of chess. He was going to have to think about coming out of retirement. He smiled as he passed a pet shop window, full of birdcages, the colourful little creatures hopping from perch to perch. He was about to walk in when a horn sounded, behind him, making his head turn.

A car he knew well sat purring against the kerb, a silver-grey Daimler. The passenger door popped open, revealing a new owner. Mulberry smiled up at him, leaning across the seats.

"Do you need a lift anywhere?" She grinned at the Satyr and reached into the back seat producing a beautiful cage with two tiny birds hopping around inside.

"I found this in Kochab's old apartments. I just thought we could drive somewhere and you could…" she looked at the cage, "…Do that thing you do so well."

Morningwood laughed and climbed quickly into the car, taking the cage on his lap and leaning across, kissed the Nymph in the driver's seat.

"I know just the spot," he said as he closed the door.